Caldera

Bruce W. Perry

Acknowledgement

I appreciate the use of the following web site, and associated ones, for researching a fictional account of a Yellowstone eruption:

https://www.usgs.gov/volcanoes/yellowstone/geology-and-history

Caldera: "A large basin-shaped volcanic depression with a diameter many times larger than included volcanic vents; may range from 2 to 50 kilometers (1 to 30 miles across)."

The last caldera forming eruption at Yellowstone occurred about 640,000 years ago. It ejected about 240 cubic miles of volcanic debris into the atmosphere, 1,000 times the amount of material ejected by the 1980 Mount St. Helens eruption.

Use this link for more **Dystopian Science Fiction Adventure books by Bruce W. Perry:**

https://www.amazon.com/Bruce-W-Perry/e/B001IO9PBC

Do not pray for easy lives, pray to be stronger men~President John F. Kennedy, 1963, quoting Reverend Phillips Brooks

Duty is heavy as a mountain, but death is lighter than a feather. ~Japanese proverb.

CHAPTER 1: ZEKE SANCHEZ, OCTOBER, 2025

Zeke's motorcycle sped along the empty road, the desert scrub rushing past off his right shoulder. Indian Springs, Nevada was a few miles ahead. The desert was clean, barren, scoured by a dry wind, but he understood, heavily populated by animals and spirits. They came out at night. Nothing big on two or four legs roamed out there now, as far as he could see, from the desert floor to the distant brown and red foothills lining the horizon.

Not too many humans had the desert survival skills that he did.

But the vast Mojave Desert was nonetheless rich and alive with wildlife and spirits, the latter of which took hallucinogens like peyote, and a little imagination, to interact with.

Zeke wore only sunglasses with the long black hair

flowing off his shoulders. He had a brown suede leather coat with frills, and a headband with beads woven into it. The headband was given to him by his family's tribal leaders, along with other prized tokens, during a ceremony on the occasion of his return from Iraq years ago. He was one of the most celebrated Native Americans to fight in that war, with stories in the local paper, so many that he eventually began to ignore them.

His face was smooth, without whiskers. He had red cheeks and prominent cheekbones that when he smiled, crinkled into deep lines from the corners of his brown eyes.

Zeke was high, on good weed that he grew himself in New Mexico. When he got drowsy, around when the sun was going down, he would pull over somewhere and lay out a sleeping bag. At the moment, although he wasn't thinking about it, Zeke was about 775 miles southwest of the Yellowstone calderas, as he angled his motorcycle toward the Pacific sunset.

He liked the desert for countless reasons, one of which was that there were no wildfires in the summer or fall. Nothing burnable out there, but the Joshua Tree National Monument west of there had been partly scorched, and you couldn't count on what the future would bring. It wasn't unusual to see the wood smoke on the horizon, a broad, jaundiced-yellow smudge in the sky, from the multiple fires in California.

Nobody was out in the desert's flat pan as he raced along. It was a kind of zero country, given Nevada's and most of the other states' tendencies to put sprawl wherever they could. They had failed to scar this landscape. Its silence was unbroken, between Vegas, where he started, after a hike in the red rocks west of the Strip, and his destination, Lone Pine, California.

He'd encountered plenty of cars on the highway, people pursuing money and excitement, lost in their dreams, or fleeing debts, gangsters, jilted wives and husbands, or the law, or simply pinning the accelerator to the floor and trying to forget what just happened in Vegas.

He'd fought again with his wife Amitola Sanchez, back in New Mexico. It was about his drinking, flirting, and general roguish behavior. He hadn't learned drinking and flirting in the Army, which had nonetheless refined his techniques.

When he'd left the Army and returned to New Mexico, he'd felt purposeless and antsy. He and Amitola went back and forth between loving embraces, mutual armistices, and dramatic breakups, for years. They'd been married in 2003, and he did his two combat tours from 2004 until 2006. Baghdad, Fallujah, and Mosul. The tours were perilous and eventful; they paid for a few years of college.

By the calendar, this was ages ago–19 years. He was 46 now. But in his mind, the time between then and now had whizzed by. It was one of life's miracles that he and Amitola were still, for the most part, together. She was a beautiful Native American woman of Navajo heritage, with jet black hair almost to her waist, dark eyes, and a well-preserved, ample figure.

When they didn't get along, he would agree to be kicked out, then he'd ride his Harley on the long western routes, reconnecting with his son Shilah, the Ancient Ones, and his spirit animal, which was a red-tailed hawk.

He counted on the fact that he and Amitola would reconcile, as if it was their eternal duty. They also had a daughter, Tiva, otherwise known as Cypress, a name she had given herself, moving Tiva to the middle. His son was in the Navy; Zeke had planned to go to San Diego to see him, after Lone Pine and other stops that would be cooked up on inspiration along the way.

Zeke received a good Army pension. He'd been working lately for a company that grew legal pot in greenhouses in New Mexico. He thought about all these things as he sped along at 70 m.p.h.: the dead, lunar desert of Iraq, with no beauty to compare with the Mojave; Amitola standing in the front yard of their ranch house, pushing the long hair out of her eyes, hair with soft threads of gray that were like what you'd find decorating a horse's mane, his own eyes misting up as she grew smaller in the bike's side mirror.

Just ahead, he spotted the isolated salt box with its two lonely gas pumps. A lost, blanched-white, but reassuring building, planted alone in the middle of the desert, shimmering in a distant heat mirage.

He decided to pull over at this outpost, get gas, food.

He pulled off the highway and parked the Harley on the cracked concrete in front of the one-story, white stucco building. A flaking red-metal sign read "Skip's

Frontier Supplies, Liquor Sold."

The pearl-drop shaped, cream white gas pumps were circa 1960s, preserved as if for the kitsch-loving tourists that flocked to those parts.

Zeke walked out of the dazzling sunlight through a screen door, carefully closing it behind him. Half the interior space was taken up with convenience-food shelves and a cashier's counter; the other half was a wooden floor with tables and chairs arrayed in front of a TV screen, blaring cable news, the box leaning from a high corner of the ceiling.

Zeke noticed a shotgun propped up on the floor, against the cashier's counter. He smiled: gas pumps, dusty shelves, and shotguns. Some things never changed in the Old West, 2025 or not.

A man in tight black pants, cowboy boots, and with thin, scraggly white hair sat at one of the tables, smoking a cigarette and blowing the smoke toward an open screen. "Need gas and sundries?" he said, stubbing out the butt in an ash tray. "If you need gas it's cash only."

"Only sundries. A couple of bottles of cold water, please. Got any sandwiches, my friend?"

"Roast beef or pastrami, on white or rye."

"I'll take the pastrami on rye, mustard not mayo. Boy, am I starved." Zeke looked for a place to sit down, experiencing a brief vertigo. Between the pot, the heat, the long trip, and the resultant unavoidable dehydration, he felt ever-so-slightly tipsy. It would pass with food.

"Coming right up friend. You'll find the water in the

refrigerator in back." The guy seemed genial, but with an old-coot toughness lying just beneath the surface. You'd have to form calluses, Zeke thought, given the types that would show up at this place at all hours.

The man stood up unsteadily. He was unshaven, wore a featureless white T-shirt, and had forearms covered in Navy tattoos. He shuffled over to behind the counter, then he removed a loaf of rye bread, cracked open plastic cases of condiments and sliced red meats, and began to roughly slap together Zeke's deli sandwich.

Zeke sensed a stab of empathy; clearly, a woman who used to help run this place was missing. Some sadness or regret was betrayed by the sluggish unwillingness of the man's movements, and the slapdash way he put the otherwise thick sandwich together.

The TV by the ceiling showed a female reporter doing stand-up at the entrance to Yellowstone National Park.

"As geysers erupt, land deforms, ponds boil over, and animals flee, scientists from the USGS and local universities continue to monitor the magma levels rising within the three calderas of Yellowstone," she said, staring gravely into the camera under the klieg lights.

"They still obsessing over that?" Zeke said.

"I suppose so. It's all they'll cover these days," Skip said. "I guess I could switch stations."

"Yellowstone's always making noise," Zeke said, settling down in a chair. He crossed his legs and cowboy boots. "That's what Yellowstone does, makes lots of steam and little earthquakes. When the big one comes, we'll know it. We won't need to tune into CNN or Fox. How long have you been in this place, by the way?"

The man gazed up to the ceiling, pondering the past. "In total? I've worked here off and on since 1960. Edna, my wife, she passed two years ago. We ran it together. Plumb near 65 years."

"No kidding."

"Yeah, I like it. Time stands still, you might say. We tried different places, but we always came back. It looks deserted now, a little bleak, but I get a lot of business from the folks traveling back and forth from L.A. and Las Vegas."

"Let me guess, they have more money to spend on the way *to* Vegas than coming back."

The man paused, as if wondering if Zeke was pulling his leg or giving him grief, then he chuckled in a way that was more of a grunt. "Suppose so. Can't spend much here, though. I thought of putting in some slots."

He put the finishing touches on Zeke's sandwich, then he looked up at the TV. "I've heard enough about Yellowstone and that damn volcano," he said. As Zeke stood up to go fetch his plate, relieving Skip of waiter duties, the older man reached under the counter and clicked the TV off.

CHAPTER 2: KIATSU

Small, nimble Kiatsu believed in heeding warnings. She was risk averse in all matters. She was aware of this attribute, and she realized it made her reserved in situations where others were more daring and gregarious. She was unapologetic for this personal trait.

She was quiet and fastidious in manner, and preferred to wear clothes of bright, primary colors, including dresses. This made her seem quite more Japanese than American, particularly in demeanor.

The safety of her children was paramount. She viewed the world as a sort of garden, which could also morph into a minefield that imperiled them. Kiatsu could be viewed as paranoid, but she saw her approach as falling into an evolutionary imperative, the sow protecting her cubs.

This cautious attitude extended to her own safety; if she was to die or be injured, no one would be around to protect Jake and Abby.

Brad Garner, her husband, was off to Chicago on a business trip; before that, it was Seattle, Los Angeles, Miami, and Houston. The peripatetic dad; the one who was never there.

Brad was solid, loyal, a great provider. She didn't complain excessively or bemoan his constant absences; that wouldn't fit her reticent and dignified nature. However, he knew he was gone a lot, and did things to make up for it, like come home with gifts and apologies. Those at times feeble-seeming gestures were not always accepted with the proper appreciation, Kiatsu thought.

Kiatsu knew of high-powered couples who *both* had jobs like this. They drove and off-loaded their kids to nannies, thus abrogating their principle responsibility to be parents. She would have none of that–strangers, mostly not properly vetted, taking over as parents. There was the matter of safety and hazard again.

She was in Pocatello, Idaho, relaxing near a lake. The kids were horsing around in a nearby forest that was part of a recreational park. Her father Takeji Saito, who lived nearby in a big Western-style house on 10 acres, had emigrated from Nagasaki, Japan in 1952, earned an electrical-engineering Master's degree from MIT, and was a partner in a semiconductor factory in Idaho. Kiatsu Saito kept his name; he was retired, wealthy, and at the very end of his life.

He never talked about surviving Nagasaki and the

atom bomb of August 1945, except to mutter occasional pithy, solemn references, or bitter imprecations, if a photo or an anniversary came up. The experience was buried inside him, like a serious illness one has overcome in their youth. He was silent and evasive about the topic, as if it represented a personal failure.

He'd been driven, single-minded, successful, and had all but left, except for maintaining some Japanese-cuisine traditions–he liked a saki now and then–his former country behind.

Kiatsu knew he'd been deeply affected by that horrific catastrophe. She thought of this as she slowly swung beneath a tree in a square of sunlight. She sometimes thought she was more obsessed with this dark event in history than he was, or that she had inherited an essential ingredient of its terror, a fragment of its trauma.

They had a few other things in common; people said she'd inherited his brains and driven nature. They had also both married westerners; her mother was named Mary Pence, and Takeji had met her in Massachusetts and soon married.

Kiatsu wrote a haiku when she was a child and the school had published it in the local paper. It was about a nuclear attack. Especially as a child, she would try to imagine being in a city that was leveled by such a blast, scalded by a light brighter than the sun, pummeled by a wind worse than the most powerful hurricane.

Takeji never told her the details; why didn't he have any physical scars from the massive explosion and fires?

So she was left to imagine what it was like, reenacting the scenario as a dark fantasy right up to adulthood.

The tragedy at Nagasaki occurred on August 9, 1945 at 11 am. The harbor city had 195,000 inhabitants; 40,000 were killed almost instantly, and another 30,000 died within a year, of acute burns, injuries, and radiation poisoning. A tragic irony surrounded this event; it was another topic she didn't feel free to take up with Takeji.

Nagasaki was the secondary target of the American pilots flying a B-29 with their payload of the "Fat Man" atomic bomb. The first target was nearby Kokura, Japan, but it was cloudy and the pilots couldn't center on their "aim point," so they moved to obliterate another city; a seemingly arbitrary tactic that Kiatsu couldn't dispel from her mind. Thousands and thousands of people meet a horrifying end, because some clouds didn't drift out of the way at the right moment.

Better to think positive thoughts. She kept swinging in the warm sunshine, enjoying the moment, wondering where her children might be, as their voices had minutes ago faded into the foliage. There were no particular dangers here, she thought; they'd had a nice visit with Papa Saito, as they called him.

Even though the sky was blue and cloudless, she heard thunder in the distance; loud, low rumbles like jets shattering the sound barrier. It was curious; she stopped her swinging. When her white sneakers touched the ground, she could feel its trembling and shaking.

Kiatsu ran for the woods, calling out for Jake and

Abby, unable to stifle the alarm in her voice.

CHAPTER 3: SLATER

"Get your butt outside," Max Slater muttered, hunched over a computer monitor where he'd been locked in place since 2 am. Nothing he was doing would change what Yellowstone was doing, he realized, so why stay chained to a cubicle?

"Situation desperate, not hopeless," he mumbled, attributing the grumpy mood to fatigue.

It was now 11 am. Yellowstone's landscape shook, rattled, and rolled beyond the window, in a prehistoric state of agitated, convulsive upheaval. Slater and two women, what remained of his staff at the Yellowstone Volcano Observatory (YVO), were located in a building not far from the West entrance to the Park in Montana.

This reminds me of the build-up dynamics at Mount St. Helens, he thought, despite the significant differences between a caldera and a stratovolcano...

Slater was born in Yakima, Washington, in 1981, one year too late for the epic Mount St. Helens eruption, and roughly one year too late to meet his father. His dad, Philip David Slater, was a civil engineer who was killed trying to flee a pyroclastic flow in his pickup truck.

Slater's childhood was close enough in proximity to hear the stories about his dad, look at the photos, dream about the giant volcano, and form an obsession with it, which eventually influenced him to become a volcanologist.

A pyroclastic flow has the same lethal effect on the people in its path, whether it originates from a stratovolcano, or a magmatic occurrence erupting from three huge calderas...

Slater sipped the lukewarm Styrofoam cup of Dunkin Donuts that took up space on his desk, then set it back down. The watery Joe he'd bought impulsively off the highway was the only thing keeping his eyes open at the moment.

The YVO, a cluster of academically nondescript rooms normally housing up to half a dozen researchers and their computers, was almost empty.

Hours ago, Slater, its "scientist-in-charge," had told everyone but Monica Lovato, another geologist, and the administrator Katy Morgan, to go home, "out of an abundance of caution." This translated, unspoken, to "while you still have time to save your asses."

The Yellowstone volcano had generated mountains of foreboding data for weeks, mostly in the vicinity of the third caldera near Yellowstone Lake.

Steam vent releases–otherwise known as hydrothermal explosions–blasted throughout the 3,500 square-mile park, not only from Excelsior Geyser or Old Faithful, but from new vents never before encountered, hurling huge rocks and spewing fountains of scalding water into the western blue sky.

At first, he thought, only two days ago, this specific activity constituted the eruption of record. The event is not magmatic; it's a hydrothermal explosion ranking with the one that occurred about 13,800 years ago in Mary Bay. These latest phenomena have evolved into the biggest Yellowstone geologic event in the Holocene epoch, or the last 12,000 years. What was happening now, however, had changed into a more interesting but potentially cataclysmic magmatic event...

Hundreds of earthquakes rattled the terrain, as they had for weeks; about 10,000 of them in the last six weeks. Several of them were in the 4.0 to 4.5 magnitude range (in any other month, most temblor clusters involved 1.0s and 2.0s).

All the GPS monitors they had distributed throughout Yellowstone had pointed to significantly accelerated ground deformations, which were bulges in the Park's surface caused by the building pressure of molten lava and volcanic gases.

The huge resurgent domes of Sour Creek and Mallard Lake, which had lain hidden for centuries under old lava deposits and thick ground cover, were exhibiting evidence of movement for the first time in the modern era, bulging by several centimeters during the last 14 days.

Each centimeter is only 0.4 of an inch, but imagine several centimeters of movement of the entirety of the earthen crust beneath your town, house, and feet.

Slater swiveled in his chair, toward where Monica stared defiantly and somewhat sullenly at her computer screen. He scratched his gray-streaked beard, which lacked the luster of her disheveled, shoulder-length brunette locks.

Every time he looked at her, he missed her more, which he reassured himself was caused by stress and fatigue, not a broken heart.

He never should have said he wasn't ready to marry her, he lamented, he never should have let it go to an argument, and tears.

"Why don't you go, Monica?" he said, earnestly injecting some affection into his voice. "Now. I'll close up here, be right behind you. It's not looking good."

They'd split up the night before, after a 10-month relationship, yet they were obviously still sharing the West Yellowstone ranch house. Slater wrote off last night's fight, fueled by too much red wine, to the crazy stress of their positions, the substantial hot seats they occupied; trying to convince the authorities and the public that Yellowstone wasn't poised for a cataclysmic, species-altering eruption.

He sensed an odd combination of professional and emotional tension. He thought they'd make up; he was sure of it. Breaking up had to be a fluke. He was going to miss her kinetic thought processes and shapely curves, and the thought of her absence made him morose and lonely.

That shocked him; he viewed himself as a stoic, a rock, someone who bounces back and finds another woman. Not this time...

He stood up and closed his laptop, shoving accessories and a cellphone into a small backpack.

"We'll all go together. Katy, shut down and get your things. Let's get the hell out of here."

Monica Lovato had a PhD in geology from USC in California, but she'd wanted to live in Montana and study Yellowstone. She'd been there two years, during which she fell for Slater, all but against her will. She'd planned to immerse herself in her career, Montana's considerable beauty, Yellowstone's rich scientific features–she specialized in caldera volcanology–but *not* get involved with men.

Slater hadn't initially fit into the driven young lady's plans, but she'd ended up going with the flow, when the chief YVO scientist avidly pursued her. A specie's choice of mate and biological future aren't always under its control, she'd reasoned, as if she was a sleek female member of a wolf pack or an elk herd.

She didn't answer Slater's call to flee. She thought it might be adventurous to be the one who "stuck it out," went down with the ship. He seemed to want to run away, a natural human reaction that nonetheless was not scientific or courageous.

She feared that it didn't take a geology PhD to

conclude that Yellowstone was poised for a major magmatic eruption, issuing from the Yellowstone calderas. That hadn't occurred in 640,000 years. She was firmly on that page. Slater wasn't, yet.

She was also pissed at his attitude last night. "I'm staying, for now," she finally answered, in a measured tone.

Monica had seen it from their truck the day before. New deformations in the land were visible to the naked eye, splitting open like pustular infections, oozing molten lava and sulfurous gases.

Monica also watched them on several webcams that were displayed on her computer screen. Some of the webcams had already been taken offline by hydrothermal explosions, and burnt up by lava flows.

The Park had since been emptied of its thousands of visitors, and the resulting traffic jam still crushed the exit routes in Wyoming, Montana, and Idaho.

Slater, Katy, and Monica, realistically, couldn't flee the region fast enough without a helicopter. Monica realized this, and Slater did too. They had a Jeep parked outside. It wasn't as if the USGS had a helicopter in waiting for them.

That was the privilege of the Yellowstone Club people who'd already hightailed it out of there, she thought distantly. Wealthy, entitled types, informed by data largely gathered by the YVO.

# #

During her tour by truck, Monica had found the Park eerily empty and primordial, with its steam releases, inextinguishable flames, ceaseless earthquakes and gaseous stenches. She had noted that Yellowstone Lake had tipped even farther south, pouring water into forests on its south shore, with landslides thundering down the basalt cliffs of its shorelines.

Slater went to the window to look at the sky, feel the sun on his face, where he watched an amazing flock of thousands of birds–loons, falcons, eagles, herons, ravens, cranes, countless songbirds–the latter the most resilient of species, fly in a southwesterly direction, away from Yellowstone.

This ominous scene of wildlife exodus was a disturbing omen, for sure; the bison, deer, elk, wolves, and bear had already disappeared. These weren't passive, impulsive species; they did things for reasons, following their instincts, which were deeply rooted in their DNA and more finally tuned compared with a human's.

The wildlife knew the shit was hitting the fan, in other words.

"We sit in front of our computers all day, digesting reams of data that never stops coming in, but the real answers lie elsewhere," he said to the window.

"What did you say?" Monica said, finally removing her thick-framed glasses and crushing a fist into a reddened eye, also strained by long hours and the unfolding drama outside, where the Park resembled a young planet in its birth throes.

Monica and Slater had fielded dozens of emails and calls from the press, which was encamped at the Park's western entrance, like a worried brigade of mourners, with about 200 shoulder-held video cameras. The YVO staff had also been badgered constantly by officials from the Homeland Security and the Defense departments.

Katy Morgan was handling the emails for now. All Slater could do was work with his partners at the USGS to reset the alert levels, which seemed oddly impotent, to their proper terms and colors–"WARNING," and "RED."

Among other things, the alerts warned commercial aviation away from the airspace above Wyoming and southwestern Montana.

Despite its lame-seeming, bureaucratic tone, especially with a volcanic emergency exploding around you, the "alerts" had a logical role to play. The Mount St. Helens eruption on the morning of May 18, 1980, which had inspired Slater's embrace of volcano study, had ejected a colossal cloud of superheated gases and particlized debris eight miles into the atmosphere, *in only 15 minutes.*

Even 35,000 feet wouldn't have been be a high enough altitude for aircraft to evade it. They had the same problem, but at a much larger scale, with Yellowstone.

Only two hours before at the YVO, Slater had gone back to his computer and set a new alert to WATCH, which meant "Volcano is exhibiting heightened or escalating unrest with increased potential of eruption, timeframe uncertain, OR, eruption is underway but poses limited hazards."

That was *conservative,* given what his data had told

him, and now that he'd upped the alert to WARNING, he thought the previous alert might have made him liable for damages, or at least criticism, in some manner. Fatigue, and paranoia; one begets the other.

The "aviation color code" was now RED, meaning "Volcano is exhibiting heightened or escalating unrest, with increasing potential for eruption, timeframe uncertain."

Geological dimensions were beyond the typical scale of human imagination; for a scientist, magma that rose to within five miles beneath the earth's crust was "close," even though the same distance *above* the crust almost reached Mt. Everest's summit.

640,000 years ago probably predated the first Homo Sapiens, Slater thought, while leaning against the window sill, but that date, which was when the last caldera-forming Yellowstone eruption took place, is barely a whisper in geological time.

Slater, trained in these prehistoric time scales, now had to wrap his head around fast-moving events that were happening in the next minute, hour, and day. He didn't think he could do it; that sort of scale wasn't in his DNA. Countless lives were at stake, however. Possibly, a civilization. He felt ill-equipped, inadequate, small.

He knew these "alert" settings were formalities, but that was his job, to show scientific constraint and deliberateness. He went back to his cubicle, snatched the cup of crappy coffee off his desk, chugged it, discarded the crushed cup into the wastebasket. Went back to the window.

Given the possibility of a caldera eruption, dwarfing the otherwise spectacular explosions and destructive consequences of Mount St. Helens (including huge ash clouds, pyroclastic flows, and lahars, truly a complete menu of volcanic disasters itself)–Slater thought it was a good idea that they should evacuate not only the Park, but a large peripheral zone of interstate residential areas, including the nearby resort town of Big Sky, Montana.

Defense officials wanted to know if the whole thing was going to go, cataclysmically. Slater wouldn't know decisively until perhaps 15 minutes beforehand, if he was lucky.

Now you see it, now you don't. More than a million souls have to be evacuated...or not. Wait, or not wait.

Still, the Pentagon lady hounded him, partially burying the present emotional distraction; Monica's general vibe of dismissal and hostility.

Then they felt the floor shake violently. Seconds later, all three turned their faces toward the window to stare at a black column of volcanic matter violently ejected and shafted upwards into the crystalline sky, followed by a second massive column of ejected debris, arching over Yellowstone Lake. It looked like a colossal hose jetting out magma, from Hell.

Katy, Monica, and Slater grabbed stuff off their desks and sprinted in a mad dash for the exit door, knowing in the back of their minds that escape efforts probably amounted to *too little, too late.*

CHAPTER 4: GARNER

Chicago O'Hare Airport, Terminal C, a cheek-by-jowl crowd of harried passengers rushing to flights.

Brad Garner was carried along this sea of humanity, a few people wearing masks to protect against potential pathogens, others sitting merely feet away from the human river, stuffing their faces with pizza and burgers, downing beers and cocktails in airport franchises at 11 in the morning.

Multiple airport flatscreens showed either CNN or Fox News, as if accommodating all political flavors. Everything was about Yellowstone, a Cat-5 hurricane and F5 tornado wrapped into one.

Brad found a place beside a window and called Kiatsu, reaching her after a few rings. Blinding sunlight bathed his face through the thick pane, displaying a clear blue day above the crowded tarmac.

In contrast, the flatscreens showed a colossal plume of volcanic debris exploding into the sky above Wyoming and Montana. The reporters and anchors had begun to flee the area, mostly in an utter panic.

"Go West," he urged his wife nervously, pressing the phone to an ear. "Just get Jake and Abby into the car and step on it. Get on that highway west." *Go, go, go!* he thought to himself. *Now!*

His wife and two kids were in Pocatello, Idaho, with a rented Nissan Versa. He heard Kiatsu's calm, vaguely faint voice on the other end.

"Okay, they're getting into the back seat now. I know where I'm going. We're waiting for Papa Saito."

"What the fuck!" he thought. Papa Saito is 94; he'll be a burden. Garner knew that she wouldn't listen to him, at least when it came to her father. He felt impotent and helpless, more than 1,000 miles away.

"I have an alternate route in mind," she added.

"Just go west, don't delay," he blurted into the phone, eyes darting around the terminal at the fretful groups clustered around the TV screens. "The prevailing winds go west to east; that's the way the ash will go." *I hope,* he thought, also realizing that the ash would be distributed in concentric circles for hundreds of miles around the epicenter. An eastward direction being merely a tendency.

"I'll be in touch," she said, with preternatural calm, a vigilant, but almost flat tone. He loved her for her beauty and level-headedness, but right now, he *wanted* her to be nervous; urgent and moving as fast as she could.

The flights from Chicago were all cancelled or delayed, even the ones heading east. They were waiting for federal guidance; aviation alerts were issued fast and furiously. The cable-casts showed volcanic vents opening at Yellowstone; giant twisting columns of roiling magmatic ash and debris, the dark color of loam. Then the video output broke apart and went static and dark.

The airport viewers, faces titled upward, arms crossed over their chests, were silent and awestruck. The apocalyptic scene, this time, didn't originate from Japan or a remote Indonesian island; it came from about 1,000 miles away northwest, in Wyoming and Montana.

The unease and fright in their expressions reminded Brad of 9/11, when the towers began to collapse, but the consequences of this event were far worse, even as both tragedies transcended international borders.

"Kiatsu, good luck, I love you–go fast! Send me a text as soon as you can!"

"I will. I love you, too." The call was cut off. He heard gasps and groans from the crowds bunched beneath the TVs. When he looked up, he saw live footage of someone–a broadcaster–aiming a camera at an oncoming pyroclastic flow. The camera view bounced around. The black, swirling avalanche of molten debris, dwarfing the trees, quickly overtook the speeding vehicle and its videographer.

No audio was broadcast–no breathless play-by-plays or screams–only silent footage, which shattered, frazzled, and disappeared. Garner wondered whether the person who held the camera knew they were going to die. How couldn't they? In the sour pit of his stomach, he thought of his own family stuck in a rental car on a crowded highway as these pyroclastic flows jetted in all directions from the supervolcano.

He quickly walked toward an Alamo rental-car facility; he had no other plan or logical course of action. Sitting on his hands was not an option. He walked to the desk and requested a vehicle that he would drive out west and drop off in San Francisco, a purely random choice. He planned to drive relentlessly, until he finally intersected with his family members.

He struck the counter in front of him sharply with a VISA card, and the young man rattled off a precooked spiel of options, such as extra collision insurance and a bigger car, until Garner finally interrupted him: "No extras, I just want to rent the damn thing, and I want a decent vehicle with a full tank of gas."

"Of course, sir," the young man said blandly, as if it was any old day at O'Hare, which for him apparently, it was. "Would a RAV4 do for today? The SUVs are on special this week."

"Yes, it will."

"Okay. You can proceed through that door, and show the paperwork to the Alamo staff waiting there. They'll give you the keys."

In less than half an hour, he was on the outskirts of Chicago, driving west on the main highway. A sullen rain drummed the windshield, through which he had a blurry view of closely knit red lights. The dark highway cast a yellowed gleam.

Next to him, on the passenger seat, was the cellphone and a medium-sized backpack that he used for luggage. He kept nervously shooting glances at the phone, for its blinking signal telling him that Kiatsu had sent him text messages, but nothing came.

The screechy windshield wipers mocked and irritated him; he twirled the knob on the console but found nothing, neither music he liked, providing a necessary distraction, nor commentary that wasn't shallow or insipid.

He kept driving, driving, into the wet, mournful midwestern night.

CHAPTER 5: ZEKE

Zeke Sanchez watched the dark blue squad cars pull off the highway into Skip's Frontier Supplies. He was all but certain they wouldn't pursue him, but his paranoia sensors, which he often relied on for survival, had sent him clear warnings. He couldn't be so sure that the peyote he carried didn't make him legally liable on the federal books.

He'd also made a fairly substantial sale on the outskirts of Vegas. He still carried the cash in his satchel.

It was better to vacate the region, and he quickly altered his plans and headed north.

He did not, at first, think about the erupting volcano at Yellowstone. He had a friend who once camped in Hawaii within a mile of an erupting volcano; he didn't want to move and ruin his vacation. Zeke was more preoccupied with connecting with his daughter Cypress, and he figured he'd "play it by ear" when it came to Yellowstone's calamitous events.

Zeke was a thrill-seeker by nature. But also cautious. *Keep your nose to the wind, and always stay one step ahead of the shit,* he thought, feeling more comfort and ease well up as he left the Nevada red rocks in his sideview mirror.

Cypress Tiva Sanchez, whose Indian middle name meant "dancer" in Hopi, was a nurse in a hospital in Twin Falls, Idaho. Twenty-one years before, Amitola and Zeke had almost lost Tiva, when she emerged from Amitola's womb with the umbilical cord wrapped twice around her neck. She was blue as ice and not breathing, but two doctors removed the cord, which was like a predatory snake she'd been born with, then they revived her from the great beyond with chest compressions and an oxygen mask.

She spent her first week of life outside the womb in an ICU.

Zeke was in Iraq at the time. He thought of that tumultuous period as he flew along northeast on his bike, with plenty of gas in the tank. Instead of seeing a robust, glorious newborn on the iPad they used to connect with home from Baghdad, he'd watched a beet-red, critically ill infant inside of a clear, oxygen-saturated enclosure fight for her breaths, her little chest rapidly moving up and down like a frightened bird's. It broke his heart; his eyes misted over as he drove along the hardscrabble, arid terrain towards Idaho.

He recalled those images whenever he got testy with Tiva; as when she rebelled that time in high school by drinking vodka with her friends and wrecking his car, or when she showed him disrespect by refusing to forgive his sins, or return his love and affection.

Once she began nursing school, then working in the hospital, she grew up and matured quickly, however.

Nothing he could say from Iraq, when Tiva was born, would console Amitola, but they both found their way out of that special hell, a place where you could do nothing but pray, which he did in spades.

His own religion was a unique one he'd invented on his own, made up of a love of the natural world, his trips on peyote, and prayers to the Ancient Ones. He'd always hated neckties, and found most conventional Sunday sermons clumsy, vapid, and tedious.

He thought he'd surprise Tiva. They hardly ever spoke, and though he owned a cellphone, he considered them an obtrusive annoyance. Besides, if he texted or called Tiva, he thought she would make up an excuse to become unavailable.

She was always either working or protesting something, which sometimes made her appear vainglorious.

She was petite, attractive, covered in colorful jewelry, and she dressed in a glittery fashion that made her seem mostly Latina. Though she had a strong spiritual connection with Zeke, they shared a kind of life force or *chi*, she considered him a self-indulgent rogue.

She knew about his sporadic womanizing. He wasn't going to live that down in her presence. So he wouldn't announce his visit. He headed north into a burnished blue horizon, against a dark line of hills and a spacious desert that appeared recently evacuated. The sky was not yet shrouded by a disaster that he'd shrug off for now, like that friend of his who ignored Kilauea's lava.

Life was fleeting, he thought, the dry wind in his hair, the dregs of the off-kilter mixture of weed and coffee still limning his mind. The heat off the road baked his forehead; the sun was unrelenting, his sunglasses casting the desert in a greenish, radiant glare.

He'd seen plenty of 19 to 20-year-olds die in Iraq. He decided he wasn't going to turn around, no matter what was happening with the supervolcano, until he connected with Tiva and determined that she was doing alright, and wasn't in danger. It was an imprecation from the blood, an instinct he would allow to play out.

He was going to bless each day, each hour, based on their own merits; it was better to be Zen, then to fear the consequences of his impulsive decisions.

He rode all day, until his backside and lower back were sore, remnants from an old war wound. It was caused by an improvised explosive device which threw him violently from a vehicle. He treated the wound with pot, yoga, and desert walking. The painkiller meds he'd gotten from a doctor once, which caused a daily, creepy dependence drifting over him against his will, were discarded long ago.

He noticed that the traffic thickened as the vehicles traveled south from Idaho and Wyoming. He knew they were fleeing the Yellowstone event. He thought he should call Tiva after all. He pulled the motorcycle off the road and parked. Got out, stretched.

He drank water from a canteen. "Shoot," he muttered to himself, smelling the fumes already from the slow-moving pickups, SUVs, and semis creeping along on the other side of the interstate.

"I need another path to follow." He decided not to dig out the cellphone buried in his belongings, that there'd be no service out here in the boonies anyways.

He would take a detour west on a smaller road, then head to Twin Falls, Idaho by a more circuitous route, which foretold clearer sailing, with all the panicked tourists and residents using the main interstates.

He swung his leg back over the seat of the Harley and started it up, the engine emitting its own oily smell but still performing well in the heat. He'd seen no other signs of the squad cars from outside Vegas. He felt free, a liberating mood that often carried him away, when he'd put some space between himself and other humans.

He parked the bike in some flat sandy gravel much farther off the road, made up a bedroll on a place that appeared, for the moment, to be free of scorpions and red ants, then face-planted. He slept deeply for an indeterminate time. It may have only been an hour; the light was still flat when he awoke, the sun blazing in his face.

He felt a pang of guilt for not calling Tiva yet, or his

son Shilah. He noticed a broadening, dark-brown storm front on the horizon.

Shilah had also rebelled against his given first name. He went by Teddy–Teddy Sanchez–because during a history course in school, he'd become enamored with the towering, driven, and impulsive figure of Teddy Roosevelt.

His daughter liked the name of Cypress, keeping Tiva as her middle name. Zeke didn't have any problem with these creative revisions; they were all part of carving out an identity for yourself.

He thought of all these things as he rolled up his bedding, strapped it to the back of his bike, and placed a call to Tiva, leaving a message: *This is you know who, your padre. I'm flabbergasted that you're not available to hear my voice in real-time, but just wanted to let you know I'm coming honey! Stay put, we're going south together...*

Zeke was an avid fiction reader, when he took the time. Watching the cellphone screen power down, he laughed to himself about the writer Kazuo Ishiguro calling cellphones in one of his novels, "oblongs."

The sky had become gauzy with dusk, and the tropospheric particles blanketing the horizon looked more like a terrible smog than a growing stain. He was losing time; he gunned the bike onto the county road, soon hitting top speed. He crossed the border into Idaho.

The only cars he saw were all going south at twice the speed limit. Then, before the sun came down over the stark scene, he saw two Chinook troop transporters, led by a third aircraft, an Apache, flying north along the desert floor, casting dark, darting shadows on the sandy ground. It reminded him of Iraq. He was filled with a foreboding sense of dread.

He spat off to the side, as though he could expel the dread down onto the baking black pavement, with its gasoline slicks and gritty road dust.

As he topped a hill, the lights of a town at the bottom of a long descent appeared. He figured he was 20 miles outside of Twin Falls, Idaho, where Tiva was within 270 miles of Yellowstone. *Maybe she's already left,* he thought.

He had to get to her, now urgent, desperate, ridden with a father's protective guilt. The Harley's engine whined as the bike hit 80 mph, the wind punching his face with its whiff of sulfur, darkness sifting down over a roiling, jet-black horizon.

CHAPTER 6: KIATSU

Kiatsu ran hard past the back of the house, where Papa Saito stood on the back porch, steadying himself with a cane. "It's a disturbance at Yellowstone," he said mildly, as if, at his age, he couldn't be bothered by it. "An eruption. I heard it on the radio."

He only listened to the radio, an artifact from his distant childhood. Understatement had arrived in his brain, Kiatsu thought, as a byproduct of the advanced aging process.

"I must get the kids," she cried out, still on the move along a grassy lawn that Saito kept trim and dark green. "Get yourself into the car."

"I'm not going. What forever for?" she heard him mutter.

She pivoted around. "We have to leave this region,

now!" *You idiot!* she thought, stifling the outburst.

The rumbling in the ground came in waves. It caused her to stumble as she ran downhill towards the park where her children had gone. She wasn't good anymore at sprinting, she thought idly. We let ourselves atrophy, then when we truly have to run, we can't.

She found Jake and Abby wandering out of the fringes of the woods.

"Get into the car, quickly! Don't hesitate, don't ask questions."

"But what's wrong? What are we running from?" Abby cried out. *You're acting as dim as Papa Saito,* Kiatsu thought.

"A volcano, an eruption. We can't stay here."

An eruption, Abby repeated, as if it was a mysterious and vaguely nauseating skin condition, which didn't concern her.

Her mother steered the two children toward the parked Nissan. She'd only snatched a canvas bag containing three water bottles and a little snack food. *No time* repeated in her mind like a sinister bird's cry.

They found the 94 y.o. man standing beside the parked car.

"Go," he said, waving his hand, as if at a fly. "I can ride it out here." Kiatsu didn't have time to argue. She thought he conveyed the typical samurai's stoicism and discipline. The admiral who goes down with the crippled carrier at the Battle of Midway.

"Okay," she agreed, still torn about the decision. "You have lots of food in the fridge. You have running water."

She felt a twinge of intense guilt, a tugging against the preservation of her own children and herself.

"Bye, Papa" she said, standing next to the open driver's door. "I love you." Papa Saito saluted her, with a wry smile on his face. He peered into the car, and waved vigorously at the children, a mischievous grin on his face.

"Why isn't Papa Saito coming?" Abby trilled, in an irritating and predictable way, Kiatsu thought, as she started the ignition. They shot out of the driveway, the tires even leaving a little patch of hot rubber on her father's pavement. The image of her father was somewhat obscured in the rearview mirror by road dust. He seemed solemn, and accepting.

"Because this is his house, and he'll be alright," she said over her shoulder. She'd grabbed too few provisions, but at least she didn't feel like she'd left her dad too little to survive on. They had a bag of apples and a box of peanut butter crackers, stashed in the back seat. They had three-quarters of a tank of gas. Simple facts and objects grew disproportionately important in her mind; cash reserves in her wallet, the gas, finding open markets; their physical safety.

They didn't have a pistol in the car, nor did Brad, her husband, believe in keeping a registered handgun in the house. In her agile, skeptical mind, always leaping one step ahead, she knew that in a stricken land, some humans can also become the problem. The principal danger.

Tears came into her eyes, driving through a still bustling, populated neighborhood, when she realized she'd consigned her elderly father to death by natural disaster–or perhaps not. She could never have allocated enough energy on the road to also keep him alive.

Sad rumination had to come later, or not at all; she urged herself to remain vigilant, on task.

Go west, Brad had said. She floored it through town, to the entrance ramp for the interstate, and to her frustration the traffic slowed on the choked highway. News was out. Everyone had felt the tremors; everyone knew Yellowstone had "gone off." If this route slowed more than it had now, she would go off the highway, use a more local road, hoping that fewer people could "think on their feet" and dare improvise an alternative.

The last thing she was going to do was trap them in the vice grip of a traffic jam, to the point–worse-case scenario, she thought–where they had to abandon the car, and join aimless wandering hordes on the side of the highway.

She would not accept that high-risk option.

These thoughts crowded her mind as they drove southwest along the Snake River, then the traffic abruptly stopped. They hadn't gone 15 miles, when the traffic slowed to 10 and 5 miles per hour. Her window was down; she heard a commotion ahead. She saw a man, with short black hair and a nondescript T-shirt, exit a vehicle in front from the passenger side, and run down the breakdown lane. From the back of his pants, he pulled out a handgun.

She put her hand to her mouth fretfully. They heard two loud noises, like someone hitting steel with an axe. Gunshots. Her hands were slick on the steering wheel; Abby was drilling her with questions that she was for now blocking out.

About 40 yards ahead, she saw a dirt road that followed the river, intersecting the highway through what looked like a cattle fence. She decided to take it. With one glance in the rearview, she accelerated into the breakdown lane.

The small town they'd just passed was called American Falls.

CHAPTER 7: SLATER

Slater exited the YVO building with a sinking sense of fatalism. This was a magmatic eruption in the Yellowstone Caldera; a massive, churning plume of heated, pulverized debris already rose 15 miles into the sky, blocking out the sun. The volume of ash and rock fragments that the supervolcano vomited into the sky would ultimately be measured in hundreds of cubic kilometers, he thought. It would alter weather patterns worldwide.

Monica and Katy sprinted after him over the heaving, cracked concrete, buffeted by waves of rapidly heated, sulfurous wind. They reached the Jeep, Monica in the front, Katy in the back, doors slamming; Slater fumbling with the keys, starting the engine, wrenching the vehicle into its lower gears with a painful grind.

They sped out of the empty parking lot, heading for the West Yellowstone exit and Interstate 191.

Sensing the nervous sweat trickling down past his ribcage, Slater thought they might not last the hour, but he kept his mouth shut. *The minimum temperature inside a pyroclastic flow is enough to broil a pot roast.* If they couldn't outrun these flows in the Jeep, they'd be incinerated, as if by a nuclear blast.

He wallowed in pointless guilt. He was responsible for two more lives, and he'd delayed their exit. He'd shared the responsibility for hundreds of thousands of lives in the Rocky Mountain West region, and he should have sent a blizzard of explicit warnings 24 hours ago.

Typical bureaucrat, crushed by the inertia of policy directives and procedures.

All three of them had places in and around West Yellowstone, the current epicenter of attention for perhaps every geologist, geophysicist, and major news outlet in the world, yet it was home to less than 1,000 inhabitants. But West Yellowstone was poised to be wiped off the map at any moment by pyroclastic flows from the eruption, and/or buried in up to two meters (80 inches) of toxic ash.

They didn't have time to stop at any of their homes or apartments, for practical or sentimental reasons. Neither of them owned a dog or a cat, which was just plain lucky.

"Where are we going?" Katy yelled from the back seat. Slater felt bad for her, the 22 y.o. who seemed considerably younger than he or Monica, a recent academic acquisition by the USGS who could have worked anywhere in the country.

She wasn't married, and didn't have a live-in boyfriend, as far as he knew, so she wasn't leaving lovers or dependents behind. He continued to doubt their chances, an attitude which caused him more than a brief self-loathing. Expunging that negativity from his mind, he pressed on the accelerator, glancing quickly at the fuel gauge. Half full.

"All I'm doing is putting as many miles between us and Yellowstone as possible. That's *all* I can do, at the moment."

Then he contemplated the nature of pyroclastic flows, an awful conglomeration of molten rock, and superheated gases and particles, which could reach 700 degrees F. and travel up to 40 mph. But their movements and dynamics were influenced by gravity; they rocketed down the steep slopes of volcanoes, and followed downhill contours like valleys.

This was a caldera-scale, subterranean explosion, but it might not produce pyro flows that could go more than a few miles. He prayed he was right.

The rearview mirror showed several exploding vents, frenzied columns of superheated debris that added more volume to the turbulent eruption clouds that seethed over the horizon.

"It's too late for airports or helicopters…or is it?" he said to Katy, as if to answer an unspoken question.

He had a friend, Jimmy Halstrom, a helicopter pilot

who did some fly-over work for the agencies in the Rocky Mountain West. They called him Greenhorn, because he originated from one of the cities back east.

He was worth a try–Slater had no other options. Now the Jeep negotiated a chaotic main drag in West Yellowstone, cars and trucks cutting each other off and pedestrians scattering like terrified, wingless birds.

He stared myopically out the mud-smeared windshield. The mid-day sky had darkened to a flaming red shade of dusk. Wafers of white ash fluttered down like cruddy snowflakes.

Pickups and passenger vehicles, haphazardly stuffed with coolers, guns, clothes, tarps, and bewildered dogs, clogged the main artery going through the town.

People darted around the sidewalks and streets with an aimless, abject terror in their eyes. *They better have a plan,* Slater thought. Pushing the panic button is easy; living through this, or meeting your maker with grace, is not.

The latter outcome was in the cards for West Yellowstone's remaining citizens, unless they had access to deep underground bunkers, with copious food, water, and oxygen supplies, which of course, the vast majority of people didn't.

"I need to make a call!" he said to Monica. "Can you drive?"

"Sure I can! Anything's better than sitting here passively, and watching the world come to an end."

On her cellphone, she had apps that connected with Yellowstone monitors, the ones that were still functioning, that is. Seismographs that existed and transmitted signals five minutes ago, generated seismograms that displayed on her screen.

Slater looked at Monica consulting her data; he wanted to know. He was a scientist first and foremost.

"What are the readings?"

"We've had at least 7.0 on the Moment magnitude scale." That was twice the typical energy release of the thousands of quakes that happened within the park during a typical year. It explained the damage they observed around town; collapsed roofs, piles of brick rubble, ropes of black smoke from several home or business fires, all of this evidence of damage dwarfed by the giant volcanic clouds that swelled above the tiny town.

Slater swapped places with Monica, as the Jeep stood running in front of the local post office. Down the block, several men stood in front of a car dealership brandishing shotguns and assault rifles. A couple of armed guys were patrolling the roof of a building that housed a pawn shop, a credit union, and a popular restaurant.

"What are they thinking? That they're going to fend off volcanic debris with rifles?" He jumped into the passenger seat, then Monica backed up and pulled the Jeep into a slow-moving caravan of desperate escapees.

"Do they think they're at the Alamo? In another 24 hours, there'll be nothing left to protect here."

Fortunately, he still had cellphone service. Another modern vestige they can't count on lasting, he thought, punching in the call to Greenhorn. The pilot didn't answer, so he left a brief message.

"We'll just keep on going to Big Sky," he said to the others, watching the bumper-to-bumper traffic crawl onto the 191-north entrance ramp. Beyond that, he didn't have much of a coherent plan, except to find shelter and dispel this dread that pervaded his soul.

"My Uncle Roy has a bunker," Katy declared from the back seat.

"Where does he live?" Slater asked.

"Outside of Bozeman, about 90 miles from here. If we just book it up 191, we might make it," she said eagerly, exuding a contagious confidence. Max was beginning to sulk, watching the unprecedented catastrophe unfold, their options for survival rapidly diminishing. He looked back at Katy.

"If we got there in time, would he take us in?"

He understood the type. Idaho and Montana survivalists and preppers, just waiting for the calamitous event they'd assiduously prepared for. They closely counted and tracked rounds, calories, ounces, and gallons, and seldom would accept just anyone into their silos and bunkers, unless you could substantially contribute to their provisions, and protection. Family and best friends only, *if* them.

They were looking pretty smart right now, he thought, but only the deepest buried, with the longest lasting provisions, were going to survive these conditions.

"Uncle Roy would take me, and anyone I'm with,

like you two."

"You sound sure of yourself."

"I spent summers during my childhood with my Uncle Roy and Aunt Bonnie. We went horseback riding, quail hunting, did camera safaris. We flushed a grizzly sow once in Wyoming. Riding down along the Bighorn River. Uncle Roy didn't move an inch as that sow bluff charged us. He'd already chambered a round, but never fired. The sow stood on her hind legs, then walked away. It was thrilling, unforgettable. We rode out of range of this bear domain, then we camped out by the river. We drank whiskey and told stories. He's a wonderful man, a straight shooter."

A message appeared on Slater's cellphone, which rested on the dashboard.

"It's Halstrom, the pilot," he said. "Greenhorn!" he yelled into the phone, now pressing it to his ear. "Where are you?"

"I'm in McAllister, about to take the bird up. How's it going? You hanging in there?"

"Barely, we're soon to be stuck in traffic. 191 north."

"I've got a narrow window, as in minutes, before I'm in a no-fly zone. I'm taking the bird west, hope to get to Spokane before nightfall. Isn't this a genu-ine shitstorm?"

"It is. We're all improvising. You got any passengers? Anybody going with you?" He could tell Halstrom was driving; he could hear the distraction in his voice, the rushing wind through a window.

"Jeter."

"Who?"

"My dog."

A pause; he could feel the deep vibration of an earthquake right through the tires and the chassis; that one was a 5.0. The shaking persisted. The air through the open window stank of sulfur.

"Can you take three more?"

"I think I could, but it will have to be fast."

"Wow!" Katy said from the back seat. Slater had the phone on speaker. He felt a wellspring of hope, an intense fondness and premature sense of debt owed to Greenhorn.

"There's a place I can probably set her down near Lakeview on Hebgen Lake. But I can't wait; you'll have to be there. No wrong turns. Ten, fifteen minutes max..."

"We'll be there in less than 15 minutes." Slater turned to Monica. "That's less than 10 miles from here. You turn west on..."

"287...I know where it is," she snapped.

"We'll be there!" he yelled into the phone again, with his eyes locked to the calamity unfolding outside the window. The swirling, gaseous clouds had already risen tens of thousands of feet into the atmosphere; they were beginning to rain a dense ash storm onto the darkened land.

"Go as fast as you can!" Greenhorn yelled over the traffic noise through his own vehicle window. "I'm flying a black MD 500 chopper."

"We'll be there!"

Off the entrance ramp to 191, the traffic began to creep. People were abruptly turning and accelerating into the breakdown lane. It was "every man for himself," Slater thought, and it hadn't taken longer than a few minutes into this catastrophe to reach that point.

"We don't have a choice!" Monica muttered, as if only to herself.

She glanced quickly over her right shoulder, and suddenly braked, before she made the aggressive move to swerve into the breakdown lane; a squad car shot past them with its blue lights on, chasing the "violators" who'd turned into the far-right lane and onto the gravel-shoulder of the highway.

As soon as the squad car sped past them, Monica gunned the Jeep into the breakdown lane, the thick tires churning up a cloud of dry dust as they accelerated.

"We have eight minutes!" Slater barked.

"Don't remind me!" Staring ahead, she saw the pursuing squad car parked perpendicular to the lane where she was driving, and a banged up Dodge pickup forced off the road. They both blocked her further passage.

No time to waste; no time to stop. She leaned forward on the accelerator.

Seven minutes to the rendezvous with the helicopter pilot.

CHAPTER 8: ZEKE

As he raced along on his motorcycle, the daydream, which relieved Zeke's mind from the dull or noxious monotone of reality, was about a woman. He didn't feel bad that she wasn't Amitola. He figured, his wife probably dreamt about other men in her fantasies, so he hadn't committed a felony.

This is what he was dreaming about, a recollection of true events, to be exact. Zeke had once hiked a trail in the Utah slot canyons that happened to be popular with young people looking for love. He knew that, simply because the trail had a lot of young single women and men who seemed to be on the prowl. He turned the corner on this trail, and lo and behold, there was a gorgeous Latina with a big, friendly smile and a low-cut T-shirt that flattered her ample figure.

The shirt spelled "Love" in sparkles across her breast. They struck up a wonderful conversation as they loped along the trail, then he asked her if she wanted to have a beer with him afterwards.

He smiled as he drove the bike and nurtured the memory. She had a margarita instead of a beer. She happened to be living out of a well-designed white travel van for two weeks. He made marvelous and prolonged love to her in the van, after they'd had the patio beverages.

Here he was in his 40s, giving to and receiving pleasure from a lovely woman all of 26 y.o., and those images, of her olive-toned skin with splashes of darker sun tan, of the massive eruption of libido she provoked in him, crowded his thoughts for several minutes as he flew along the desert country.

She confided afterwards that she had a boyfriend who served in the military, but that it was not *too* serious a relationship. Zeke felt bad about that, but not *too* intensely. Life is fleeting.

\#   #

He accelerated down the hill into the Idaho border town, then pulled over to call Tiva again. She still hadn't answered his phone call, or left a message with him.

A generic food-booze-and-sundries convenience store sat off the parking lot where he'd left his bike. He opened a screen door and stepped inside the building. A young lady looked up at him from the counter, where there was an old-fashioned cash register.

"I'm closing in ten minutes."

"Okay, just looking for some water and snacks. I won't be five."

"Are you getting the heck out of here too? Yellowstone's blown all to hell! They said thousands are dead already! I have to pack up my pickup–I'm going to Northern California."

Zeke thought her fears and casualty figures might be a tad overstated. He *hoped* they were.

"I've got a family member in Twin Falls. That's where I'm headed," he said, as he pulled a couple of cold plastic water bottles out of a utility fridge. "Do you have any water in cans or glass? More sustainable."

"No," she scoffed, as in, how can you think of consumer-product sustainability under these circumstances?

"How's the cellphone service here?" he asked. He brought the waters to the counter, adding salted cashews and beef jerky to the purchase.

"We have service. It's all good. Listen," she said in a calm voice. "I don't need any money for these things. Just take what you need."

"No worries. Everyone needs to be paid fairly for their goods and services."

"No, really. Just take what you need and go. That's what I'm going to do. I don't even know if this joint will be standing when I come back. *If* I do..."

"Many thanks, but take this. You'll need it on the road." He pulled a twenty out of his wallet, and inserted the folded bill into the breast pocket of her bluejeans coat.

"I hope you find your family. This is really scary," she said.

"Her name's Tiva, Cypress Tiva. I think she has a baby blue van with a luggage rack on top. You didn't happen to see one come through here, did you?"

"Nah, almost every other kind of vehicle, though. There're all coming from the east; almost no one's going *towards* Yellowstone and the east, but you."

"I have to make a call." He gave her a high five. "I'm Zeke."

"Darla."

"Take care of yourself, alright, Darla? And thanks for the drinks and grub." He tossed a couple of pre-cooked hot dogs and a high-cacao chocolate bar into the small brown paper bag.

"I have to get my dog Camille in the back, then I'm gone. You're my last customer."

He heard a door bang outside, gruff voices, footsteps.

"Happy trails, and best of luck to you," he said, heading for the screen door.

"Good luck!" she called out.

He left through the screen door he'd entered. Two young bearded men came towards the door, a pickup parked nearby.

"She's closed," Zeke said.

"The door's open," the first man quipped. He had a weird beard that was carefully manicured so that it was square shaped. It appeared antiquated and over-groomed, Zeke thought, like an old daguerreotype of a Civil War veteran.

They sauntered through the open door.

Zeke took out his "oblong" and noticed that he had a return call, from Tiva's number. He paused and listened to her message. It was nice to hear her voice. It came through loud, clear, and invested with purpose and clarity, literally like a voice from his past that demanded his attention. She was working the late shift at the Twin Falls hospital. So she hadn't escaped yet, he thought.

He left a message that he would meet her at the hospital, and that it was important that they evacuate together. Any rhetoric from him, with insistence and authority in the tone, would cause her to behave in an opposite way, he reminded himself. She was *that* stubborn with her dad.

\# \#

The two men walked up to the counter, after Darla had already told them she was closed.

"I need two packs of Camel's, honey," said the guy with the square beard. His companion turned and headed for the refrigerator in back.

"I told you, I was closed. Sorry. The register is locked." She was in a rush to get in the back and take Camille to her truck.

"You can take care of us, sweetheart," the guy said, then out of the side of his mouth, "Ricky, get a twelve-pack, will yah? And see if they have any vodka ice tea and kielbasa!"

"Please go," Darla said, standing at the end of the counter, away from the cash register.

"You don't mind if I go behind the counter and serve myself? Cigars and cigarettes? You got any matches?" He moved toward the area behind the counter. "Hey, you know, you're not bad, not at all. What's your name, sugar plum?"

"That your truck outside?" The voice came from where the screen door was half ajar, held open by Zeke. "I mean the one rolling down the hill right now."

"What?" the other guy, Ricky, said, striding out of the back of the store, a twelve-pack held under his arm like a football. He looked out the window. "Shit!" He ran past Zeke, who held the door for him.

"You gonna help him, fella?" Zeke said to the square beard. "Truck's half a block away by now."

Clutching two packs of cigarettes, the man strode over to the door and slipped past Zeke, who shut the door behind them. The man stopped, reached into an inside pocket of a denim coat, and removed a retractable knife.

Zeke heard Darla lock the door from the inside. He was still holding the small paper bag of food and water. He stepped back on the sand-covered concrete, as the man turned to face him. Zeke put on his sunglasses and removed one of the hotdogs and began to eat it, chewing the food slowly.

"I know what you are, a collector of fine, antique knives," he said. "I know one when I see one."

"You made that truck go down the hill, by taking it

out of gear, didn't you, hero?"

"I have a really cool knife back at my bike, a Jim Bridger one, I'll show it to you," Zeke said, still chewing slowly.

"The fuck you will," square-beard man said, and flipped his wrist, clicking open the retractable blade. His smile was more like lips pealing back on teeth, and he seemed to be pleased with his ability to punctuate a sentence by snapping open the knife.

Zeke finished the hotdog and wiped his hands on the plastic wrapper, tossing it into a nearby barrel. "Peace brother," he said, holding up two fingers and smiling.

In a flash, he poked them into the man's eyes, pinned the hand with the knife against the man's hip, kneed him below the ribs, and disarmed the knife by twisting the stranger's wrist extremely backward. The cocky miscreant howled. The blade clattered onto the cement. The man sunk to his knees in the parking lot, cursing angrily and covering his eyes with a hand.

"You should work on your crappy manners, stranger," Zeke said. He fetched the man's knife from the ground, as Darla rolled past them in a small Toyota pickup, with an eager looking dog padding around in the back. Zeke threw the knife into the desert as he walked back to his motorcycle, the man still moaning and cursing off to the side of the empty lot.

CHAPTER 9: KIATSU

With its busted concrete and collapsing gullies, the utility road along the Snake River had been left in disrepair, as if to dissuade drivers coming off the highway. She drove the Nissan hard, nonetheless, feeling the bumps jolt and shudder the wheel shocks and the chassis beneath the floor. She dreaded a flat; she hated the violent sounds, the dust rising from the floor to make a filmy cloud, permeated by the weak sunlight.

Kiatsu slowed down, to 25 mph, not wanting to disable their only escape vehicle. The road turned to dirt, riddled with washboard shaped ruts. The river flowed off to her righthand side and below, to the north. If it was only wildfires they were escaping, she thought, they could go down into the river, in a pinch. The shoreline of the river, where cottonwoods thrived, lay beneath the road, then the terrain flattened out, with, seen through her sunglasses, a radiant curtain of blue, cloudless sky.

She forced herself not to look behind them, to the east, where epic ash clouds quickly approached, a colossal black stain on the horizon. She had to think of her own morale, too. The thought of black, lethal clouds made her heart sink, and triggered the dread mushroom cloud that seemed to haunt her father and her own nightmares.

She thought of the shots they heard on the highway. It was already happening, desperate, angst-ridden people, acting violent. One has no solution or defense for that.

To the south, stalled cars idled or crept along the highway. She'd made the right move, to go onto this local "road to nowhere." Fortunately, its surface smoothed out, so she didn't have to worry about a flat or a broken strut. Still, they couldn't go faster than 30 mph, and they needed to be going 70 mph.

"Mom, I'm hungry!" Jake said.

"Eat the peanut butter. Eat the apples," she snapped. "You know, Jake. You have to be more of a man now. You have to help me, play an important role."

"I know," he mumbled, faintly disappointed at having to grow up.

They passed pedestrians on the road, forlorn solo walkers or groups of three or four men. She sped past them. She wasn't going to stop for anyone, except for a mom and her child, if obviously in need. They had little room for more, regardless. That was a no-brainer; she wouldn't stop for any aggressive-seeming males.

She sped up past a group of men slouching by the roadside. They threw a bottle at her car; it clanged off the rear bumper.

"What was that?" Abby cried, concerned.

"A bottle, you dope," Jake exclaimed, as though he'd already gown up faster, and meanwhile formed a calloused nature. "They chucked a lousy bottle at us!"

"Why?" she asked, in a pained voice.

"They want us to stop, because they want to use our car," Kiatsu answered bluntly. "It goes fast in a forward direction, also in reverse; it can take right and left turns. It has a tank of gas. It's priceless."

"Priceless," Abby repeated, as if trying out the word, the sound and meaning of it.

A reliable car on the open road is gold now, Kiatsu thought, glancing over at the interstate, still snarled with traffic. People were abandoning overheated cars and trucks; running out of gas. They were coming over to her road, on foot, her nameless rough road along the Snake River.

She thought again of her father in Pocatello. She didn't think of Brad. He was out of danger, probably worried sick about his family. She'd almost depersonalized her husband, because he wasn't there to be with and help them, and he had no way to aid their minute-by-minute survival, which crowded him and everything else extraneous out of her mind.

For the moment, bumping along in the car, she thought of Papa Saito's remarkable life, and whether or not he was dead, and whether he had found peace at the moment of death, and contemplated Nagasaki when it came.

Will the better angels emerge from these stranded people, she thought, or their worst natures?

She thought she saw, in the distance, a group of men building a barricade across their dirt road. She hoped it was only some kind of shelter, from the elements and the heat. But she planned for the worst.

"Duck down," she yelled back to her kids, accelerating the car drastically.

"Why?" Abby asked.

"Just do it!" she snapped. "Jake, duck down in the seat with your sister!"

"Do what Mom says, numbskull," Jake said.

"Oh shut up!"

"Here, hang onto a stuffed animal," Kiatsu heard him say.

It crossed her mind that the old rifle that Papa Saito had placed into their trunk would come in handy. The rifle was his old Japanese Army infantry weapon, a family keepsake.

She didn't want to use it. She didn't want this predicament to morph into *that* scenario.

Any exchange of gunfire would pose another threat to Jake and Abby. But sometimes, she imagined, it came down to us or them. You had to deploy firepower, a notion that could only make her laugh at herself; all 110 pounds and having fired this weapon once, with her father, into a pile of dirt.

Once they'd passed the men building their crude

barricade–thankfully, the Garners weren't harassed–she put a couple of more miles in, speeding along, then pulled the car to the side of the road. She turned off the ignition, stepped out of the driver's side, and popped open the trunk. She removed the unusually heavy rifle, which sat next to the steel tire-changing kit, and placed it on the front seat, where she made sure the rifle's safety was on.

She picked her cellphone off the passenger seat and put it on the dashboard, as it alerted her to new unread messages. They were from Brad, she thought. She didn't have time to listen to them, or read the texts. This time she looked at the rearview mirror; the horizon bloomed awful gray matter, massive mushroom clouds of a burgeoning substance like talcum powder.

She skidded back onto the road, the ground dipping off the righthand side into a shrub-choked riverbank. They were nearing the half-a-tank level, and she anticipated closed fueling stations or massive lines at the open ones. She would just have to get gas as soon as she could, and meanwhile put another 200 miles between them and the doomed, benighted region.

Inexplicably, she started crying, softly, out of exhaustion, but she hid the tears from the other two.

CHAPTER 10: MONICA

She yanked on the steering wheel and the Jeep tore through a rickety barbed wire fence and suddenly they were on hard, scrubby flat ground. She'd missed the squad car by about a foot. The officer, who she could see in the sideview mirror in the breakdown lane, scowled at her, with one hand on his holster, but he had his hands full with the pickup driver. His image quickly vanished in a cloud of road dust. She hit about 40 mph, banging through ruts, rocks, and sand, until finally she relaxed and let up on the accelerator.

Slater had been yelling "Slow down!" and other stuff she wasn't focusing on. They had to get to Hebgen Lake. Less than 6 minutes and the helicopter would be gone. She believed the pilot; he wasn't going to wait more than a minute. He, his machine, and his dog were literally toast if he didn't get into the sky and head west on schedule.

It should be obvious by now that the airspace over about a thousand miles of western states was a no-fly zone, she thought.

Monica sped along the rutted road, staring straight ahead, feeling the sweat on her hands, until she spotted an opening ahead in traffic. The drivers were cutting each other off; road-rage skirmishes erupted off to the side of the highway.

"No room for gallantry," she said, "or maybe all the gallant men are gone." She looked at Slater, "Nothing personal."

"No worries," he said. Slater thought Monica was still mad at him; maybe she hated him. Her emotions could be binary and extreme; loving, then turn on a dime, and act as if she despises him. It was personality type; she felt things strongly, she couldn't hide her emotions. He was a "high-functioning introvert," an old girlfriend had once called him, so he had trouble processing the strong-willed Monica, and the layers of her varied emotions.

He had trouble processing the behavior of the majority of females. It was probably too late for him and Monica together, even if they survived the next half an hour.

The Jeep lurched into a roadside gully, then back up the slope on its other side, hammering the underside of the vehicle with a stiff jolt, then in one fell swoop–"Hang on!" she cried–she cut off an overloaded

Toyota pickup as its irate driver leaned on the horn. They were back on the highway.

"Wow, that was cool, Mon," Katy yelled from the back.

"Great move there, baby!" Slater blurted out.

Four minutes left.

She kept going, swerving across three lanes to take the Hebgen Lake Rd. exit. For the first time, she thought they'd make the rendezvous with the helicopter pilot Halstrom. If she saw a speeding cop behind her, she wasn't going to stop, not for nothing.

Vehicles were parked all along the sides of the road to and alongside the large mountain lake. "This is no refuge or escape outlet," she muttered to herself. "They're all deluded."

"Or desperate," Katy said.

"You're telling me," Slater said.

Behind them, not 20 miles south of their position, West Yellowstone was engulfed and incinerated by a pyroclastic flow from Yellowstone, the equivalent of a tornado of ash, carrying an interior temperature of 700 degrees F. It traveled about 40 mph. It would kill hundreds of people in the town, instantly. No one could survive an encounter with it, and death was certain.

"There's Greenhorn!" Slater yelled, pointing through the soot-smeared windshield at a small, black helicopter making its way at a low elevation, over the shore of the lake. A crowd of people massed on the shoreline beneath the aircraft, pointing and waving their arms. None of them would be taken aboard, however desperate they were.

"They all want a lift out of here," Slater said. "Which is obviously impossible. Monica, go over by that pier. I have a flare!"

Monica steered into a driveway, through a parking lot, and slammed hard to a stop in front of a metallic pier that extended several yards from shore. The helicopter was still at least a half mile away. The ash fell heavily; it gathered in pale brown drifts.

"Those people," Katy said from the back seat, a hint of detached wisdom in her voice. "I don't blame them. They're terrified, like us. They're trying to protect their children and their loved ones."

Slater looked back at her but didn't say anything. A shadow fell over the lake, swirling with ash. He thought the helicopter could stay aloft in it, for a short time, although he'd never flown one.

"This is our last chance," he said. "The event is magmatic, catastrophic, and we're too close to the epicenter. Cars aren't protection; neither are buildings or homes or...lakes."

"This is obvious to me," Katy snapped, irritated. Slater stepped outside, near where they were parked beside the pier. He fired off a flare gun; its payload arced into the darkening sky, then flashed brightly, misting red as the lit-up vapor drifted down.

Hundreds of people on the shore stared at them. Slater didn't feel guilty, like Katy. *Guilt* was a cheap emotion to him, at the moment; he was merely acting to save a precise group of humans from almost certain annihilation. This man in the helicopter had already risked a lot for them, Slater thought. He could have been long gone by now.

"Grab your stuff, and let's get the hell out of here! Let's go, onto the pier!"

"I'm not going," Katy said, in a blunt way that signaled she wouldn't be swayed. "You two go without me."

"What do you mean?" Monica said. The helicopter, a fairly new McDonnell-Douglas MD 500, flew closer towards them. He'd seen the flare; he'd seen his targets.

"You heard me," Katy said. "I'm not going to get the VIP helicopter ride, while everyone else here, including kids, tries to survive on the ground. Or perishes."

"It's not a VIP ride; it's a last resort. At any rate, we don't have time to argue." Slater yanked his rucksack out of the back of the Jeep. It contained good but basic essentials, nothing fancy: medical kit, water bottle, Swiss Army knife–but it wasn't the best "go" bag he could have assembled. It didn't have food, emergency blanket, antibiotics, ammo, pistol.

Do what you can, with what you have...he thought.

"I'm staying," Katy repeated firmly.

Monica stared at her in the back seat, then seized her own small backpack.

"You're serious, aren't you? You're going to survive this intense ash fall right here, in the Jeep?"

The MD 500 accelerated toward the end of the pier, then slowed, hovered, the loud, metallic rotor blades churning up the purple water on the lake below. He held the hover position, just feet from the metal pier, as long as he could. The pilot waved at them all urgently, from the cockpit.

Slater ran with his bag to the end of the metal pier. Halstrom had to be highly skilled, Slater thought, to hover in position, to give the grounded people a fighting chance. At least two of them.

Halstrom leaned over and unlatched the door. "Step up using the landing skid," he screamed. The door hung open awkwardly; the turbines roared, the lake churned, the wind stiff and relentless.

Slater seized his bag and hucked it inside the chopper. He looked back once at Monica and Katy, who were still earnestly talking. Then he awkwardly hoisted himself up onto the landing skid; for a moment, it looked like he was going to pitch into the lake. His legs dangled and flailed towards the water, then he got his left leg up onto the skid.

Monica and Katy watched from the other end of the pier.

"Take the keys," Monica said, with a tone of resignation. "And get out of this place, north and west as fast as you can drive." Katy took the keys wordlessly, stuffing them into a coat pocket.

Monica grimaced, caught in a moment of indecision. "Come with us, Katy. This is foolhardy. We have room. We'll try to save more people, once we get clear."

"I can't," Katy said quietly. "Get over here!" Slater screamed from inside the helicopter, hands cupped over his mouth.

"Okay, I'm coming," Monica yelled back, then she kissed Katie hard on the forehead. "God speed, okay?"

"Yuh." Monica turned and jogged toward the waiting chopper. Katy hopped into the driver's seat of the running vehicle and backed the Jeep up. She planned to head west on the road alongside the lake.

Monica ran to the end of the pier. She didn't want to look back. She didn't want to make eye contact with Katy. A mob of people surged along the edge of the water nearby.

The pilot couldn't hold the hover position for a minute longer. Monica tossed her backpack to Slater, who held the door open for her. She stepped up onto the landing skid with her left leg, took Slater's outstretched hand, then pulled hard and rolled onto the floor inside. Slater closed and latched the door behind her.

Greenhorn pulled out of the hover position and into a rapid ascent, leaving the lake behind them. The mob surged onto the empty pier, pointing and waving. Monica pushed herself to her feet, then slumped back into one of the three passenger seats. She felt like a cheat, leaving others behind, the last survivor to get a seat on the lifeboat.

The dog lay placidly panting at the pilot's feet.

Monica could see Katy, the Jeep, and the crowd grow rapidly smaller. She kept watching, the guilt and remorse feeling like an anvil on her chest. They were colleagues and friends. They'd begun confiding in each other. She sensed that Katy was somehow right, deep in

Katy's heart and soul, staying on the ground was the right thing *for her*, even though it seemed suicidal.

Everyone had to follow their own conscience, she thought, until they forgot how.

Below, a young woman and a child climbed into the back of the Jeep, the passenger door closed, and the Jeep drove quickly away from the milling crowd.

A fog of drifting ash and rock fragments smothered the shoreline, as the aircraft rapidly gained elevation. It looked like a curtain being drawn; they could see mountain slopes as the pilot arced away from the lake. The people and the randomly parked vehicles and the few cars that still moved, like Katy's, vanished for good.

The MD 500 accelerated west through the ash, the headwinds battering the windows and body of the helicopter with a grit as fine as sand.

CHAPTER 11: GARNER

St. Louis, Kansas City, Topeka, he'd clicked them off, driving through the night. The cellphone lay beside him on the passenger seat. He'd asked Kiatsu for updates, but had received none. He understood the communication silence; she was busy driving for their lives, but he was nonetheless desperate for news. He wanted to nail down where they could meet, even as it seemed absurd and illogical, as they were more than a thousand miles apart. Brad in Kansas, she in Idaho.

He wanted to be reassured that they were safe.

He focused the energy and angst of his obsessions into the driving, the tension flowing through his foot to the accelerator. He wouldn't stop, except once for gas and the soggiest hamburger, from a roadside Burger King, he'd ever eaten. He'd never visited any of those

Kansas cities before, a trivial fact he idly noted when driving over a dark, gleaming highway in a light rain.

The radio was on part of the time; random pop music and classic rock, then news stations with hyperactive DJs and wire-services reporters talking about the supervolcano. He usually switched out of them, back to the music. He'd turn the radio off, and he'd veer off the highway onto random weigh stations occupied by faintly ominous tractor-trailer trucks parked in the shadows. He'd check his messaging app, and finding no new messages, he'd speed back on the highway, flooring it at 75 to 80 with renewed confidence, because not much of the traffic was going west.

Denver was next. It's surprising what vast swaths of the continent one could cover with a full tank of gas, he thought, staring bleary-eyed through the windshield at the rug of black road illuminated by the headlights. He booked it across the "fly-over" states; the cornfields, the farms, the exurbs, the strangely empty 21st century Great Plains, with its ghostly traces of absent buffalo herds, a lonesome image of wildlife dreamt up as he stared through the wet window at the weakly lit roadside.

He saw solitary homes on this road through Kansas, small towns with impossibly flat terrain and expansive acreage of empty fields, save for fences and the occasional storage silo or tractor, lying between buildings.

He thought of the Clutter family and Truman

Capote's *In Cold Blood*, a book Garner read in middle school that terrified him. The radio offered no solace and ineffectual distractions, so he turned it off and let his mind wander to the youthful road trips he'd taken across the American landscape.

He'd reached eastern Colorado, which had a fecund smell in the night air, with freshets of manure mixed in with the rich grassy odor. This part of the state was like Kansas and Nebraska; same landscape and traditional, conservative folk. The Front Range of Colorado was more outwardly changeable and flashy; outdoorsy citizens and oil and cannabis entrepreneurs with more money to spend.

He thought he should stop in Denver, call Kiatsu, get some sleep. A few hours. He thought of when he was in college in New York City, the thrilling 1990s version of the city, and he drove all night with another fellow for spring break in St. Pete, Florida. They parked on the beach, and he walked out on the sand and face-planted on a towel, deep REM sleep, and woke up drooling. On the same trip, they parked overnight on a campus in New Orleans, and were woken up at dawn by two red-necked campus cops, who roughed them up a bit.

The rain had stopped; the sun came up in a grainy light that misted over the Kansas horizon. He noticed the air was flecked lightly with ash, already. Spreading out from what happened 650 miles or so northwest of his location.

He approached a jarring roadblock on I-70, a harsh pool of bright, pulsating blue lights. His fatigued brain couldn't process it. He drained the dregs of cold coffee from a styrofoam cup, feeling a dread of fecklessness, that what he could do to rescue his family added up to zero.

He lowered his window; a burly cop with an orange vest leaned into him.

"What's your destination?"

"Denver. Then north."

"No one's going north. We're rerouting traffic to Denver, only if you're a resident. Otherwise, you go south, or turnaround. There's a pull-off on the median strip for that."

"What's happening up north?" He felt hemmed in, a low-level vibrating panic.

"What's happening? Military and rescue crews only, that's what's happening. And we're keeping an eye on a wildfire south of Denver. I recommend that you turn around, go back to Kansas, Iowa."

"I can't turn around, I'm looking for my family."

"You and everyone else. Alright, go ahead. We're holding up traffic. You still can't go north. Don't even try."

The ash had picked up, like a brisk snowstorm. The policeman walked away, adjusting a mask on his face. Garner could go through Denver, posing as a resident, he thought, then head west on I-70, if there were no roadblocks. Fat chance of that. He was a rat in a maze with only one direction to go, south, and his family members were still at least 700 miles away.

As he pulled away from the roadblock, the cellphone

came to life on the seat next to him, chirping and brightening in a way that made him think of Kiatsu; reassuring news and her soft, calm voice. He quickly snatched it off the seat, still negotiating the maze of the roadblock and its chaotically placed orange cones.

Men and women waved him on with lit-up batons. He thought of covering Colorado in two hours, then heading north through Utah.

It was only some automated warning; a dully worded message about local stay-at-home warnings. He was trapped, only a few miles out of Last Chance, Colorado.

CHAPTER 12: ZEKE

Zeke pulled into the Twin Falls, Idaho medical center parking lot. The ash fall had already darkened the sky into an unsettled gloom, just before sunset. He watched a store, several blocks away from the hospital, being looted through a broken storefront window.

The wayward teens that take advantage of emergencies, he thought. Every town and city had them, and they were all too ready to pounce when the opportunity presented itself.

Standing next to his motorcycle, he looked at his cellphone for messages, but it abruptly lost service. "Useless oblong, never comes through when you need it," he muttered to himself. Maybe the small town, more than 260 miles from the volcano's epicenter, had nevertheless been forced to power down.

He was able to retrieve Tiva's last stored message: "hi dad I can't leave now. working."

That didn't give him much to work with; he anticipated resistance from Tiva as he strode across the parking lot to the entrance, pulling a buff over his mouth and nose. The airborne debris was like crappy bits of insulation set loose by a demolished building. It gathered on his shoulders, which he annoyingly wiped off, before holding the door for a man pushing a blanketed woman in a wheelchair.

The weakly lit foyer inside had an elevator and a stairwell. He took the stairs; Tiva's station was on the second floor, the Emergency Room.

He felt bad about tracking ash into the hospital, but everyone who'd been outside for any length of time was now covered head to toe in a thin layer of it. And this ash fall isn't going to stop anytime soon, he thought. As long as Yellowstone erupts, and it had an inexhaustible store of magma to puke into the earth's atmosphere, the ash would continue to pile up and smother the surfaces of everything.

He thought he knew as much about volcanoes as any common layman. This could last weeks, months, a year, then he forcibly dispelled the foul rumination as he pushed through a pair of swinging doors, to face the dull sheen of fluorescence on scuffed linoleum.

He came upon a large open hallway, smelling faintly of disinfectant, with several people slumped in chairs along the sides waiting for doctors. The ER had a central desk with a receptionist seated in the middle of it. The place was busy, just short of frenetic. It *was* an ER, things could be crazier than they were, he thought.

The nurse behind the desk had an expressionless face, a competent but not cocky vibe.

He stepped forward, yanking down the already dusty buff.

"Tiva Sanchez? I'm her dad."

"You mean Cypress."

"Yeah."

She looked away, consulting a stack of papers on her desk. "She's due for a break"–then to a nurse who stood behind her–"Can you get Cypress for a moment, if she's not now with a patient."

Zeke glanced around the windowless, and what appeared hermetically sealed, environment. That had its advantages, in terms of providing temporary shelter from swirling and unbreathable ash, but it also kept everyone from monitoring how bad it was outside the hospital. Ignorance was bliss.

Zeke was aware he still smelled like weed. Standing in the ER amidst these hard-working healthcare workers made him feel vaguely miscreant. The waiting patients appeared enervated and apathetic, except for one worried mom, who sat next to a teenager in a soccer uniform. Sprained ankle, Zeke thought, and she brings her to the ER? In the old days, we'd stick it in the river, or go home to mommie and get an ice pack.

"Can I get anything for anyone? A drink?

Munchies?" He felt like he needed to pitch in, not knowing, but guessing, what Tiva had in store for him.

"That's okay, Mr. Sanchez," the desk receptionist said, parrying his offer and mildly upbraiding him.

Two men came rushing in with a prostrate victim on a gurney, all three of them covered in an obnoxious layer of ash, which made them look like coal miners. Tiva came walking briskly out of the back, gave the men directions, then smiled wearily at Zeke. He hugged his daughter, who wore blue scrubs with a loose white coat thrown over them.

She had a stethoscope dangling around her neck, and her black hair was tied back. She was her mother's daughter in almost all ways; short, compact, willful, and attractive.

"Good to see you dad." That made him feel all warm inside. "You smell like pot. Are you stoned?"

"Not anymore. I came all way from outside of Vegas. The volcano is nothing to fool around with, baby. You can't wait it out; you have to run. Let's leave now!" He realized, with the scent of pot and the road dust he carried, having recently passed out on the open desert, that he was an unlikely advocate for clarity and responsibility.

Not to mention his family baggage; Tiva tended to act like his heroism and honors from Iraq were interesting biographical facts, but not relevant to the things she cared about.

"I have to stay. We have patients. We can't just up and go. That would be unconscionable."

"Understood, but this town will be evacuated. The National Guard will bring buses and trucks." *If they can still run the engines, he thought.*

"When that happens, I'll evacuate with the patients. Thanks for thinking of me, dad," she said, the latter part with less conviction than would typically accompany those words.

He looked around the busy ward with a grimace of concern. "Listen, Tiva, honey."

"Cypress, but that's okay."

"The window of opportunity is closing. Soon, we won't be able to escape. The ash will be too deep; things grind to a halt. We can take your car and my motorcycle, if we leave now. We can also take other people, if you want. But we have to split, *vamonos.*"

"Sorry Zeke, no can do. I've got to go back to work. I've got a break in about half an hour. We can get coffee, if you're still here..."

"Have you looked out there?"

She was already walking back to the ER with a purposeful gait, and she ignored his question.

He took a deep breath and watched her, bewildered. She was a girl, a teen still finding herself and experimenting, the last time they'd spent some time together. Now she was a focused, faintly defiant young woman, with an important role and responsibilities.

She'd outgrown Zeke, with his footloose and nomadic tendencies. He thought of her decades ago, struggling for breath in an ICU while he looked on helpless in Iraq. He got a lump in his throat.

Okay Cypress Tiva, he said to himself, *now you've put me on the spot, and there's no way I'm going.*

He went back downstairs through the ash-tracked stairwell and opened the exit door halfway. The parking lot was dark and thickly obscured. Then all the town's lights went out. He heard shouts, a dispute, glass breaking, coming from the furry darkness down the street.

He saw shadows of fleeing, marauding people; vehicles with their headlights on moved slowly through the murk. He assumed more looting would commence. Felony crime had also gone up recently in America. Now the criminals saw another opportunity.

The hospital's generators growled to life; the facility's lights quickly came back on. He pulled up his face protection and strode across the parking lot to his motorcycle, making sure to secure the essentials from his saddlebag–including a hunting knife, the subcompact Beretta, a tactical flashlight of 3000 lumens. And of course, bags of weed and peyote.

He sensed chaos coming. He was used to it; this was a sixth sense he'd acquired in Iraq, one that often warned his company about ambushes. He was like a wolf who could sniff trouble in the air, even though his spirit animal was truly a red-tailed hawk.

So much in life was about situational awareness, and being prepared.

He fetched the hunting knife with the ivory-colored handle, and the sub-compact Beretta. He pocketed them both. The rest of the stuff went into a handy go-lite backpack.

He carried the handgun because he liked the feel of it in his hand, and because, after all, crime was way up in the U.S.

After recovering his things, he headed back to the ER to plead with Tiva. In vain, he thought. He wasn't sure she would have left, even if she worked in West Yellowstone. She was a gallant sea captain, going down with the ship.

He added cycling goggles above his buff. The ash fall was awful and almost blinded him; he knew this was just the beginning.

Twin Falls might be more than 260 miles from Yellowstone, but the volcano had come to the town.

It would eventually bury two thirds of the U.S. in dreadful ash piles; only inches would cause vital machines, factories, utilities, and aircraft to seize up and malfunction. Some cities would get 40 inches.

He heard more glass breaking in the parking lot; a guy was smashing his way into a car with a crowbar. The feral-looking 20-something was one of a gang of five, ransacking ash-covered cars for any valuables they could loot.

Zeke took his gun out, considered firing it into the air to disperse the vultures, then he didn't want to waste 9-millimeter ammo. Speaking of situational awareness, things were going to get worse than this, he thought, small town or no small town. It would be bedlam under the cover of impenetrable darkness.

He jogged back to the hospital entrance and up the stairs, thinking about the vulnerability of the medical facility's generators. They had air vents, and weren't impregnable to the fine, dense particles that filled the air. He always had to shovel snow away from the vents, when he took care of a generator in the New Mexico mountains once.

He heard loud, disorderly voices in the stairwell behind him. He went halfway through the swinging doors to the ER waiting room, when all the lights in the ward went out.

CHAPTER 13: KATY

The noise from the helicopter faded as the machine arced into the dark clouds, its red tail-rotor light vanishing into swirling brown particles. Katy felt a tug of regret, a kind of disagreeable, insatiable hunger, but she knew she had done the right thing.

She had two people in the back seat who depended on her.

Not that the helicopter is 100 percent safe to begin with, she thought... she still felt alright with two feet firmly on the ground, even as they nervously pumped the Jeep's accelerator and the brakes.

The woman in the back held a male toddler in her lap; she brushed the sweaty, dirty blond hair out of her face. She stared silently outside the window, quietly relieved, but she appeared overcome by a fearful awe.

"What're your names?" Katy barked hoarsely. She was overcome by emotion herself, the momentous nature of survival decisions made on the fly. "You and your child's?"

"Kendra," the woman said weakly. "His name is Christopher."

"Katy."

They fell into an awkward silence again, as Katy motored along Hebgen Lake Road. She vaguely knew the road traveled west for several miles (good), then it turned north to connect with another interstate (not so good). She wanted to put as much lateral distance between them and Yellowstone as possible, but sensed the odds were against them.

Katy felt a lonely abandonment, chiefly, a scar that had lingered since childhood. Busy academic lives can paper over a lot of what happens to you in life.

Once years ago, on a crowded beach north of Boston, Katy's mother had looked away for a moment to chat with a young lady, allowing 4 y.o. Katy to wander and lose herself in the throngs of oblivious tourists. Katy was lost for an hour, wandering aimlessly between towels, then standing in a light tidal spillage, her little feet sinking in the mud, taking turns bawling and scanning the hive of strangers in vain.

Her mother was more distraught, thinking her drowned, but somehow, Katy still recalled the core emotion of abject fear and abandonment. It would periodically return, nudged awake by external stimuli, an evocative event.

She brought forth the old pain, as the helicopter disappeared into the sky's murky gloom, even though she had initiated that rejection with her own actions.

Her conscience had overruled her childish baggage.

"Damn," she cried out, then noticed Kendra's look of consternation in the rearview mirror. She slammed on the brakes, backed the Jeep up into gravel and shrubs, then jerked the vehicle into the opposite direction, almost cutting off a sedan filled with people. One of them gave her the finger. Two pickups dragging campers had blocked the road ahead, their drivers somehow absent, having panicked, left the area, or succumbed in some other manner. The rutted, gravel roadside offered just enough room for the Jeep to turn around, speed up, and reach the intersection with U.S. Highway 191.

"Where're we going?" Kendra cried out, still cradling the little boy, wrapped in a zipped up hoodie.

"I'm getting back on the highway towards Big Sky. I know where to go there; everywhere else here is a dead end." *Leading to our probable deaths...* she thought.

"Won't the highway traffic be stopped? What will we do then?"

What do you want, the VIP escort? Katy bristled at Kendra's weepy dependency, the extra pressure she applied.

I'm the one who let the helicopter go to save your ass!

"I can't move forward on that road. I know of a shelter. That's where I'm headed. I know of a place in

Big Sky," she said, boosting her own morale. "I'm going to stick with what I know."

Frantic pedestrians had crowded the lake's shoreline, while the windblown ash, with a sickening pallor like dead skin, gathered in piles and coated the placid lake. People had shouted through Katy's window, begged her to stop, slammed their palms on the hood of her car. Where were their own vehicles? Out of gas, trapped behind the campers? She had empathized and understood their grim prospects for the next 24 hours, but she couldn't stop for anything.

She cried softly, a tear streaking down one reddened cheek. The thunking windshield wipers, smearing ash, mocked her.

She *did* have a shelter in mind; she wasn't simply placating the young mom in the back seat. The small building sat at more than 8,000-feet elevation, not 50 miles away. The north lane was moving on U.S. Highway 191, an answer to her prayers. The southbound lane was snarled in stop-and-go traffic.

A good Samaritan stopped to let her into the northbound traffic; most people were fleeing the eruption south, toward Utah. Katy knew her first choice, a seat-of-the-pants one, was flawed but preferable, as opposed to being mercilessly trapped in traffic, as thick ash storms and even pyroclastic flows bore down on the landscape.

Within an hour, they drove slowly up the deserted access road at Big Sky, Montana. She stopped at one point; a small, steadfast elk herd crossed the road in front of them, followed, not a minute later, by two wolves. It wouldn't take long for the wildlife to reemerge from their hiding places, she thought; most of the people had left, fleeing for their lives.

For some reason she thought of her mother, Jeanine. How she drove her to all the soccer games, and promoted her academic pursuit of science. Jeanine had died young, in her forties of ovarian cancer, as if in delayed punishment for losing Katy on the beach. Katy had dealt with the awful pain of that loss, while only in high school, by burying herself in sports and academia, as well as in a circle of friends who liked to smoke a lot of pot, a habit she hung onto now. She even had a baggy of good weed with her; she didn't think of it as an addiction problem, but she understood that it made her even more shy and introverted.

She was more comfortable with her volcanology data and studies, which had literally blown up in all of their faces at the YVO. She supposed that they could use the dope as a painkiller, if needed later.

"How old is he?" she asked.

"Him? Chris?" Kendra said, unsteadily. "I don't know, exactly."

"You don't know?" Kendra looked out the window silently, ash mixed with high-elevation snow, blowing horizontally.

There was no food up here, Katy thought absently. The resort's elevation was 7,500 ft. above sea level, to begin with. They didn't have farms and orchards; normally, all food and drink was trucked in. In this realm, they grew and cultivated tourists.

Where would they find food to live on? It was October; the higher slopes of 11,160 ft. Lone Peak were already covered by a thin layer of snowpack. *There has to be plenty of food stores to scavenge,* Katy thought. Most of the resort's occupants had probably left only with what they could carry.

"When's his birthday?" Katy repeated. She paused the Jeep, idling in the parking lot next to a hotel. She wracked her brain to remember where the fire road, which she had in mind, began. She would have to off-road a bit to find it; first, there were the hotels. Food and water.

Luckily, the Jeep had four-wheel drive and could handle the rock-strewn, gouged-out slopes, when it came to driving up them. For now, she shut off the Jeep's engine, noting that it still had two-thirds of a tank of gas.

"Why did we stop?" Kendra asked plaintively.

"I'm going to see if we can find provisions in this hotel. We shouldn't go to the shelter without some. You can stay here, with your son, if you want." Katy didn't see anyone else, at the moment. Kendra looked out the window again, faintly mouthing words.

Have a plan, keep moving forward, Katy repeated to herself...She wanted to dispel doubts, which she could feel creeping to the surface, such as: a blocked fire road (could she find the correct route, and navigate it?); and a locked, empty shelter. She got out of the vehicle and stood next to the Jeep. The October air was cold at this elevation.

One other car meandered around a large parking area, but the hotels were only sporadically lit. Having skied here many times before, she knew there were several hotels, clustered all around the lower slopes of the mountain.

Katy leaned into the Jeep to address Kendra, pensive in the back seat.

"How old is your son? Come on, you can tell me. We should be honest with each other. I mean, it affects the kind of food I grab. Like, is he totally into solid foods yet? Does he eat junky, or good food?" Katy really didn't know anything about caring for toddlers and children.

"He's not my son," Kendra said, looking away blankly at the parking lot.

CHAPTER 14: KIATSU

She drove the Nissan on U.S. highway 84 west, near Burley, Idaho. She knew she needed gas. The ash fall had darkened the dusk. Her children, Abby and Jake, were unusually quiet; she thought they were tired. She was exhausted, propelling herself forward like an automaton, yet aware of the danger of bad decision-making when you're weary.

They crept in traffic toward a rest stop that had eight gas pumps and a diner, but it was hopelessly crowded.

She looked at the rifle lying next to her on the seat, distastefully, but with the sense that at least she could defend them. It was the rifle that Papa Saito was trained to use to repel Americans if they invaded the Japanese mainland, a massive invasion that never occurred, due to the atomic bombs.

She vaguely thought she should practice firing it again. *What are you thinking Kiatsu?* She upbraided herself; she wasn't a shooter. She was a defender, not an aggressor.

Abby perked up when she sensed the car slow. "Where are we going, Mum? I'm starved."

"We ran out of crackers and apples an hour ago," Jake reported sullenly, his voice furry with fatigue.

"A pity," Kiatsu said, going over in her mind their diminished options. "We do have canned food, which I'll get out when we pull over. They also seem to have a place selling food."

The rest stop had a rear exit onto a local road. Perhaps the open countryside is better than the highway, she thought. They still had a cellphone, plugged into a charging gizmo that worked off the cigarette lighter, the lighter an archaic remnant of the 1950s to 1970s, when salesmen and housewives smoked a lot in the car.

She unplugged the phone and handed it back to Jake. The gradual need for gas caused her great anxiety.

"Jake, I want you to search for gas stations north of here, in small towns. Use the Map app on the phone."

"They have gas here."

"But the lines are endless, with no guarantee that their supplies won't run out." The line of vehicles ahead of her had their right-turn directionals on; everyone had the same idea, viewing the rest stop as some kind of reliable refuge and supply depot.

People were clinging to old habits, she thought, when they should toss out their preconceptions and think outside the box. *Survival.*

"C'mon Jake, I'm giving you a mission. Find all the gas stations in small towns, between here and the Canadian border."

"What? Canada? That's not close! It's like, up near the North Pole!" He took the cellphone anyways, exuding a pleasure that his mom depended on him for a task that could make them safe.

"Oh, alright."

"Thanks, hun." Kiatsu took the exit and drifted towards a pack of cars still looking for a parking space. She spotted a piece of dried up grass off to the side, unoccupied, and parked on it, negotiating the car awkwardly over the turf. It offered open access, if she drove across another section of manicured lawn, to the local road behind the diner.

Ash blew heavily, swirling through the beams of her headlights. When she shut off the lights and the engine, the parking lot fell into a murky dusk, interspersed with whirligigs of swirling dust.

She watched people stack up in front of the gas pumps; it looked like an hour wait, at least, based on her scant observations. They were lucky to have working pumps.

The way people patiently lingered in front of the pumps, typed in their information, fiddling with their credit cards and fuel dispensers, seemed quaint. It was behavior designed to make people forget they were still

230 miles southwest of a super eruption.

She spotted a man who stood in the cargo bed of his pickup. He seemed to be selling portable cans of gasoline, to only a small group of people. She thought it was worth investigating, and turned to her children.

"I'm going to try to buy gas from that man–then we'll go into the restaurant, see what food we can scare up." The latter clause just popped out of her mouth, making her feel more like a westerner, and less like the displaced woman of Asian origin.

"A hamburger," Abby said. "I really feel like a burger."

"With cheese on it," Jake said. "Cheddar, not Swiss."

"Jake, we'll get you both hamburgers," she said, opening the driver's door. She studied his face, his eyes narrowed with concentration on the Map app, mouth pursed in determination. She loved him for his dedication, bending toward the task.

"I want chips, and a banana with the burger. Medium rare meat," he barked. "I've found these towns we should go to, all with gas. Not in Canada."

Montana stood between them and Canada, anyways. The westerly direction was their primary option. When she didn't say anything, words crowded out by the conflicts of competing options, Jake said, with his voice rising, "Food, Mom! Remember?"

She smiled, for the first time in hours, then turned toward the truck and the diner. She held the car keys in her hand, not thinking it was necessary or preferable to lock her kids in the car.

"I'll be right back."

A motorcycle pulled up nearby; the rider was helmet-less, broad-shouldered, wearing a tasseled leather coat. He had rich black hair flowing down over his shoulders, but he was covered in ash. He yanked a scarf down and removed his goggles. He began to brush himself off, with a patient grimace.

He rested his hands in his lap and surveyed the parking lot, as if disapprovingly. They were all in the same boat, she thought, crowded into packed spaces and scrounging for supplies.

She walked, as if out of a dark snowstorm, into the crowded diner, where they had already placed chairs on top of tables, closing up. They weren't making food anymore, but they had a fridge containing pre-made turkey and ham sandwiches–already hearing her children's complaining voices, she bought six sandwiches, for provisions, and dropped them into her bag. Her children had to learn to cope in a burger-less universe.

The diner only took cash; she was running low. She had the sense that the world had slipped into a restricted state, with old cold cash accepted, and perhaps bartering, as hour-by-hour survival predominated.

When she came back out into the ash storm, which felt like coarse sheets of dead moths, gathering on her shoulders, her slacks, the tops of her shoes, she didn't think of it as particlized magma, the contents of a giant exploded caldera, but more like obnoxious pollution.

She thought of her young father, wandering

glassy-eyed along the river where injured people in Nagasaki took refuge (he never talked about it), and how the lethal radiation was not visible to the naked eye, whereas she was all too aware of the epic disaster that had befallen their region, and its all-too visible and palpable toxins.

She approached the pickup where the man was selling his gas; the shorter line still seemed doable.

The man stood amidst his gas cans in the back of his truck, like a hawker of miracle cures in the nineteenth century. She got into line behind a half dozen people, as hundreds of cars idled before the fuel pumps. The man sold four gallons of gas, including the can, for sixty bucks. *The going rate*, she thought, *Good old free enterprise.*

The tall motorcycle rider stood in the general commotion wearing goggles and a buff pulled back over his face. "Take advantage of shortages, and desperate people," he said to her, his voice rich, but somewhat muffled.

"Indeed," Kiatsu said. "And yet, I need gas, and I could use the can later. I think I'll compromise on the price. But of course, you drive a motorcycle."

"My daughter has her car. Where're you going?"

"As far west as I can."

"That's wise. We better get going," he said in that muffled voice. "No time to spare."

"Good luck," she said, fishing three twenties out of her wallet.

"Happy trails."

"Happy trails to you," she replied, fondly recalling the American folk song. *And till we meet again.*

The man standing in the truck, who wore ski goggles and a medical-looking mask, pocketed her money, then squatted down and passed her the heavy gas can, which she gripped by the handle and brought down to the ground by her feet.

"Can you carry that yourself?" the motorcycle rider asked. He'd pulled down his buff temporarily. He had an amiable, approachable voice.

"Yes, thanks." It was his turn to buy gas.

"I'll take one can of your liquid gold, and it better not be bilge water."

"No worries, partner. Coming right up."

Kiatsu shuffled away across the parking lot, lugging the gas, watching her shoes leave prints in the layer of crap that covered everything. Then she struck her forehead with the palm of her hand. *Dammit!* She didn't have one of those cones that was needed to dispense the fuel. She put the gas can down onto the pavement. She handed the food through the car window to her kids, then reached to the floor and popped open the little fuel-tank door.

"Need some help with that lady?"

Shouts came from the far edge of the rest stop, then two pops in the dark that made her flinch. Gunfire.

"Oh shit," the man who had spoken to her said. He stood next to an old, battered SUV, wearing a wool cap and a thick beard. One of those cones she needed stuck out of the mouth of his own gas tank.

"I suppose so," she said, looking nervously toward where the gunshots had come from. "If I could borrow your own...do-hickey."

She needed to get inside the car and out of that ash fall, which blew in her face. People's voices were muffled, as the foul blizzard only became more blinding, covering the roofs and windshields of the vehicles.

"In that case," the man said matter-of-factly. "I've been waiting in line forever. It seems like it should be my turn." He wandered over to where the can sat at her feet, picked it up, and brought it to the rear of his car.

"Hold on right there, Mister. That's my gasoline," she said in a measured, yet weary tone. "You can't have it."

"Who says?"

"I do," the motorcycle rider said. He was standing with a young woman nearby. "Put it back where you found it, Bozo."

The man watched him silently; then, "Mind your own business."

"This is my business." Zeke put his right hand down to the bulge in his side pocket. His fingers on that hand twitched in a barely perceptible way. The lady stood next to him with her arms crossed across her chest, wiping away blobs of ash that gathered on her hair and cheek.

The man sneered, turned, and snapped open the rear cargo door of his SUV.

Zeke walked over to where the gas can sat on the ground, commenting calmly, "I'm going to return the gas to its rightful owner."

Just then, the bearded man with the ash-covered wool cap stepped back and brandished the shotgun he'd taken out of the car.

"Leave the can on the ground," he said. Zeke paused momentarily, as if sizing him up.

"Jesus dad," his companion, Tiva, said. "Let's get out of here. The ash is making it hard to breathe!"

The man waved the shotgun around insolently, aiming it in the general direction of Zeke.

"We're making a little trade," the man said, with a hint of menace. "Me and the lady here. She can use my funnel; I borrow some gas."

"Buy your own," Zeke said. "It's a free country."

The man laughed bitterly. "It was until about four hours ago. Then the cap came off the geyser, and now it's a new world."

"Put that thing down. You don't look like you know how to use it, and you're going to hurt someone."

"Oh, for God's sakes!" Tiva said. "We don't have time for this pissing contest." The two men stared at each other, ash drifting between them like a screen. Zeke's hand drifted down around the metallic bulge in his side pocket.

Then a fourth voice was heard. "Put the gun down now, Bully Man. Slowly." Kiatsu stood at an angle to the man in the dust-covered wool cap, aiming Papa Saito's infantry rifle at a target somewhere around the man's chest.

"Are you kidding me?" The man laughed, but less

confidently this time. The ash swirled around in the darkness; they looked like white shadows, a tense tableau. She walked slowly towards him with the gun held upright, finger on the trigger; her eyes unblinking, but she strained to control the shaking in her legs.

CHAPTER 15: SLATER

When the helicopter had reached a 3,000-foot elevation, the clouds parted intermittently. Slater sat buckled into his seat. Greenhorn grimaced silently as he flew his way through the dismal, murky turbulence. The spaces in the clouds offered fleeting glimpses of what unfolded in West Yellowstone and beyond.

At least three towering columns of Godawful magmatic vents had opened in the park; one of the columns collapsed like the failed superstructure of a building.

Slater watched, transfixed, still feeling somewhat guilty, even though they were far from out of danger. He knew Monica blamed him for Katy, for not leaving earlier with her, for not effectively using his authority to get her on the chopper.

Katy made up her own mind and she was iron-willed. If anyone should have understood that, he thought, it was Monica.

The collapsing column had become a pyroclastic flow. This was his field of academia, which didn't leaven the horror, but further cemented his attention. When do volcano scientists get to see real pyroclastic flows? he thought. Almost never.

He thought of his father, and this made him want to stare more fixedly at this lethal geologic development.

A solid line of cars, in the pyroclastic flow's path, snaked up Highway 20 from the West Yellowstone entrance. He watched everything unfold, as if it was a static-filled TV screen in the dead of night. A slow-moving nightmare.

When Mount St. Helens had erupted on May 18, 1980, Slater's father had raced down an open country road. He didn't have traffic to contend with. He hadn't left early or left himself enough time to escape; yet, harshly judging his father's fatal miscalculations was not only tactless, Slater thought it would jinx them.

A thick avalanche of black, airborne debris surged forward below, falling upon and devouring the forests and terrain, like a tsunami composed of superheated air and rock fragments. The people trapped in traffic didn't have a chance, or options.

A thousand feet high and five times as wide, the pyroclastic flow overtook the lines of hundreds of vehicles, which some people had abandoned to flee across an adjacent field. They didn't know what a pyroclastic flow consisted of (in this case, a good thing), or, Slater thought that they wanted to die on the run, standing up, and not like trapped sitting ducks in a stalled vehicle.

The survival rate will be zero, he thought. *700 degrees F., 370 degrees C., a mile wide. Instant death, by vaporization*. He watched the flashes of the gas explosions as the giant, fast-moving cloud enveloped the traffic on 20.

He could make out the running people in the field, too well; the clothes that they wore, their gender, body type, age; the color of their hair. It was unseemly to watch; he averted his eyes.

This reminded him of years ago, watching the video footage of people leaping from the burning World Trade towers in New York City. It was more than an unhealthy fascination to watch; it was heartbreaking, and tactless.

He turned away, as the helicopter vanished into the clouds, as if someone had let the curtain down. The visibility was nil, a hazard intensified by the mountainous terrain. Greenhorn's border collie hadn't quite detected the air of tension; she lay nearby, as if relaxing on a barn floor.

"Where are we going, Jimmy?" Slater asked.

"Your guess is as good as mine," the pilot answered hoarsely.

"You mean, we don't know?" Monica's voice conveyed a mixture of annoyance and fear.

A shudder vibrated through the chopper; Monica and Slater hung onto to straps that protruded above their seats, and the collie scrabbled across the floor and rolled, ending in a furry heap at Slater's feet. They were completely enveloped in the filthy maelstrom, the main cloud of ash, Slater thought, since they were surely too high for pyroclastic flows.

"What about Jeter?" Halstrom screamed, frantically looking behind him for his dog.

"He's okay," Slater said. "Can you use the radar?"

"I'm on the stick, pal. The ash could shut down my motors, at any moment! It doesn't take much!"

Merely a flock of birds can bring down passenger jets, Slater thought, a melancholy mood retaking his spirit. He exchanged an anxious glance with Monica; she looked as helpless as he felt.

At the same time, he was aware he bore witness to a profound geological event, the defining one of his lifetime. Also, the agent of perhaps the end of his life. In another dark flight of fancy, he thought he was like a doctor peering into his own guts after a bad abdominal wound, noting the anatomical details. This was his field; the nature of this supra-regional catastrophe.

He'd stared at ancient lava and magma deposits through electron microscopes. Now the very same substance swirled just outside his window, and it was trying to kill them.

"Go as far west as you absolutely can," he said, sounding pathetic to his own ears. Unable to mask the dread. He felt weak and obvious, like a panicked passenger screaming to the driver, "Step on it!"

"This bird isn't designed for that altitude, above the clouds!" Halstrom screamed back. "No one's in the air now. There's a reason for that!"

They had another glimpse of the ground beneath them, a break in the thick, sooty fog. It was all mountains and valleys; not a shred of civilization was visible. Eastern or northern Idaho, in the mountains, Slater thought.

"Poor Katy!" Monica yelled, with a kind of delayed bitterness. "She was left behind like that. I'll never forgive myself. Or us!"

"If she found an open road, she might be okay," Slater said.

"Really? Well that lets us off the hook!"

Halstrom looked back at them, the chopper now bucking like a small bronco. Slater held onto Jeter, who lay at his feet and remarkably kept his cool.

"I've got to set the bird down, soon! If the engine shuts down in this shit, I'll lose all control of my navigation."

They might have been in the air for 40 minutes, Slater thought. Hardly time to cover 85 miles, at 160 mph. But they've been going slower than that in this turbulence.

"Try to make the Washington border!" Slater yelled, with undisguised wishful thinking.

Then the helicopter made a descent that was so fast and unexpected that Slater's head went back and struck the window behind him; he swore and felt the lump and stared at his fingers. The others' voices sounded hollow.

He vaguely thought they were going down somewhere in Idaho north of the Sawtooth wilderness.

CHAPTER 16: GARNER

He smelled the smoke first; the dark horizon glowed orange.

He was on Highway 25, headed south towards New Mexico. Rumors of a wildfire; no details yet. The traffic was sparse, given that he was not that far from Colorado Springs and Denver. No one seemed to be moving, as if a self-imposed "shelter in place" had evolved.

Road blocks had forced him south, but he still held out hope for a route that went west on Highway 10 to California, then up the coast. Maybe Kiatsu had made it to Seattle; he felt useless, driving almost aimlessly, still hundreds of miles from his fleeing family.

He was, of course, supposed to be with them. But he'd "needed to work." He'd passed on the Idaho trip, willingly. As if Jake and Abby were not important, or getting in the way of his ambitions. Garner raked himself over the coals with guilt, until he had an unquenchable desire for a drink. He needed fuel, then he passed a road sign–Gas, Food, Lodging. *All three,* he thought, *in about that order.*

The ash gathered like a thick snowfall; when he slowed for the exit, he thought by instinct he would skid and slide through it. He recalled his last full conversation with Kiatsu, her gentle pattern of thoughts, the curt assurance he'd conveyed about the reasons for not spending the week with his family.

A movie he'd recently watched led off with a Mark Twain quote, paraphrased: *It's not what you don't know that will get you, it's what you're so damn sure of that's dead wrong.*

He drove down the county road toward the filling station, only a few other headlight beams stabbing into the darkness. *I can act too sure of myself, as if I'm always trying to prove something. Prove I belong with the top dogs. That's what executive suite office life does to you.* He had a high six-figure salary (with bonuses) in a tower in New York City. The money let him off the hook.

The demands of the job provided a certain excuse, insulating him from family obligations. He never attended Jake's soccer games; Abby's swimming and horseback riding lessons were always attended and supervised by Kiatsu.

She was a devoted Mom, but she never wanted to be labeled a "soccer mom," having her own lab-researcher career.

He turned into a nearly empty parking lot; the wipers clawed at the clinging ash. They mocked him with their monotony. He glanced at the cellphone, no messages, then let it fall onto the passenger seat.

He thought he might buy one of those small flasks of Dewar's or Jack D, which they kept behind the counter at filling stations. It was a bad habit and a thirst he mostly had no excuse for. *Don't get sauced, idiot!*

When he parked, a young guy stood outside the entrance door to the Chevron station, locking up. Garner noted his vehicle's three-quarter empty tank, then walked across the parking lot.

"What's up? Can I get some gas?"

The young man, who wore a hooded sweatshirt and a Denver Bronco's baseball-style cap, looked down at the fistful of keys, one of which was inserted into the door lock.

"I'm closing up. We have to evacuate."

"Due to the wildfire?"

"Yes sir." He finished locking the door, looking up impassively. "Didn't you hear? The Calder fire, it's threatening Cimarron. I'm a volunteer firefighter; I have to go."

"I see." They stood together, ash falling all around them, blowing into little unkempt piles.

"You know, it's bizarre we have ashfall all the way from Wyoming and Montana," Garner commented, apropos of nothing. "But a local wildfire that's producing its own ash."

"It is what it is," the guy said, juggling the keys in one hand, as if he had second thoughts.

"Well, thanks for your time," Garner said, "We should be getting out of here, breathing this stuff is the pits."

"You empty?" the man asked him.

"Not quite, almost."

"Alright, four minutes. That's all I have. Pull up to pump four." He unlocked the door, yanked it open, and jogged inside the station to switch on the fuel-pump dispenser.

"Thanks buddy, I..." Garner ran to his RAV4 and started it up, drove up to the pump, filled the tank as fast as he could (he didn't have to produce the credit card). The man came out of the station, waving Garner off.

"Don't worry about it," the guy called out. He locked the door again and ran to a pickup that was parked nearby.

"Thanks! Thanks so much!"

Garner followed the pickup out of the parking lot, and took the turn back toward the highway. He thought better of it, and did a U-turn in the direction of another road that would take him south through Taos and Santa Fe.

Having a full tank made him feel like he had accomplished something.

He pulled over into a vacant space of gravel off to the side of the road. He switched off his headlights. Yes, he had cellphone service. He wanted to send more messages to Kiatsu; at the very least, he ached and hungered for a status message.

He called, but once again only listened to his wife's sultry, congenial voice. Then he sent a text: *Let me know where you are, if you can, and if you are safe!! I'm far west of Chicago and coming north asap. Where are you? Text if you can. I miss you. Endless love, Brad.*

If he could only receive one reply. He felt the crushing weight of loneliness in the dark, the guilt still throbbing and festering.

He stepped out of the car. He could only see one other set of headlights light up some woods in the distance, rise up as a car mounted a hill, and vanish. He wiped the dust off his windshield and headlights. He checked the cellphone again; service, yes, but no messages from his wife.

A wave of fatigue overtook him. He got into the back seat, stretched out, and put his head on a backpack, pulling a coat up to his chin. *We don't know how weary we are until we close our eyes.*

He thought of his own father, John Henry Garner, who'd passed away in 2020. He'd known Brad's kids for only a few years. John Henry worked in the defense industry–first for Raytheon, then Lockheed. He was born in 1934 and had Brad late, when he was 45. He spent a year fighting in the Korean War; he never talked about it.

He didn't share war stories with his son, who learned to never ask about Korea. It seemed a wall had been put up, and Brad accepted it. Brad had an early memory of watching jet fighters and bombers take off and land at a military air-force facility in California, where the public could sit on grass and look out over the facility. They used to eat tuna sandwiches and sip a powdered Tang drink.

What Brad thought about when he closed his eyes, along with his wife and children, was the man who came home when it was dark and poured a drink; but if he got home earlier and Brad was outside shooting baskets, or firing a tennis ball off the side of the garage, John Henry would put a briefcase and suit coat down and play with his son. They'd play catch or shoot baskets together.

He thought of his father's spirited but awkward jump shot clanging off the backboard; the time he squatted down in the catcher's style and took Brad's pitches off his shins and knees, without complaint.

Brad fell deeply asleep. It was still dark when his snoring woke himself up. He switched an interior light on, and it seemed like the vehicle was covered in dead moths. When he got out, he rearranged the stuff in the back seat, then he hopped into the front seat and pushed the power button. Nothing happened.

"Shit, Dammit! The engine's gunked up," he said out loud. He tried the power button multiple times, then he tried to call AAA on his cellphone, as well as any local service station, but couldn't get through to anyone.

It was as if the local towns were locked down, out of service.

He got out of the car with his small backpack, noting that his cellphone had a 62 percent charge left, and it was 2:45 am, Mountain Daylight Time, in New Mexico. He started walking, thinking that he was hungry, that he would probably hitchhike for the first time in decades, and strangely, wondering what ordeals his father had suffered in 1954 in North Korea.

CHAPTER 17: KATY

"What the hell do you mean, not your son? Is he your nephew?" Katy paused outside of the Jeep, in the shadow of the empty hotel.

Kendra hesitated a moment, almost embarrassed.

"No, I found him."

"You found him? Like he's a discarded cellphone, or something?"

Now defensiveness entered Kendra's voice. "He was abandoned. What was I supposed to do, leave him?"

"Do you know anything about his family?" Kendra's stare had become catatonic. Katy shook her head; the woman's excuses were dubious beyond belief.

"So you left with him, basically kidnapping someone's child? And he ends up with me–so I'm hosting a felon."

"I'm not a felon," Kendra said bitterly. "You saw what it was like back there! It was fricking chaos! People panicking! Do you advocate leaving children behind?"

"Clearly, not. I've got two in the back of my Jeep."

"You know, fuck off," Kendra said. "You're not my mom…or my case officer."

"Case officer? What would you know about case officers?" Katy opened the back door of the Jeep and fetched her backpack. She needed to shove supplies into it.

"I can't imagine how the parents are freaking out at this moment," she muttered, as much to herself. "They might have just left her for ten minutes. They come back, their son's gone. That's traumatizing. They might still be there, looking for him. And I have no way to get the word out from here."

"I saw him, alone, for longer than 10 minutes. It had to have been…20…30…"

"I'm going to the Summit Hotel. It's right there, next to the Jeep. You two stay here, and don't take my stuff," she snapped. "There's no place to go from here; you won't survive the ashfall, so don't even think about wandering off with him. And yes, a part of me does regret taking you in."

"Oh!" Kendra said, fussing with the door handle. "I've got to get out of this car. It's suffocating. I need a cigarette."

"Suit yourself. But look after him."

"Yes Ma'am," Kendra said contemptuously,

struggling out of the car, standing up, and lighting a cigarette she'd fetched from a breast pocket. The ash swirled around the deepening darkness, making dirty piles against the thick tires of the Jeep.

As she walked toward the empty hotel, which had just a few lights burning in lower floors, Katy thought, planning the hunt, *that kid looks like he could eat just about anything*. She called back to the Jeep, hoisting a backpack onto her shoulders. "I'll be back in less than 30 minutes."

She rechecked her pocket for the Jeep's ignition keys. Fatigue and stress blanketed her mind; she felt her reactions and commonly sharp thinking processes idling down. She needed food, rest; they needed a few supplies, then secure shelter. She strode quickly toward the back of the hotel.

The parking lot was dingy, a mixture of pavement ice reflecting a weak moonlight, and the furious, dense ashfall. No one else was around.

She knew where the hotel kitchen was; she also realized that she was planning to loot and steal. Technically. Was it against the law to survive? Snatch some grub to feed a child? It didn't make much sense, to perish of thirst and hunger, but die a virtuous, law-abiding woman.

Katy went to an exit door that she remembered from when she had skied at Big Sky, and stayed in this hotel. She found the door locked; no surprise there. She wore a pair of glacier goggles with protection on the sides; a yellow buff yanked up over her nose. She walked away from the locked door. She wasn't going to smash glass to get in, not just yet.

She skirted a swimming pool, which in the hotel staff's haste had been left uncovered. The sides of the pool were littered with empty plastic cups and glasses that once contained margaritas, vodka tonics, rum cokes, before it was abandoned by fleeing merry-makers. Katy, in a fit of caustic good humor, brought on by weariness and the need to laugh, thought of drunk young women in bikinis bouncing away from the pool as Yellowstone began to explode.

She saw nothing by the pool that was immediately salvageable, not even chips, nuts, and salsa. If she saw a glass of melted ice water with an old lime in it, she'd probably guzzle it, despite the bity aftertaste.

She loved to swim. She'd been in the pool that time she skied for the weekend, with a guy her age named Barry. She'd met him on campus (Montana State University), and he'd asked her along on a ski date, having bagged a couple of passes to Big Sky at a filling-station ticket special. Neither one of them had any money, but they'd splurged anyways for a hotel room for two nights.

He, of course, thought he was going to get laid, even though it was their first weekend together. She felt sorry for him, a nice, fairly smart guy with a weird laugh and unknown intentions, because Katy pretty much knew she wasn't going to let him shag her.

They stood in this pool together, sipping drinks, the steam rising up around them; stars glinting over the luminescent ski slopes.

It was a good memory; she could lose herself in it, for a moment, standing in the ash that soiled the pool side. Two other people were fiercely French-kissing in the corner of the pool that night, and Katy smiled, thinking it was giving Barry ideas. Too much Public Display of Affection (PDA) for her, enough to make Barry even hornier. Then the door to the pool room opened with a jolt, snapping her out of this exhausted reverie.

A guy in his twenties with shaggy hat-head, a black, ski-bum's beard, and a gray puffy coat. He was as surprised as she was, and dropped a styrofoam cup full of coffee.

"Hey!" he said, a squeak of strain in his voice. "Where did you come from? I thought everyone had split."

"West Yellowstone. Do you work here? I'm trying to get inside for a few minutes."

"I used to work here…it's crazy as shit, what's going on, isn't it? I lived in the mountain village, but I'm driving west in my truck. Get the hell outta here."

I have a young woman you can take as a passenger, Katy thought.

"Can you keep that door open for me?" Katy asked. The man looked at her curiously.

"Yeah, for sure…sweet." He held it open for her. She gave him a half smile as she strode past him, smelling beer and cigarettes.

"You see," she said, by way of explanation. "I'm

responsible for a kid and another gal, and I thought there might be some supplies in here."

"You might find some food and stuff in there," he said warmly. "Fair pickings, under these circumstances."

She smiled more willingly, grateful and reassured, and kept on walking inside the hotel. She was on the first floor. "Thanks a lot, and good luck."

"You too!" he said. She wasn't prepared, at all, to take on another person, or plan an escape or survival tactics with this guy. She wanted to make all the decisions. She was glad when he didn't follow her inside.

She kept going through a dark hallway, then reached the front of a restaurant. She saw a clutter of abandoned dishes inside; fruit and bacon and half-eaten omelets. Glasses of water; cold cups of coffee. She sauntered in, yelled "Hello?" No answer. The kitchen entrance was in the back, where she was more likely to find complete packages of supplies, rather than the garbage lying around the tables.

It's still edible, however, she reminded herself; beggars can't be choosers. She went to the back of the restaurant, her path lit by the small flashlight she carried in her backpack. She heard the steady hum of refrigerators. *Electricity still on... but that may not last...*

There were two long stainless steel tables for food prep; she found a couple of open bags of white-toast bread–empty calories–she thought, and two partially filled egg containers. She stuffed the bread into the bottom of the backpack; the eggs on top.

She scanned the shelves–a few cardboard containers of salt and flour, which she bagged. She was conscious of her own footsteps and banging around metal pans and utensils; she felt like a home-breaker, a scavenger. She watched the kitchen entrance nervously, not sure if the disaster was old enough to justify stealing in everyone's mind.

She turned her attention to two large refrigerators. Locked! *Who locks refrigerators? Restaurants do. They don't want their employees stealing the prime rib and truffles.* Still, that was frustrating. She needed the good stuff, the fat and the protein. She left the kitchen, after emptying a stale-bread bag onto the floor.

Into this scavenged plastic bag went portions of omelets and left-over bacon and sausage. She ravenously crammed some of this rubbery leftover food into her mouth. She must have eaten three breakfasts as she rummaged through the dining area.

Then the whole building started to shake, violently. Dishes and tables crashed to the floor. She heard a loud rumble and sunk to her knees, crawling under another table as wall hangings and ceiling tiles tumbled down. *An aftershock,* she whispered to herself. A significant one, 6.0-plus in magnitude.

There's going to be hundreds of them. She felt in no particular danger, and waited it out crouched beneath the table. When it subsided, she ran out of the restaurant and back down the dark hallway with her loot.

The trembling had stopped completely, when she

reached the exit door. She decided to keep it propped open, and that they would camp out inside the hotel for at least that night or two. She chose a 20-pound dumbbell from the fitness room to lean against the exit door. When she set it up, she noticed that her hands were shaking.

Her mouth had gone dry. She heard a roar outside, like thunder. She jogged outside, past the pool, the rucksack banging against her upper back. A huge car-sized stone rumbled down the slope above her, with a cluster of small but lethal stones in its wake. The big rock, shaped like an arrowhead, thundered down the slope toward where she had parked the Jeep, splintering trees, raising a brown cloud of dust, and crashing into other rocks.

She thought she heard a woman's scream; it could have been a bird's cry. She made it around the corner of the building. The air smelled burnt, scorched, amidst a curtain of soot. The Jeep was still upright and intact, yet dented; Christopher bawled and stared from the back seat. Fragmented gray rubble lay about the area with a pallor of dust drifting away from the aftermath of a substantial rock slide. The black arrow-shaped rock rested against a gouged hotel wall and smashed window.

Not far from the Jeep, Kendra's bloody, battered body, clothes ripped, tattered, and blood-stained, lay amongst the gray stones. She was deathly still; even the wind on the slopes had ceased. The air smelled like sulfur and fire; all Katy could hear was the toddler's hollow bawling from inside the car.

CHAPTER 18: ZEKE

Kiatsu held the rifle steady on the guy with the shotgun. He hesitated, then lowered the weapon to the ground. She sensed herself breathe easier; she really wasn't prepared to shoot a person over gas. She *was* inclined to defend herself, her loved ones, her friends, violently, as a last resort.

Zeke gripped his own pistol. "Don't try anything," he said. He walked over, bent down, and fetched the man's rifle. The guy grimaced around an unruly beard, as he stood by his car and balefully eyed the proceedings.

"Too bad, you lose," Zeke said. "You have zero civic responsibility, in the way you deploy this weapon, so I'm confiscating it."

"Now that the macho posturing is over, can we go

now?" Tiva said, turning to leave.

"Thank the lady, she's not into the macho," Zeke said. "What's your name again? My short-term memory's shot these days."

"Kiatsu Saito."

"Thank you, Kiatsu," Tiva said. "I can tell you're a really nice person. You had to do that. What kind of a rifle is that anyways?"

"A service rifle…from Japan. It was my father's."

"It looks like an antique. My name is Tiva. We all should get going; it's dangerous out here."

"You gonna give me my shotgun back?" the man whined. "That's stealing, buster!"

Bluntly, "No."

Zeke turned to Kiatsu: "You want to come with us, once we gas up?"

"Yes, that would be helpful."

"We have a motorcycle and a car."

"That's my property," the man demanded, shifting his feet, as if ready to lurch forward and throw a punch.

"Tough luck," Zeke said, adjusting his goggles and fanning the ash away from his face. "Things are tense enough out here, without the loose cannons waving their guns around. You forfeited your rights, buddy. Ciao."

They all walked together, leaving the man looking bereft and resentful, standing by his car. "I'll call the cops on you, for stealing my rifle!" he yelled.

Zeke laughed as he strode through the flurries of ash. "The police, that's funny. He's got a record, I'd bet, and an outstanding warrant."

"Let it go," Tiva said, her back turned towards him. "We've wasted enough time."

Zeke was able to procure a funnel, so they could add the gasoline to Kiatsu's tank. Unbeknownst to her, he traded a little weed he carried for the use of someone else's.

Then they hit the road, heading west with the fleeing hordes, bound for Washington state and the West Coast.

Kiatsu felt safer following Zeke's motorcycle, with Tiva's four-door sedan behind her, the traffic crawling along in an endless gridlock. The breakdown lane was littered with large semi trucks whose diesel engines were choked by the dust. Kiatsu's eyes were heavy with fatigue. They averaged less than 30 mph through the frenetic storm, the monotonous knocking of the wipers smearing ash like the crushed wings of dead bugs.

She was grateful when Zeke's rear blinker clicked on, his right arm signaling "pull over."

"It's time to get some shut-eye," she murmured to her children, but they were already asleep. She shut off the car's lights. The night was black and foreboding. Although they traveled through small towns, the electricity seemed to have gone out.

"It's happening," she whispered to herself, hearing only the ticking of the cooling engine in a thick, lightless silence.

They were parked in a vacant lot where weeds poked through dust, like sand dunes skirting a beach. She craved sleep, even while in a sitting position, drifting into it willingly.

Zeke parked the motorcycle on a kickstand, then crawled into the back of Tiva's car. He put a coat under his head and lay back, with the sensation that he was falling backwards into a dark, moonlit lake. The sound of "dust on car window" was like a bird's fluttering wings; it had an incongruously lulling effect.

Zeke slept till dawn, waking to a blood-red sunrise that fought through curtains of dust and smoke. The dream, the one he remembered, was vast and realistic, unfolding in three acts.

He had a young lover in the dream, a good-looking woman quite a bit younger than he and his wife Amitola. The young woman, whom he wooed and cooed over, had a tiny infant with her. Some uncertainty about whether the infant was his pervaded his dream, which had an air of grounded reality. He was still enveloped by the dream an hour after waking. He took dreams seriously, viewing them as iconic messages from beyond, and within.

He thought a young woman would enter his sphere at any moment, in some capacity, and he also thought it strange that Tiva hadn't asked much at all about her mother, Amitola. They'd had a strained relationship; Zeke had thought Tiva had grown out of it.

He stepped out of Tiva's car, into a furry, grainy light, and stretched, gazing around at deciduous trees whose branches were oppressively weighted down by dust. He thought maybe he'd benefited by not watching or hearing the news headlines; a "news drought" buoyed his spirits.

What was there *new* to know? A cataclysmic eruption had taken place. So run for your life. And help other people, especially children.

As he arranged the buff and goggles back on his eyes and face, the dream lingered like a thick vapor in his mind, as if he had fallen in love while asleep. Dreams were serious stuff, he thought, coded messages from past lives, deep in his soul, his DNA, his background which included the Ute tribe and the Spanish invaders from the 16th century.

He would let the others gain some much needed sleep. They were, he hoped, out of immediate danger.

He shivered in the cold dawn, doubting that the knucklehead would follow them after his shotgun. Which now lay in the trunk of Tiva's car.

The wood smoke he smelled contained another warning altogether. The timber throughout the West might as well be a giant tinderbox, just waiting for a match to be struck.

He craved coffee, which he set about to make. He heard a car door open and close. It was Kiatsu. "I might light a fire," he called over to her. "Make some cowboy coffee."

"Make enough for me, kind sir."

He laughed, and that felt good, even as it came out a muffled croak beneath the layers covering his face. He found a tree, and he used its canopy to make a fire. Kiatsu wandered over to the edge of the lot and stared at the pale sun through fog.

"Did you sleep?"

"You bet I did," she said. "I have no cell service. I've tried to send a message to my husband."

"Where is he right now? Do you know?" He put ground coffee into the bottom of a metal canister, poured water over it, then began to heat up the can over the fire. He had a filter that he would push down over the boiling water and ground coffee. They sometimes called these things Italian presses, but this was a crude one, made for camping. They made dark, strong coffee.

"In Chicago, the last time I heard. On business. I think he rented a car; he was going to try to meet us. I can't tell him where we are. He must be going crazy–he might think we're injured or dead," she said bluntly.

That made her think of Papa Saito again; this time she had the inkling he had survived in his basement. He had a few of the nine lives left. He also was "very Japanese," she thought.

He viewed death as a part of life, not something to dread and deny, as they do in the west. He would repeat this proverb, translated into English: "Duty is heavy as a mountain, but death is lighter than a feather."

If he died, she was sure that he would meet his end with grace. After all, he was in Nagasaki in 1945, and he was still alive in his 90s. This thought made her feel better about leaving him; if for only the moment.

The children were still sleeping. She walked over to where Zeke made the coffee, then thought about a to-go container she had in the car. She fetched that, brought it back, and filled it up with a delicious warm brew that imbued her with a kind of false, but appreciated, optimism and energy. She saw Tiva walking over to the fire and the tree; she smiled at her.

The traffic was already moving ponderously though the fog. She smelled fire and wood smoke; it was too permanent and thick to be coming from Zeke's fire. She looked all around and noticed no evidence of a wildfire they would have to worry about, but it was another anxiety filed away in back of her mind.

A passenger car pulled over to the side, near where they were parked. A woman, very pregnant, got out by the side of the road. She stretched, and bent gingerly to the back of the car to fetch a coat. When Kiatsu's gaze met the woman's face, she looked strained, burdened, and afraid, so Kiatsu smiled and asked her whether she could get her anything.

"Is it your first?"

Yes, the woman nodded.

"You'll do fine. When you reach your destination, everything will work out." She stepped forward and embraced the lady, who thanked her, then got back into her car.

The wood smoke now singed the inside of Kiatsu's nose.

CHAPTER 19: MONICA

The helicopter descended rapidly towards a broad, open field, surrounded by copses of shadowy pine groves. Dust and ash swirled in the overcast sky as they hovered close to the ground, the wake from the chopper's rotors forming a bowl in the tall grass. The blades pierced the silence with their greasy, metallic turns.

Monica trusted Greenhorn; she didn't think they were going to crash and die. When both landing skids touched down, Greenhorn shut off the engines, all of the people palpably breathing a sigh of relief. Slater had thought, with the echo of a cliche, they had gone from the frying pan into the fire. But now that they had landed, being lost was a new challenge. The heavy ashfall continued, as though they'd landed in a blizzard.

Jimmy looked around wild-eyed for a moment. "Where's my dog? How's Jeter–where are you boy?" Then he grabbed the mutt in a smothering embrace, when Jeter stood up unsteadily at Slater's feet.

"Everybody okay?" Monica asked, eliciting a murmured "yeah" in unison.

"I'm not getting a signal on my radio," Jimmy said, as the dog moved to the side window, slowly wagging his tail.

"That was my next question," Monica said. "Where are we?"

Silence.

"Somewhere in central or western Idaho," Slater said, uncertainly.

"That's about right," the pilot said. "The boonies. A wilderness area. The Sawtooths."

They all looked out the window, preparing to stretch their legs. The ash made everything look the same; only the undulation of the terrain had distinguishing features. Slater unlatched the door and stepped down into the tall grass. Jeter followed him.

The ground was moist and spongy. He wore a pair of thick-soled, low-cut shoes, but reminded himself he had no other footwear, and they might have a long walk out of this wilderness. He didn't want to do it in wet shoes and develop a form of trench-foot, which he was prone to.

Monica stepped gingerly down from the chopper after him, covering her face with a buff. "If we're lucky," she said. "The outskirts of civilization are right over that ridge there." She pointed across the grassy wildlands to a ridgeline of peaks, gaps, and passes. *We're not equipped for that kind of trip, she thought. Hope is cheap, but I cling to it.*

"We're not going anywhere tonight, that's for sure," Greenhorn cracked, leaning out of the chopper.

"If the ash lets up a bit," Slater said. "Could you take off again? Maybe take us over those passes?"

"Possibly. We'll see what it's like in a day or two." Greenhorn called after the dog, who followed a scent that took him several yards away. Jeter must have picked up wildlife smells, Monica thought.

"We'll have to cross this field to get wood for a fire," Slater said. "Maybe we can move the helicopter to the edge of the woods."

"I wouldn't risk it," Greenhorn said, irritated in a way one can easily slip into when fatigued. "We were lucky to safely land, as it is."

Slater couldn't be sure that the grassy wildland wasn't bisected with muddy canals and bogs. It seemed like a partial wetlands, and that made their migration more problematical.

Jimmy seemed to read his thoughts: "Even if I got the state police or first responders on the radio, there would be no rescue. No aircraft are flying now, unless it's military and they go up into the damn stratosphere, above the volcanic clouds. And there are no roads out here, from what I see. I've got this arthritic knee..."

Greenhorn seemed to require a morale boost,

Monica thought. "We're grateful that you took us up in the helicopter. You saved us. I don't know what we would have done."

"No worries," he mumbled. "Fly the friendly skies of Yellowstone. Maybe the dust will die down. I'll try the engine in the morning." He dug a pack of Lucky Strikes out of a pants pocket and lit one up. He still wore a pilot's protective goggles; the ash swirled around in shoulder-high eddies as the pale, enshrouded sun sunk towards the mountain range to the west.

"We've got our feet on the ground, and we'll get through this together," Monica said.

"Yeah, we're the lucky ones," Slater said. He seemed antsy to move. "I'm going to get some dry wood and ground cover for a fire, before it gets too dark. And the ash gets too thick."

"Don't. It's already getting too dark." They made eye contact, and to Slater, she was the old Monica, the one he was close to before they broke up.

"It won't take long. If we have a fire, we're more likely to be spotted as well."

Monica wasn't counting on being "spotted and rescued," right now. *Save yourself,* she thought. *It's up to us now.*

"I'll go with you," she said. The wind riffled the grass, like the fine fur of an animal.

Then they all turned their heads toward Jeter, who'd barked a couple of times. He dug frenziedly at something in the grass about 30 yards away. When they reached the dog, his nose was to the ground, and he moved deliberately through a trail that animals had made in the underbrush. He definitely had the border collie in him, Monica thought. She was a dog person, but thankfully hadn't been responsible for one of late, so she didn't have to leave a dog behind.

"C'mere Jeter," she said. "You have to get back in the chopper with Jimmy." They could hear Greenhorn's throaty call for the dog. Jeter rejoined the group obediently, not before Monica noticed a sizable pile of animal scat on this game trail they'd discovered.

"What do you think that's from?" she asked, by way of conversation, given that Slater was no Yellowstone wildlife expert. He was an interested layman, when it came to flora, fauna, and critters.

At the moment, he was taking a concentrated interest in a handful of ash, which sifted through his fingers. He was an educated connoisseur of pulverized magma; he also had distracted himself from their plight by admiring Monica's shape from behind. *That hadn't changed.*

"That's not a deer," Monica said, inspecting the mushy pile at her feet. She hugged herself, as the shadows that had fallen over the wilderness added a chill to the air.

"Could be elk, or coyote," Slater said, venturing wild guesses. "It has to be a bigger animal."

"It's voluminous. Could be a bear," Monica said uneasily.

"Might be."

Monica stared at him with trepidation. "I'm scared

shitless of bears."

"I know you are. We've been through that before. Remember the time we went to Glacier National Park, and you only wanted to go half a mile down the trail?"

"Vaguely."

"We're digressing. Let's get some fire material. It has multiple advantages, the chief one being warmth."

"And that it wards off predators..."

"No worries, Monica." He eyed the waning light of the afternoon, the trees with their slightly muted autumn colors.

"Are you coming?"

"Yeah. But we really should carry some kind of weapon." To Slater, that sounded unusual coming out of her mouth. Normally, Monica wasn't a big gun advocate.

"If it will make you feel better, I've got a hunting knife in my pack, back in the chopper."

"A knife? Is this *The Revenant*?"

"Well, we don't have firearms, so..." He fetched the knife, then he began walking through the tall grass, towards the trees. The forest led straight towards gaps in the mountains. The dust storm showed no signs of letting up.

"You don't have to come. I should be back in 40 minutes. I'm bringing the flashlight." He called over to Greenhorn and told him that he was fetching firewood, but got no response. Jimmy had gone back to the helicopter, with Jeter in tow.

"I'm not going farther than maybe a mile, a mile and

a half," Slater said.

"I'm coming. What do you think I am, a wuss? We do have matches, right?"

"In my backpack," he called over his shoulder.

They walked about 40 yards through the grass, which was wet with dew and caked with soot. Slater looked over his shoulder to commit the helicopter's location to memory; there weren't many landmarks to use, but the helicopter's rotor blades stuck out from the ground cover and could be seen from a distance.

Three hawks flew overhead as they walked. One of them squawked jovially, as if in greeting to the newcomers. Monica found their presence comforting; she watched them soar over the chopper's position and cover the whole expanse of bottom land in seconds, until they settled into distant pine trees.

As she strode purposefully beside Slater, she realized, despite the bucolic surroundings, that they were quite marooned for the time being. And during a catastrophic geological event. This blunt realization steeled her to focus only on the next task, obtaining fuel for that night's fire.

Then use Jimmy's map to figure out a route out of there, she thought.

They had about 80 minutes left of daylight.

CHAPTER 20: KATY

Katy knelt down and checked Kendra's pulse. "Oh, Jesus," she muttered to herself, standing up and lowering her buff to rub the dread and frustration out of her eyes.

She reached down and checked the young lady's vitals to make sure, then straightened the body's legs, since the lifeless woman was contorted in the disturbing position the rock strike had left her in.

"We could have another aftershock at any moment," she said to herself.

Katy could hear Chris whimpering, then the car door opened as the youngster struggled to the ground. He seemed unhurt. "Stay right there, Chris!" Katy yelled. "You're alright. I'm coming."

She jogged over to the child, placed the backpack on

the ground, then hugged him. *The orphan*, effectively, she thought, is now *my* responsibility, until any parent is found.

She briefly recalled her own agonizing experience on the beach.

Chris stopped bawling; she felt her own tension melt away in the embrace, if only for those moments. She took the boy by the hand, first hoisting the now heavy backpack onto her shoulders.

She probed along the hotel wall with the flashlight. The huge stone leaned against the outside of the structure, like a recently unearthed fossil, or an *objet d'art.* They daintily shuffled through the rubble, and into an unlit room that had the dimensions of a small studio, including a kitchenette.

It was warm, for now, out of the wind. She put the silent boy down on an unmade bed. She pulled down plates and cups from a shelf above the miniature stove. She made them a crude, hardy meal from her collected scraps. The lights worked, as well as the burners on the stove. She quickly boiled some water, before the juice went out. "It must be generators," she said to the boy, who picked at his meal without relish.

Another shelf contained leftover condiments from a former tenant, hedonists playing in the Montana Rockies, before the region underwent its awful, violent conversion.

She found ketchup; she added blobs of this to the hours-old, gelatinous eggs, which Chris then stuffed into his mouth and slowly chewed, savoring them.

Katy ate her own, thinking about switching on the cable TV for updates. She stirred the eggs, stale cheese, and cold hash-browns into a ketchup-soaked casserole.

"This ain't half bad, you know?" she said to Chris. "In fact, it's damned good."

She swabbed the casserole with white bread painted with mayonnaise, a bottle of which someone else had eaten a third of.

"We are now bonafide dumpster divers," she declared.

The boy chewed the cold bacon strips with an awkward vigor, like a dog. Then he quipped, "Aunt Phyllis has a dumpster in her alley."

"Where does she live?"

"Fee-nix. Where's Kendra? Where did she go?"

A pause. "She got hurt by the rocks and I asked some people to take her to the hospital. She'll be okay soon." She felt bad about lying. Yet, she didn't know this lad. She didn't have a feel for his stoicism, or grasp of the concept of death. Her instincts told her to keep humoring him.

"Phoenix, ah. Where do *you* live?"

"Irvine."

"Irvine, California?"

"California. We drive to the ocean. I swim with my dolphin, Charlie. We eat butterscotch ice cream."

"I'm a chocolate chip lover myself. What's your last name? Mine's Morgan."

"Farnsworth," he said precisely. The food had perked him up.

"Chris Farnsworth," she said, getting up off the bed to switch on the flatscreen TV. "Sounds like a Marvel actor, or a pro golfer."

"I like Incredible Hulk."

It took a while to find and operate the remote, a fiddling that fondly reminded her of past hotels. The screen glowed on, and the first video to appear was a dreamy infomercial for Big Sky itself, the kind of promotional winter panorama accompanied by soothing female voiceovers.

Katy channel surfed until she found CNN; their coverage was non-stop, but there were no longer any in-field, on-the-spot reporters. Only Wolf Blitzer and the like. All the regional reporters had fled or been killed, Katy thought. She shut the tube off.

When she looked over, Chris was snoring on his back, the ketchup-stained plate dropped on the pillow beside him.

"Good," Katy whispered. She picked up the plate and brought it over to the sink, where water still ran. Feeling like she was on her toes, despite her own clawing fatigue, she began filling bottles and glasses with the tap water, before it ran out. She guzzled down several glasses, almost forgetting how desperately thirsty she'd been.

She went over to the bludgeoned wall of the studio and pulled a curtain across the broken glass and crumbled plaster and gaping hole where the rock had struck their temporary digs.

"I'm wiped out too," she said, as if she needed her

own voice to keep her company amidst the boy's light snoring, and to convince herself to turn down the dial on her nerves and get some zees.

A despair washed through her; she rubbed tears away as she thought of Kendra's lonely corpse lying outside, in a cold field of rubble. *Yes, she was sure the young lady was dead. She'd checked her vitals twice.*

She briefly considered going back for a third check, or dragging the body into the car. *If a bear wants it, she thought, it would smash the car window in anyways.* These morbid notions only wiped her out more.

She lay down and pulled the covers over her head, and it was a delicious warmth that flowed over her, against her will and in obeisance to her exhaustion, like a gentle waterfall or the sunny mineral baths she knew from Northern California.

When she woke the next morning, getting out of bed and leaving Chris asleep, the body outside had disappeared.

CHAPTER 21: KIATSU

A mass of birds flew overhead, a giant formation of geese shaped like a boomerang. They headed south, making their honking clarion calls, toward Nevada, away from the wildfire.

She couldn't hear the squawks and the cries because she had the windows rolled up, but she respected the wisdom of the flock. She envied their ability to navigate above the flames, even through the dense ash clouds. She felt puny, vulnerable, and trapped by comparison.

North of her escape route, the orange flames rose to the top of the tree-line, spouting fountains of sparks and embers. The fire, and the glowing embers, and the drifting curtains of ash made for a hellish tapestry. It didn't resemble her known world. The same nightmarish scene scorched the forests adjacent to the highway. They were, in fact, surrounded by fire.

She continued to press the accelerator and follow Zeke and his speeding motorcycle. She wondered how long he could stand the noxious air out in the open like that; not for long, merely minutes, she thought. He was all wrapped up in scarf and goggles, the dark hair flowing behind. She feared for all of their lives, for the first time believing that the odds had severely tipped against them. Her children made no noise, simply gaping in awe out the glass of the back windows.

She wouldn't have been surprised if Zeke's coat, with its leather frills along the chest and arms, spontaneously caught fire. She was visited by the nightmare vision of Nagasaki, the entire atmosphere, the air one breathes, aflame.

They'd never made the Oregon border. When he'd felt the heat on his face, like opening an oven door, Zeke had turned them south at the first opportunity. Follow the birds. But the wildfire, lit by hot, airborne ash, and consuming the vast forests of west-central Idaho, traveled too fast, Kiatsu thought. She stared with fear and disbelief in the rearview mirror, as fire licked the roadsides and pools of flying embers burst across the highway, barely missing Tiva's car.

Pulling over and resting, this time, wasn't an option. They'd all die; there was no refuge, only driving as fast as they could, and praying for their survival.

Zeke traveled in excess of 50 mph, stopping only for slowing traffic, then veering off to the side of the road to pass them. The highway had opened up considerably compared with their western route; the solid line of traffic on Highway 84 had now dissipated, as more vehicles fled the fire south toward Nevada and Utah, taking any roadway they could.

Her cellphone rested on the passenger seat. A few minutes ago, it had glowed and signaled the receipt of new messages. It was almost out of juice; she knew the messages were from Brad. If she could stop safely, she'd read and answer them. She'd tell him that she and her children loved him, and not to worry. Always remember that, *we miss you and we love you,* but don't tell him exactly how perilous their situation was. That wasn't *need to know,* that his wife and children could escape a massive eruption, only to die in a forest fire.

Visibility had dropped to nil, a murky, reddish shroud at mid-day. It was getting more difficult to see Zeke; she had only glimpses of Tiva's car behind her, then balls of flame and embers would dance across the highway, and Tiva would disappear into the enveloping smoke. Kiatsu didn't want to lose touch with her new companions; she suddenly felt lost and feckless, then admonished herself for that descent into weakness, much as her stubborn, gritty father would.

They were surrounded by tall, burning stands of timber; they passed neighborhoods engulfed in flames. She flinched and hunched her shoulders, when merely half a mile away, a filling station exploded in a bulbous fireball.

Eight minutes went by, like two hours. They might have made six miles in that time; they climbed a long snaking hill, which was less woodsy and more canyon, rocky-type terrain. Zeke's directional went on again. He was turning right, off the road, into an open area of shrubs and dirt that was full of smoke but not fire, with hills piled with rocks, like what she had seen in the deserts of Southern California.

Zeke pulled a U-turn in the gravel; Kiatsu thought that he was making sure Tiva had seen him make the turn. She had. The two vehicles pulled up beside him, then he signaled toward the rocks, restarted his motorcycle, and they followed him until he stopped again.

He parked the motorcycle, stepped off it, then collapsed onto the ground. Kiatsu jumped out of the car and ran, pulling down her own buff and shielding her eyes from the irritating smoke and ash. She reached Zeke, who was lying still on his side. She pulled him by the shoulder, so he rolled over onto his back.

"Mr. Sanchez, are you okay? Do you hear? We have to make the cover!" She yanked down on his dust-covered buff, revealing a red face covered in grime.

He opened his eyes. "Shit, where am I?" he said, licking his lips and struggling onto an elbow.

"We're in the countryside and there's a wildfire all around us! We have to go!"

Then he looked around in amazement, as if suddenly realizing the extent of their peril. "Oh shit, I must have passed out for a second there. I do that sometimes. A doc called it syncope, or something or other fainting. I know where we are; don't lose hope. Just give me a second..." He struggled to his feet.

"Where's Tiva?"

"She's right there, she's coming! Can you walk?"

"Are you kidding me? It takes more than this to knock me out." He hitched his shoulders defiantly, getting his bearings. "I don't remember breathing for about the last hour. We're going into a chamber just beyond those rocks. C'mon Tiva! Run!"

"What about my children? They're still in the car!"

"Oh yeah, crap! Get your kids now, and follow me! I'll be standing in front of the entrance to the refuge–it's just over there!" He pointed to the jumble of rocks, but an entrance wasn't visible from their vantage point.

"You mean, a cave," Kiatsu called over her shoulder. Embers swirled through the air in a hot wind. Funnels of fire exploded in tall trees only 50 yards away; they could hear a roar like an oncoming freight train.

Kiatsu gasped and ran back to the car, opened the passenger door, dragged both kids out, told them to hold their coats over their heads. She wasn't mincing words: "Go to that man waiting over there! Run for your life!"

She shut the car door. She wondered if it would burn up, then what? She took everything of value off the front seat, including the cellphone. The wind was hot on her eyes, as if, in minutes more, they would melt. She watched her children disappear into the smoke, heard yelling, insistent voices. She left the food in the back seat and ran, towards Abby and Jake.

A column of red-hot smoke saturated with embers hit Tiva's vehicle; it burst into flames. The heated gale knocked Kiatsu off her feet; she sensed heat on her back, the most terrible sunburn. Her eyes reddened, smarted, teared; she began to choke. She crawled towards her children. She fought to regain her feet, which had a strange, instant weakness. Both cars burned.

She noticed her pants and her shoes were on fire.

CHAPTER 22: BRAD

Remaining with a stalled car, in the middle of a thick ash storm, wasn't an option. At least, he kept telling himself that.

Damned useless rental! Garner felt no special affinity or responsibility for the RAV4, but it *had* taken him hundreds of miles from Chicago. He'd wait for someone to drive by, catch a ride to a service station, and see if they'd tow the car. Or he'd pass a house and ask for a lift to a station, but that wasn't looking good right now, as all of the homes he wandered past were remote, set back from the road, and dark.

They were sleeping; he'd be seen as an intruder, or they've all evacuated from the local wildfire. He didn't have a clue from which direction the fast-moving fire approached. As he wandered on foot along the side of the dark road, covering his face, still without messages from his family, he flirted with the notion of reversing direction and returning to the car.

Which plan was safer? This walking aimlessly toward the tiny village of Cimarron, New Mexico was an idiotic idea; but somehow, he couldn't stay put. He was antsy and had to keep moving, even if the prospects seemed more logical to stay with the car.

Desperate times call for desperate measures, he thought. He still had his credit cards, and he'd rent or buy a more durable vehicle, just to get out of these boonies and get closer to his family members.

He pulled the cellphone out of his pocket, poking it to life in his hand. It had juice, service, and *a message from Kiatsu! She's alive!* He stopped on the side of the silent road and anxiously read the pithy texts:

Dear Brad, We are heading west in cars and doing okay. It was a close call. At this time we are in western Idaho near the Oregon border. We're teamed up with a good, capable man named Zeke Sanchez and his daughter Tiva. Jake and Abby are fine. Now, we aim for Portland. Take care of yourself and we love you. Can you make it to Portland? I will try to call. Much love Kiatsu

She broke this message up into two texts, with her characteristic economy. He texted back, but the service had instantaneously vanished. He wanted to hurl the phone into an adjacent field, but then reminded himself that it remained his only conduit to his family, and had worked only moments ago. *Get a grip on yourself,* he thought. *Appreciate the progress you just made.*

He buoyed himself up with an image of reuniting with them in the western city, throwing his arms around them, burying his face in one of Kiatsu's warm, fashionable sweaters, which always carried a subtle scent of floral perfume.

Then he heard a tree fall and crash on a nearby hillside. He whirled around to look. The countryside was unlit and shadowy; he could only see the glow on the northern horizon of what had to be the wildfire. Glinting embers drifted through the air, or was that only ash, which fell gently around his feet with a calmness that only seemed to reflect the eye of another more furious storm to come. He quickened his pace, even if only to finish his first mile on this country road.

He thought back to when he'd last hitchhiked in New Mexico, as a nomadic and unfocused 20 y.o., more than 20 years ago. He was headed to Tucson, Arizona, where he knew a girl at the university. This was one of his first big youthful adventures, embarked on during the tail end of the bygone era of hitchhiking. He was on Highway 25 going south from Colorado. He got picked up by a semi-truck driver. The man was smoking cigar-sized marijuana joints, which the curious Brad toked on. They didn't talk much, and when they reached the intersection of Highway 10 west in New Mexico, he let Brad off.

The memory was beginning to fade, but a state trooper forbid Brad from hitchhiking in the middle of the night on Highway 10, yet oddly, given the usual severity emanating from law enforcement, he let Brad sleep that night in a barracks corridor. Being 20 y.o., Brad actually fell fast asleep in his sleeping bag on the hard floor, only to be awoken by another trooper's kick first thing in the morning.

This memory was how Garner passed the time as he wandered through the night, surrounded by trees drooping with dust, the air thick with a choking scent of wood smoke.

Finally, high beams illuminated the road. A pickup truck approached; Garner stuck out his thumb, already feeling that he'd declined a few rungs on the status ladder. He felt vaguely desperate, juvenile, and marginalized. Unjustly, he'd grown to look down on hitchhikers, as shiftless citizens "down on their luck," or even as potentially dangerous vagrants.

The truck passed him, then quickly pulled over, as though the driver had second thoughts.

Garner jogged through the gloom to the passenger side of the truck. The driver reached across the seat and unlocked the door. Garner opened the door, and as he stepped up onto the seat, the driver asked, "Where are you going?"

"My car broke down back there. I'm either going to a service station, if any are open, or as far south as I can. Thanks for stopping."

"I'm going to Mexico," the driver said matter-of-factly. She had black hair cut halfway down the ear, a baseball cap, and a faded jean coat.

"Wow," Garner said. "I figured you were a local,"

then he added, "since I was on the way to a small town and all."

The cab held a strong pot aroma, which was not unpleasant. He liked the scent of weed; cigarette smoke gave him a headache.

"You looked lost, a bit sorry," the driver said, putting the vehicle into gear and grinding the tires back out onto the empty road.

"I'll go as far as the connection with Highway 10, if that's okay. I don't want to impose on you. My name's Brad, by the way."

"Aeva." She looked at him with a mixture of bemusement and curiosity, then back at the windshield, through which one could only see about five yards in front of the truck.

"We have to go as far as we can," she said, with a clipped authority. "Non-stop. With the ash fall, the wildfires, and who knows what else."

"Given that I was walking out there, that sounds like a wonderful plan."

"You were a sorry sight," she repeated, with a half-smile. "It's been a while since I've seen a hitchhiker, especially one your age."

"It's a lost art."

Garner noticed she had small hands, gripping the stick shift and moving through the rough gears. They were surely a woman's hands, but had the dexterity of an experienced heavy-duty truck driver.

"Do you live in Mexico?"

"I did. I live in Taos now, on the outskirts, with my

partner Lucy. She's already down there. Mexico feels like a better option, with the volcano going off like it is."

She had worn, scuffed black cowboy boots, and straight-legged jeans. Her face was comely, but he sensed that out of modesty, shyness, some other motivation, the beauty had been hidden, covered up by slack, lackluster denim.

He'd thought the driver was a man for the first minute, then was relieved by her neutral feminine presence. The last thing he needed was the proverbial "stranger on a dark road" pulling a knife on him.

He was going to take this ride all the way to the border. He'd deal with the liability of his abandoned rental later.

The road was murky, thick with what looked like swarming moths in the high beams. The horizon behind them glowed; the fire grew, but they appeared to be driving away from it. That seemed like the lowest priority, given what was happening to his family, and that ash appeared to be burying half the lower 48.

"It seems like we've outrun the wildfire, for now," Garner said. He sensed the hitchhiker's obligation to make casual conversation, an instinct that hadn't prodded him in decades.

"Hopefully so," Aeva said, staring straight ahead. She had a sharp nose and full lips.

"Do you work with horses?" Brad asked.

"Yeah. How did you know that?"

"Just a guess." He imagined cowboys flirting with

her, then being gently rebuffed.

"All my customers claimed their animals before I left. I would never leave horses in these circumstances. Do you mind if I smoke pot?" she said.

"No."

She pulled over briefly, shut off the vehicle, and for a moment they sat in the dark silence. She lit up a slim joint, cracked the window an inch, and drew the smoke in with a savory manner. She offered it to him. "No, thank you. You see, I'm trying to reach my family on the cell, and I'm monitoring their whereabouts. Kind of have to keep my wits about me."

"Suit yourself." She smoked for another minute, then pinched the end of the joint and stored it in a makeshift ash tray, which was an old coffee can. She laughed to herself as she switched the ignition back on. "I was just thinking of Mexico, and hoping we can see the sun again."

"I totally get that," Garner said, as she pulled the truck back out onto the nearly empty county road. The smoke from the joint hung like a kind of aromatic lid by the ceiling. They were virtually alone. Her mood seemed to lighten, as if she was relishing memories of Mexico, and not thinking much about the stranger sitting beside her. His own words flowed more easily in the sparsely lit truck.

"I greatly appreciate you picking me up back there. Nine out of ten women would have kept on driving." She regarded him with more bemusement. He suddenly pictured her with her "partner," in bed.

"What's your partner's name, again?"

"Lucy Racine."

"Do you miss her, yet? Sorry, that was a dumb question. Of course you do."

"She can take care of herself. She has an independent streak. Anyways, my ma and my pa, they act like it's weird that I have a female partner. There's some awkwardness. This trip will go better with just me, when I visit my parents. Then I get together with Lucy. Do you miss your wife?"

"You bet I do." He decided, for no particular reason other than fatigue, not to go into the whole story.

"Do you know any good jokes?" Aeva asked.

"Not off-hand. Just silly ones that I tell my kids."

"Like?"

"What did the grape say when the man stepped on it?"

"What?"

"Nothing, it just let out a little whine."

"Ha-ha! Not bad." She was a good audience.

"Then there are the ethnic ones, you know, the ones I can tell at work. Did you hear the one about the Irishman and the Scotsman who got up and left the bar?"

"No."

"It *could* happen, you know."

"Oh no." Her turn. "What about the dude that sees a guy fishing in a puddle outside a bar. He says, 'C'mon old man, I'll buy you a drink.' Kind of patronizing and feeling superior, like. So the old man goes in with him and they sit down at the bar and order a couple of martinis. The first guy thinks he's being smart and he says, 'Say old man, how many did you catch today?' And the other guy looks at him, sips his martini, and says, 'You're my eighth.'"

"Ha-ha, very good, I like that one. I will commit it to memory, because I always forget jokes."

Another several minutes of silence went by. The windshield wipers swatted at the fitful ash that had blown in on the wind.

"It's okay if you sleep, you know," Aeva said.

"Thanks, I'll help with the driving soon, if you want."

"I might take you up on that."

They skirted the eastern slopes of the Sangre De Cristo mountains. The evening seemed endless, as though time itself had slowed. He kept checking the cell, but still no service. He felt less aimless, that he was finally getting somewhere, but in blunt practical terms, he was no closer to Kiatsu, Jake, and Abby. *They're alive, Thank God,* he murmured out loud. Aeva turned to listen. His head fell back against the head rest as he tumbled into the depths of sporadic sleep, to the monotonous dirge of the wipers.

He heard the hum and hollow thuds of the tire treads on the vacant road.

CHAPTER 23: MONICA

Day became night, as if someone had thrown a switch. They'd reached the forest on the edge of the bottom land, at least a mile from the chopper. They didn't know where they were, except in another remote swath of woods in the Sawtooth National Forest.

It was a straightforward hike through tall grasses to the trees. But Monica thought the return trip to the helicopter, as the ash fell and blocked any moonlight, was fraught and risky.

They were out there ostensibly to collect firewood, but all Monica could find was termite-eaten deadwood that was as light and brittle as balsa. Slater was reduced to cracking small branches off the lower trunks of trees. She just wanted to get back to the cramped refuge of the chopper.

She kept thinking about the voluminous pile of scat they'd seen on the way over. They weren't high on the food chain in this wilderness. They were some predator's tasty morsel; bears, cougars, wolves. The beasties thrived here, she thought. There was good reason for caution. Even paranoia.

It had been a long afternoon.

"This is stupid, collecting this pathetic wood. Let's get the hell out of here."

Slater took that remark as an insult. She thought he was acting like a cheeky boy scout, making his little bundle of campfire wood.

"You want to eat, right? Stay warm?"

"Let's just go," she said, shining the beam of light from her flashlight around the thick, dense woods.

The ash continued to drift down in curtains, covering the leaves and the ground in a luminous soot.

"Just hold the light steady, okay? I'm almost done. We've got enough for at least tonight." Then he went on, in a cheery way she found annoying: "You like soup, right? I've got some camping supplies in my pack; delicious chicken soup, pea soup, some kind of freeze-dried veggie medley..."

"Pea soup, wonderful," she said. "When I was a kid, I used to like pea soup with bits of ham floating in it." That made her think of her mother again, making lunch for Monica during the oh-so-brief "Mom" period, before she divorced her dad and went a little crazy. They ended up in a borderline shabby ranch house, next to a vacant lot in Phoenix, far from her beloved Santa Monica.

And that thought, in turn, made her feel alienated and abandoned.

"Let's get the hell out of here," she said. "I'll help you carry the wood." Her instincts told her to go, *now.* She always went by gut feelings, which proved accurate far more often than not.

Slater followed her at a short distance out of the bush, compulsively stooping to add more twigs to his wood bundle. She aimed the flashlight's beam around the dark forest, where she sensed all kinds of shadowy, random movements, which turned out to be nothing but what fear made in her mind.

The flashlight's beam began to flicker weakly.

"Jesus, batteries, don't fail me now," she said, trudging through the tall, wet grass, the brim of her hat pulled down low over her eyes. She wasn't used to being lost; she hated that feeling. She hated being out of control, in a wilderness, if even for only a moment. She was an outdoor lover, but risk averse.

They couldn't see a sign of the helicopter's fuselage, not yet. They trudged about 50 yards; the grasses were knee deep and bristling with briars and coarse weeds. All you could hear was the plodding of their footsteps, the shunting of the wind.

"Jeter!" she cried out to the dog, in a muffled and plaintive voice. "Just bark!...so I know where you guys are." No answer.

The field sloped down off to the left into a dark gully, where there were more dense clusters of trees and brush.

"We better be going in the right direction," she mumbled. "It's really hard to see our trail," which was only the depression their shoes and thighs had made in the tall grass. It was not a well-worn game trail.

She stopped, listened, aimed the flashlight onto the dark slope. She'd heard loud noises, which stopped.

"Did you hear that?" she whispered. "I heard branches breaking, footsteps."

"Yeah, I heard that too," Slater said, but without the fear and paranoia in his voice. "We might have startled some deer, or even a moose. Or even a lone black bear, a foraging yearling. Whatever, that happens all the time when I go hiking. Let's just keep going."

She took his word for it; she kept walking. The sallow, airborne ash reflected the flashlight beam like headlights aimed into the rain.

More crashing came from the brush below, followed by a drawn-out, throaty groan. A heavy, ponderous body smashed through undergrowth, beneath them in the dark, but they couldn't make it out.

A low, anxious tone: "That was no deer."

"Just keep walking," Slater whispered. Her pace quickened. She thought she smelled piss. The jittery column of light bounced around the long, slanting grass, surrounded by darkness.

"That hunting knife you have," she said. "Give it to

me."

Then she spotted the chopper's rotor blades, a distant shadow leaning at an angle. They were about half a football field away.

"There it is, the helicopter! Jimmy, it's us! Call out if you can hear us!"

"He can't hear us," Slater said, looking behind them nervously. "He's probably inside, but at least we know where the chopper is. Better than banging around like a couple of lost lambs out here." Slater resumed a nervous chatter; now Monica knew he was as scared as she was.

"I caught a ride once with a hired driver in Bozeman. He used to be a guide in Yellowstone. We were talking about bears. He told me, 'It was the moose, not the grizzlies, that used to give us problems. One time a grizzly walked right past us on the trail. We just stepped off and let him go by. *He* didn't care.'"

"Wait a second," Monica said, stopping. She aimed the thin, wavering beam back down the slope, into the brush, into the dark hollow where they'd heard the crashing sounds. Branches snapped; then a flurry of heavy footfalls clambered through the inky underbrush.

Indistinctly, Monica could make out the huge brown bear, waddling out into the open, with its hulking shoulders swaying. Its shifting bulk appeared almost amorphous in the shadows, all 700 pounds of fur, head, ears, and front quarters. The shoulders swayed back and forth; the huge head moved up and down. She heard deep grunts and growls in the empty night.

She made a desperate calculation; it might take them, at a brisk hike, a minute and a half to make the helicopter.

Don't run, she thought, even though she had an irresistible desire to sprint at full speed to the chopper. Every fiber in her being cried out *Run! Run for your life!*

But she'd also been told, *don't run from a grizzly, unless you want to send the signal that you're breakfast, lunch, and dinner for Ursus Arctos.*

She froze, holding the light on the animal, as if against her will. Slater hissed, "Monica, don't agitate him. Just move!"

The grizzly stood up, all seven to eight feet of him, then huffed loudly and snapped its jaws, a terrifying noise she'd never heard before. The bear began to rub its back on the bark of a tree, before it settled back heavily on all four legs again.

Slater pushed away the hand clutching the flashlight.

"We probably got too close to a carcass. Just keep walking. It's not a sow, and I don't see any cubs around." They strode quickly toward the shadow of the rotor blades, Monica's heart beating like a hummingbird's, sweat coursing down her ribcage.

The ash storm fell thickly. They listened for the footfalls; seconds went by. She could only hear their own plodding footsteps, their raspy breaths.

A deep, reverberant growl emanated from the darkness. Heavy footfalls struck the soggy ground behind them. *It's charging,* she thought. *It's going to catch us.*

Hollowly, in the background, she heard Slater yell, "No! No bear!"

Within seconds, she thought: how far away the chopper still was, and how Mother Nature had equipped the brown bear to be an almost perfect killing machine. It ran 40 mph; the apex predator could cover a cluttered forest floor like an Olympic sprinter, even while weighing almost 800 pounds.

She noticed that she had stopped breathing, as though she forgot to exhale.

It was already too late. She looked down, one hand gripped the flashlight, the other sweaty hand clutched Slater's hunting knife. It was fight back, play dead, or play dead and fight back, or die.

CHAPTER 24: ZEKE

The funnel of fire powered through the forest, setting treetops, vehicles, and roofs ablaze.

The ridges burned along the northern horizon of Idaho. No home was spared; the cars and trucks were reduced to charred metallic hulks. That included Kiatsu's Nissan Sentra and Zeke's Harley Davidson, both burned into greasy, scorched chunks of metal. The ruined bike lay pitiably on its side, its tires melted like black goo over the stylish spoked wheels.

Seconds before the wildfire roared over the dirt lot, Zeke sprinted back to where Kiatsu had collapsed. Her shoes were on fire; flames flickered along the fabric of her trousers and sweater. He put out the flames with his coat, as quickly as he could, then lifted her up and carried her back to the cliff-side chamber they used for shelter.

He'd known about the cave before; its location was the reason he had pulled off the highway. Tiva, Jake, and Abby were huddled as deeply as they could crawl into its craggy depths.

Red-hot embers flew through the air; he closed his eyes and wondered if his own hair would spontaneously burst into flames.

Zeke set Kiatsu down on the dirt floor of the chamber. White smoke wafted off the burned fabric. Her eyes were closed–then they fluttered open, expressing confusion, fright. She was still breathing, her chest faintly moving up and down.

"She's going into shock," Tiva said.

Tiva had a portable medical kit with her. They made sure all the flames were extinguished on Kiatsu's clothes. They made a pad of coats on the floor of the cave. Then Tiva went to work with dressings and medications.

Outside the entrance of the shelter, an unfathomable firestorm had blown through, leaving a scorched earth: exploded, melted vehicles and trees reduced to brittle, smoky charcoal. It had the duration of a brief summer storm, but the aftereffect of a fire bomb.

Jake and Abby were mute and appeared traumatized, but Zeke reassured them their mom was going to be okay. They had to find a hospital soon, though; there is only so much sugarcoating you should do with children, he thought.

Zeke was worried about Kiatsu's serious injuries, but

realistic; they'd survived the wildfire, by the thinnest of margins. If he'd missed getting them into the shelter by five minutes, they would all have been barbecued in a 1,500-degree F. blast furnace.

The thought made his own legs tremble, as the adrenaline of the aftermath coursed through his veins. He scowled, imagining his charred, ruined Harley.

He stood at the entrance to the chamber. Ghostly wisps of white smoke drifted from the forest, where burned trunks hissed like eggs in a griddle.

The kids remained uncharacteristically silent behind him, although Zeke knew they had a thousand questions.

"I'm gonna get some food and water for us, guys," he said, anticipating at least one of their unspoken thoughts.

"What about the car?" Jake said. "Is our car ruined?"

"It sure is my friend. We're going to find another one, though. We'll be able to catch a ride with someone, and we'll get your mommy to a doctor." *Or "scavenge" a working vehicle, as in steal, as soon as possible, he thought.*

Zeke wandered over with the children and knelt down beside Tiva, who sat cross-legged next to Kiatsu, wrapping her wounds in gauze and tape.

"How is she, darling?"

Tiva grimaced, concerned. "She has bad burns on her extremities and feet. Obviously, she needs critical care soon. With burns..."

"It's the infection risk, I know..."

"How's the car?"

"Toasted, along with my Harley-Davidson! A 1,500-degree fire, that won't take long to annihilate everything in its path. The wildfire's gone to the west of here, so I need to go look for alternative transportation. There might be a car or truck down the road that still runs. I hope...fingers crossed..."

"We can't stay here forever. We've got to get moving fast. This lady needs help. Maybe someone out on the highway will give us a ride?"

"Maybe." Zeke stood up, dusted himself off. Kiatsu looked as austere and motionless as a marble saint.

She had not cried out in pain. He didn't understand that; burns are extremely painful, he'd heard the moans of wounded soldiers three times her size, before the morphine kicked in. She may have been blessed by unconsciousness; she may have been going into shock. They could use some of his stronger weed as a painkiller, when and if she woke up.

All Tiva could do was apply some antibiotic cream and burn gel, dress the wounds with gauze and tape, and when Kiatsu was awake, administer some ibuprofen, even though they were running low on water. Only one canteen left.

He watched her carefully, quietly reciting an invocation to his own Gods, the Ancient Ones from the Great Plains.

She was a calm, fine woman; she didn't deserve it, he thought. No sir. Life metes out its arbitrary blows irrespective of whether the person is good or bad. Fires and volcanoes are equal opportunity killers.

They would pull each other through this, he thought. They'd put their heads down and find salvation at the end of the road. He was glad he'd found his daughter...

From what he'd seen, Kiatsu possessed a chaste, almost divine stoicism.

The wind picked up outside, stoking the flames that finished consuming the burned vehicles. Singed upholstery and burnt wooden pieces of blow-torched homes skittered along the ground. The ash, still drifting in thickly from the east, sifted over the wreckage like piles of flaky skin.

He adjusted his goggles, pulled up his buff, and carefully picked his way through the wreckage, still feeling bad about the carcass of his motorcycle.

Questions plagued him: If he found a working vehicle, and the keys (*lucky strike!*), where was the closest hospital? Boise? That was still too far away; at least 150 miles, he guessed.

It's doubtful we'll find a doctor or an open clinic that can deal with burns, he thought. At least we have Tiva, and her medical kit; her knowledge and expertise.

He wondered how long Kiatsu had, before she succumbed to her injuries. He was vexed, fretful. Maybe he could find a doctor using his cellphone, but when he pulled it out of his pocket, it had no service. *Useless oblong!*

That couldn't happen, Kiatsu dying, not with Jake and Abby at her side; he couldn't stomach that agonizing outcome.

Every car or truck he could see in the area was burnt to a smoldering hulk. Thirst clawed at his dry, sore throat. Water, transportation, medical care, in that order, he thought.

A few vehicles snaked through the smoldering wrecks, fleeing west. They ignored his attempts to flag them down. Given that he was soiled and powdered head to toe in cinders and dust, he understood why no one would want to pull over for him.

He must look like a walking-dead zombie, he thought, coughed up by the apocalypse.

He walked west along the highway and a grassy easement, bordered by a chainlink fence. Beyond the fence was a long dirt driveway, which led to a partly demolished home. About a third of the structure was collapsed into piles of charred timber, but the rest of the house, and an attached garage, appeared intact. He found a space in the fence where a car or truck had previously plowed through it, then he made his way up the driveway.

The structure's contents were still salvageable, he thought. He would explore it, and cop some useful supplies. He continued to cough spasmodically, craving water, and wondering what the noxious air was doing to his lungs.

He searched the connected garage, peering in its window. He was disappointed, but not surprised, to find it contained no vehicles, motorcycles, or bikes (which wouldn't be of much use to him anyways). He turned his head and called out, "Hello! Anyone home!"

No answer. When he tried the side door to the garage, it was locked. It had glass window panes. After a search for a rock that was taking too long, he finally used the butt of his pistol to break the window. Then he reached inside and unlocked the door.

He found a prototypical exurban clutter of things: a lawnmower, wadded up garden hoses, trash cans, and a flag that was wrapped around its pole and shoved into a grungy corner of the garage, amidst the spider webs and teeny piles of dead insects.

A yellowed old Frigidaire was shoved in next to a wooden workbench. He peeled back its adhesive door. It wasn't powered up, or cold. He found a bottle of spoiled milk, a foul-smelling carton of rotten eggs, an aging six-pack of Rainier beer, and two gallons of department-store water.

This was the kind of water that he used to ridicule as bogus, because all they did was fill up cheap gallon bottles with tap water, slap a fancy label on them, then sell them for four or five bucks each.

Now it was liquid gold. Bingo.

He'd save the water and share it with the others, but he instantly cracked open a Rainier and guzzled down the flat brew, which was a perfect panacea for that clawing thirst. He'd bag the other five cans as well.

After a brief search of the rest of the garage, he resorted to unwrapping and removing the flag from its staff. It was an antique, tattered Old Glory, its frayed edges making him think it had flown for a part of the administration of Woodrow Wilson.

He tied a knot to make a bag; this was good enough for the mile or so he had to walk, back to the red-rock hovel, where he was afraid they expected him to drive up in another cozy vehicle.

He left the garage and lugged his provisions back up the driveway, with the harvest thrown over his shoulder, using the staff for a walking stick.

We'll come back to this house, he thought. It might be partly burned down, but it still could still have more water, food, medical supplies; you name it. Hell, they might just use it as a shelter for the night, at least until they could find some wheels.

Then he heard it: the loud, unmistakable *rup-rup-rup* of a helicopter's turbines, high up and hidden in the clouds above them.

CHAPTER 25: KATY

Katy was shocked to find that Kendra had been dragged away from the hillside. She didn't think it was a human that removed the body. It was not as if ambulances were active at night in the area, at this moment of mass panic and evacuation. She thought of looking for tracks in the ash, but decided to be Zen about it.

C'est la vie. There was nothing she could do to affect this outcome.

She'd slept only a few hours, but deeply. The early morning shadows lengthened over the cold terrain. She repacked her things, leaving Chris to sleep wadded up in the covers.

The gouge in the wall of the abandoned hotel had made their temporary refuge unfit to live in, she'd decided.

This was a gut decision, as a stiff wind down off the mountain, which climbed steeply from the hotel, had torn her crude covering off the wall. The room was cold, damp, and moldy. An ominous banging of metal pipes came from the other side of the walls.

It still had some advantages: a double bed with blankets, running water, electricity, oven burners that worked, although she didn't expect these amenities to last long. She could attempt to erect a more permanent patch for the hole, she thought, but she just didn't want to stay in the hotel permanently.

Katy reasoned that the cabin farther up on the mountain was a safer and more reliable refuge, one unlikely to be invaded and claimed by other stragglers. For that reason, a gut feeling that principally guided her decisions, she didn't want to seek out other rooms in the hotel.

She was afraid that the hot ash, still falling steadily and swirling in the heightened winds, could ignite a structural fire. She was afraid of marauders, and confident she would find the small, high-elevation lodge unoccupied, for at least the moment.

Now, it was only a question of getting there. She had to go up 1,300 feet in elevation, as the lodge was located at 8,800 feet above sea level. Higher altitude was generally nothing to her; she tolerated it well. She didn't know how Chris would do, or how she would handle Kendra's death with him.

He was being passed between adults like a hot potato, and she thought his unformed emotions and mind must be in a spin. At least he was sleeping.

She hoisted her backpack and walked outside to the Jeep. Wearing gloves, she scraped and dusted off all of the windows and the hood. The ash had become caky, like wet flour; the air was cold and unlit by sunlight. She had the buff pulled tight around her face, and she tried not to breathe deeply. She wore a ski hat, but she might have to lend that to Chris, who didn't have her layers.

She leaned the backpack on the front passenger seat, then she went back inside the hotel to collect all of her scavenged food. This was another problem she had with leaving the hotel; it was still a reliable, even boundless, source of food and water. She could always return to it for harvesting expeditions, she thought, by walking down the fire road from the slope-side lodge.

She didn't know how long they'd be stuck on Lone Peak, the summit of which went up almost 4,000 feet from the hotel.

Survival involved having a plan, winging it, then changing the plan if that wasn't working. Always, a plan. Always, adapting.

It wasn't rocket science, but it took a crafty spirit, a fit body, and a generous serving of luck. They had gas, food, water, shelter, she reasoned, things could be a whole lot worse.

She returned to the hotel room, where she found Chris sitting on the side of the bed, appearing dazed and out of it.

"Good morning!" she said, trying to sound chipper.

He hesitated a moment, then said, "Where were you?"

"Taking my stuff to the Jeep. I'm going to get the food and water now. Do you want something to eat?"

"No. Do we have to go?"

She didn't have the energy, and wasn't in the mood, for the 20 questions. She wondered how mothers did it every day.

"We have to get out of here, you know? Those stones are coming down the mountain and hitting the hotel. And it's cold in here. But we're going to a really nice place. Why don't you have something to eat, and put your coat on."

"Oh, alright." They seemed to have the faint beginnings of rapport.

He climbed off the bed sluggishly, as she worked the ski hat down over his head. She noticed he had the sniffles, and for the first time, a rather worn pair of high-top sneakers.

She thought again of his parents; by some off chance, she could find them. They must have his suitcase full of backup shoes and clothes. The responsibility for the vulnerable can bring on a headache; Katy sensed the dregs of one.

She moved quickly around the kitchenette, stuffing the food remnants in a bag. "When was the last time you saw your real parents, I mean, before you ended up with Kendra?" He thought for a moment.

"We stopped at the lake to get some water," he mumbled.

"Hebgen Lake–so they can't be too far away," She said. Actually, they're probably dead, she thought sullenly.

She imagined her colleagues in the helicopter, all of the days she had spent hanging with Monica and Slater while monitoring Yellowstone. Simply living out those days together, when life was merely characterized by ordinary zeal and disappointments, not minute-by-minute survival.

She thought Monica and Max were a good couple, perhaps too bright and intense to live in complete harmony. Knowing Monica's hard-headedness, Katy knew they fought a lot. Knowing Slater, who'd hired Katy for a virtual dream job, she knew he was brain smart, but perhaps not woman smart. He didn't have a sense for when to let it go, chill out.

Then, it became apparent to Katy that they'd broken up…Katy made Chris a stale bread and peanut-butter sandwich as these homely thoughts flowed…Katy hardly had time to contemplate whether the breakup was permanent, and would affect the atmosphere at the YVO, when the shit hit the fan at Yellowstone.

She suddenly felt intensely lonesome, wishing she had a man around who cared about her. Maybe it would happen someday, soon, if she lived through this.

Chris followed her outside to the Jeep, slowly munching on the sandwich. He wasn't crying or whining that they were leaving the hotel–*thank you*, she murmured.

She thought of Monica, the look on her face, as she

departed on that precarious looking chopper. A mixture of guilt, regret, and fear. Well, Slater and Monica were forced together *now*, whether they liked it or not.

She put Chris into his seatbelt in the back seat, then she slipped into the driver's seat and started up the Jeep, feeling awash with relief as the engine coughed and sputtered on. She switched on the windshield wipers; fucking monotonous ash already piled up on the hood.

She thought of the death and mayhem they'd barely escaped, from the pyroclastic flow; she briefly entertained the ghastly image of being inside a 700-degree tornado, and what went through one's mind for the second before they were carbonized to dust. Then she forced herself out of these woeful thoughts, and went back to work, driving the Jeep slowly over rutty, bare ground.

She wouldn't be doing this if all they had was ordinary wheels. *Thank God for four-wheel drive, and half a tank of gas.*

She drove past the point where something had dragged Kendra's body away. Chris hadn't asked about her; he appeared to exude the uncomplicated acceptance of a child. The Jeep's thick tires bit into the stones, gravel, and mud of the fire road; she dropped it into four-wheel drive, as the road rose into a 20-percent grade.

She drove slowly over rocks that lay at the periphery of the rock slide, then they turned into another switchback. She felt some confidence; the hard-working Jeep otherwise handled the grade flawlessly. She'd be at the lodge in possibly 30 minutes. It would be sturdy, and have creature comforts. The side of the road was bordered by stands of lodgepole pines, lining gullies that people loved to ski and snowboard into, now covered in fallen needles and ash.

She spotted the green metallic roof, the railing of the moderate-sized lodge's spacious outdoor deck. They reached the cleared slope of this mountain, and she parked within about ten yards of the lodge. She turned off the engine; she noticed a light was on in the building. *That could have been left on by whoever exited this place after the eruption,* she thought.

"Stay here for a minute," she said. Chris sat quietly in the back seat, nibbling the final bites of the sandwich that had kept him quiet and not overly inquisitive.

She exited the car and walked halfway around the building, shivering in a cold wind that sleeted an early-season snow. She wished she had another knit hat, as Chris wore hers. Everything was murkier in the early morning light, because she also wore protective shades with leather add-ons on the side.

Behind the lodge, she found an ATV parked near a deck post of the dwelling. At the foot of the vehicle was the satchel that Kendra had been carrying.

CHAPTER 26: MONICA

Jeter barked furiously and incessantly at the window, virtually frothing at the mouth. The door was latched tight. The huge grizzly, ignoring the collie's growling and snapping, nosed around the long grass and shrubs outside of the MD 500.

He looked up now and then, impassively curious, lumbering over his realm, taking his time and appearing more distracted than ferocious. After about 15 minutes of foraging, with Jeter apoplectic, he finally ambled off into the bush.

Sprinting for the chopper, Slater had dropped his backpack first, then Monica. The bear fell for the unintended bait, halting its charge to search for anything edible in the discarded baggage. He'd batted them around with his giant paws and torn open the packs and scattered their contents, but he quickly lost interest. By that time, Slater and Monica had dove into the interior of the helicopter, just before Greenhorn latched the door behind them.

Jimmy had a pistol out, but he didn't seem inclined to use it yet. He wasn't sure he had enough ammo to take down a 700-pound male grizzly, nor that they needed or had the ability to harvest bear meat at the moment.

Slater wondered if the bear's charge had been a bluff; he didn't want to think of himself as having nearly left Monica to be mauled and devoured. At any rate, they'd escaped by the skin of their teeth. After several minutes, Slater went back outside and collected the scattered belongings and the barely recoverable backpacks. Jimmy followed him with the loaded handgun. Slater also recovered at least part of the firewood, which he'd dropped when the bear charged.

Soon, he had a fire going, several paces from where the helicopter had landed. The fire, with flames weakly consuming a modest pile of moist wood, lit both of Slater's and Jimmy's tired faces. It was hardly big enough to dissuade a large predatory mammal from returning.

They didn't think the bear was going to come back, because it hadn't been rewarded for its efforts, or been "fed." But when Slater began to cook soup and other grub in a small camping pan, sending a chicken-broth aroma wafting through the surrounding bush, Monica was nervous and opted for staying inside for the evening.

Jimmy was buoyant; he had good news. He'd discovered a "clogged motor-oil hose," and scrubbed or dug out ash deposits that had infiltrated other parts of the MD 500's Rolls Royce engine. He went on and on about the mechanical processes he'd delved into, until Monica, still exhausted and shivering from the grizzly charge, asked him for the "dummy's version."

An initial test of engine start-up had worked, he replied. He planned to take off the following morning.

The inner rejoicing was hard to contain; she also didn't want to be devastated if his plan didn't work.

He said he wanted to head south, then follow the highway as far west as he could fly. He sounded far more upbeat about the helicopter than he had the day before. He clearly was a mechanical genius–she admired that because she didn't know any true-blue fix-it guys.

Monica took the news as a fortuitous sign that they didn't have to hike out of this wild place. *Anything, anything! to avoid going back into the backcountry, with the bear constantly in the back of their minds, if not on their trail. There were gray wolves, mountain lions...*she didn't want to think about it anymore.

The relief induced her to collapse and zonk out in a cramped corner of the passenger area, using Jeter's furry back as a pillow.

# #

The rotor blades slowly turned, gradually gaining speed as they pierced the morning silence with their greasy, metallic din. Greenhorn wore his head gear, sitting in the pilot seat with the three other passengers behind him. They'd already untangled the landing skids from the tall grass and shrubs.

The aircraft lifted and arced away from their temporary, remote sanctuary. Monica sensed her heart leap. She wasn't thinking at all about a further crash risk; she wasn't going to let that enter her mind.

The aircraft quickly gained hundreds of feet of altitude, racing over the dense, green wilderness at a cruising speed of 100 knots (about 115 mph). The view filled Monica with awe and foreboding; they would have spent weeks out there, attempting a perilous hike-out. The rotor wake had left a well-defined circle in the grasslands; she watched it gradually get smaller, surrounded by hundreds of miles of unbroken forest.

How puny they were down there, she thought, how thin their margin of survival. She felt safer, if only artificially so, as Greenhorn jetted along in "the gold-standard MD 500E," as the pilot proudly described it.

They reached 1,000 feet of elevation, then 1,500 feet, which was the ceiling before the visibility dropped to nil. There were no roads or towns from horizon to horizon, the dark, rolling carpet of a vista broken only by a distant lake. The sky was marred by billowing brown clouds, a constant reminder of Yellowstone's eruption about 300 miles east of their location.

Lightning flashes appeared in angry clouds draped along the eastern horizon; the supervolcano had created its own weather, systems that stretched for miles on end in both directions. Due to the massive layer of particles deposited in the troposphere, the aboveground dome where weather occurs, the winters to come would be arctic, bleak, and lengthy, for most of the northern hemisphere.

At the moment, Halstrom was flying blind through an increasingly murky airspace. He descended back to the treetops, following the contours of the land, west towards Oregon.

"We're in the Sawtooth National Forest," he called back to Slater and Monica. "I camp and hike in Joshua Tree, and I used to think that desert park was big. This Sawtooth is bigger, at least a million acres."

The helicopter gained more altitude, and they flew over the empty, dark purple lake. It was windblown with countless tiny rivulets, but there were no signs of boats and vessels. "No one wants to fish in a shitstorm," the pilot grunted. "I'm sure that's Alturas Lake. It's about 30 miles north of Ketchum. That's good, I pretty much know where I am."

"How's the fuel?" Monica asked, not wanting to be peevish or complainy, but interested.

"Low to moderate. We have enough. I'm 50 miles from Boise."

Slater made a quick calculation–if they were 50 miles from Boise, Idaho, then they were about 480 miles from Portland and the west coast. They could be in Boise in half an hour.

"Can you refuel in Boise?" he asked.

"That's the plan."

They'd finally seen signs of civilization, with a few widely separated fishing and camping settlements visible. The landscape looked like a slept-in blanket, a deep green rug of lodgepole pine, Douglas fir, and Engelmann spruce forests, flowing in dips, ridges, and valleys. To the north, a jagged range of snow-encrusted mountains rose above 10,000 feet.

Monica admired the vistas out the window, basking in the feeling of being whisked to safety, and a restored sense of order.

"Ever been in a helicopter before?" Jimmy called over. They'd reached forested hills on the other side of the lake. Startled white birds erupted from the treetops. The MD 500 disappeared into the clouds that nested in the following valley.

"Twice," she said. "Once on an aerial tour of Yellowstone. Another time on a tourist's ride in Florida, with two friends who had dropped acid. Now *that* was a trip!"

He laughed incredulously. "How sober was the pilot?"

"As sober as I was. That was a stage I was going through. You know how it is when you're young, you have all kinds of friends. They don't always make the same choices you do. I was pretty boring, a nose-to-the-grindstone academic. They were drug enthusiasts and experimenters, but I wasn't. I wanted to see the Atlantic ocean from a distance, and soberly. I was way too paranoid for that kind of stuff…drugs…I was just a kid, starting graduate school in California." She caught Slater listening to her.

"I never did acid either," the pilot said, merely happy to shoot the breeze about youthful indiscretions. For the moment, it seemed like they were in the clear.

"I smoked pot in my time, and I love to drink those microbrews, probably too much."

He looked back at Monica, as if to double-check that she was listening, still with his head-gear on.

"Do you have a wife, Jimmy?" she asked, in a loud voice over the engine.

"I did, Gretchen. She passed, four years ago. She had M.S. We have a son Brandon. You remind me of her, a little. Pretty, smart..."

"I'm really sorry to hear your wife died," she said. Slater put his arm around Monica and kissed her on the cheek. She turned and smiled at him. The dog lay at their feet, slowly wagging his tail. It was a small space. They all felt secure as they sped over the untamed forests.

"Where's Brandon now?" Slater asked.

"Baja California. Works for a seafood company. I'm going there, once we get our butts out of this cluster–"...he didn't want to ruin the vibe by cursing their current state..."this fix we're in."

"We can get to Portland, rent a vehicle, drive down to Southern California," Slater said hopefully. Then he thought of all the responsibilities, as a scientist, he'd left behind. He'd run away from them, like a man who's abandoned a child that has become delinquent. A catastrophic eruption had almost killed them, but had now killed, doubtlessly, thousands of others. His official warning had been late, inadequate in a pathetic, bureaucratic way. He suddenly felt demoralized; his head rested on the window, which gently vibrated.

Dark green forests, gullies, a small creek, flew by beneath his feet. The engine sounded loud and he held his head in his hand for a moment.

"Are you alright?"

"Just a little headache," he told Monica, his head turned. "I have to find out what's happening, analyze the data. I have to make a prognostication, and report it." Ash deposition depths, geographical distributions, probable duration of eruption, population estimates of displaced people, fatalities, and affected major Metro areas. Hundreds of thousands, perhaps, will die in a handful of weeks. The loud engine hammered at his temples.

Nature wins, he thought. Mankind can only minimize the damage and loss of life, and then only if cooler heads prevail.

The landscape beneath them became scorched, coal black. Hillsides covered in black ash, trees toppled over into matchstick piles of charcoal. They passed a home burned to the ground, vacated, an oblong, debris-filled pool still aquamarine in color.

Tall flames writhed along the blackened borders of forests. Tendrils of the wildfire pooled on hillsides, climbing the slopes as if reaching upwards with molten arms. They flew over the burned hulks of vehicles arrayed along a road; the ground-level smoke thickened. The helicopter, which had previously skimmed the forest canopy, climbed another 800 feet in half a minute.

A cloud mushroomed into the western sky. The chopper cleared a ridge and dipped toward a highway again, one that aimed toward Boise. In a clearing, surrounded by rocks, they saw a man, a tiny man, alone, waving what looked like a red blanket. He shook it furiously, like a flag, when Jimmy turned the aircraft 180 degrees and gave them all a better look.

"That's the first person we've seen today on foot," Monica said. "He needs help."

The pilot wore a blank look that expressed unwillingness. "We can't go pick up anyone who needs help down there. I'm only designed for three passengers."

"We can fit a few more."

"We're not a medevac search-and-rescue outfit! Including fuel, I can carry a max payload of 1,500 pounds. I'm already at about 1,000, and we'll be at max when I fuel up."

Slater took a deep breath, exhaled. He was tired of leaving people behind. They'd let Katy go; she would have been in the chopper now, payload limits or no payload limit.

The man waved his arms, using the international distress signal, flag clutched in one of his hands.

"We can at least see what he needs, maybe it's an injured child."

"What if it's a ruse, some kind of bait," Jimmy abjured. "Desperate times. You never know what's going on down there. There's also a wildfire, and we've got to get to where we're going, *vamonos.*"

"Please?" Monica said. "Only five, ten minutes?"

Greenhorn shook his head world-wearily, as if in response to a recalcitrant child.

"Alright, alright, alright!" he shouted over the engine, relenting. He put the helicopter into a descent. Nearing the ground, it unearthed a messy cloud of dirt and black ash.

Zeke Sanchez ducked, covered his eyes, and ran toward the chopper as it settled into the open lot, not far from the burned and scorched Harley.

CHAPTER 27: KIATSU

She'd gotten on her feet and shuffled to the chamber's entrance, when she heard the loud rattle of an engine. The air was foul outside, with sepulchral blankets of smoke arrayed along the earth. She held her arms out, as if she was about to fly, because it was too painful to keep them close to her body.

The young lady Tiva had said, "don't move." But she was tired of laying on the hard floor of wherever they'd taken her, and she thought if she didn't move, she would die there. She mobilized all of her willpower, brought herself to a sitting position, then with the other two, including Jake, holding each hand, she stood up, fighting the dizziness and nausea.

Her feet moved, as if they were someone else's and she was observing them from outside her body, then she saw the helicopter, its rotor blade turning and the group of people talking beside it.

She felt too weak to talk, so she didn't discuss the matter with the young nurse: how could they possibly have summoned an emergency medical helicopter, under these marginal circumstances?

Her arms and her legs throbbed, although Tiva had given her something with water. Zeke stood outside with three other people. She moved closer, with Jake and Tiva. Abby wandered behind her. They'd kept telling Abby that her mother wasn't going to die, she's just sick, but Abby knew Kiatsu had been burned.

She could hear the conversation, fragments of it, as the blade of the helicopter kept turning. It dispersed the white smoke, but kicked up a cloud of fine grit. Zeke pointed over to her, "She needs critical care." Then he turned to look at her again, as though she was going to be reprimanded for leaving the shelter. If she hadn't left, it might have become her crypt, forever.

Perhaps there's an afterlife, and Papa Saito is there, she thought. But she had no conventional religious principles and thought the view of the afterlife a fanciful one. She thought that all of life was what she was experiencing, now.

"I don't have room for two more," the pilot said. "I can't carry the weight, without lightening the payload some other way." Kiatsu concluded, Zeke wanted Tiva to accompany her.

The world spun; she felt light-headed and intensely thirsty. "I'm sitting"; she knelt to the ground. Her arms were still out like wings. She thought of the iconic war photograph of the young Vietnamese girl who'd been injured by napalm, running naked down a road; a photo you couldn't pry your eyes from, a heartbreaking one that summoned all of the evil injustice of war.

You looked at the picture and you wanted to know what had ultimately happened to the girl. It stirred your humanity.

Now she understood, perfectly, why the child had held her arms out like that.

# #

"I'll stay," Monica said.

"You sure?" Jimmy said.

"Yes, if it means you can take her to the hospital."

"Okay, the injured lady comes with me. We aim for the hospital in Boise."

"With the nurse. With Tiva," Zeke said. It was all happening without Tiva's input, and that bothered her, even if it was the right thing to do.

"And you're going to stay here, Dad?" she asked.

"Ah, no. I'm gonna get my ass to the coast, with the kids," Zeke said.

"I want to go with Mom!" Jake said. "Me, too!" Abby cried.

"Alright, I'll stay," Slater said. "Can the kids go, if I stay on the ground?"

"Yeah, I think we're alright," Jimmy said, after making a brief calculation of weight. "I have minus you and Monica, which I take it is almost 300 pounds, then the two small-ish ladies and the two kids, that about evens it out. But let's go–we don't have time to dawdle." And nobody's arguing or bickering, which is the best thing, the pilot thought.

They carefully led Kiatsu to the helicopter, and she and Tiva got in; the two children followed. Zeke, Slater, and Monica stepped back several paces, the rotor blades cranked up, and the helicopter lifted off, the grit swirling and intensifying the already dry and malodorous airspace.

Zeke and Monica waved and turned to leave and walk back to the shelter, to fetch their possessions. Everyone had hardly said anything when they'd separated–the tension was high, the time was too short, and the wildfires still raged not five miles away.

Strapped into her seat, Kiatsu watched through the window as the three people and the smoke and the burned cars shrank from view. She glanced over at her children. The helicopter ride suitably distracted them.

"Are you in pain?" Tiva asked. She was strapped into the seat next to Kiatsu's.

"Of course I am," she answered, smiling weakly.

Tiva rummaged around in her medical pack, which sat open at her feet. "I'll give you something."

"I'm lucky to have you. You are an angel," Kiatsu whispered, closing her eyes and letting her head fall back.

CHAPTER 28: GARNER

Brad had taken the wheel, after Aeva had pulled over in the breakdown lane. When he exited the car and walked around through the headlight beams, he noticed that the soot was deep enough to leave footprints in. They were 950 miles from the supervolcano, and he wondered what the region west of the Mississippi would look like only one week from now.

The local wildfire had left wretched, blackened stumps of trees in its wake, sullen piles of rubble where only the foundations of charred homes remained. Traffic was light; the region was beginning to feel deserted, with only the intrepid, predatory, and desperate still plying the roads.

A potent aroma of weed pervaded Aeva's thick coat, as she walked past him to the passenger side. She smiled at him wearily, a pretty smile that helped to melt the tension between strangers.

He put the truck into first gear awkwardly, feeling the old stick vibrate in his fist. The steering wheel felt leaden. He sensed the desire of Aeva to fold up in the seat and fall deeply asleep. She was temporarily leaving their fate in his hands, with the trust shared between the bereaved.

"You alright?" she murmured, turning her head to look at him skeptically.

"Yeah, I'm alright. It's just very different than the rental I was driving, like a cement mixer versus a fairly new RAV4. It's been a while since I've driven a truck."

"Yuppie, huh?" she chuckled.

"Yeah, yuppie. Guilty as charged."

Then: "Wow, I haven't heard that term in a while. Yuppie. What about...woke ubergeek?"

"What?" She closed her eyes.

He drove along the unlit road, keeping the speed conservative, conscious of the two-thirds empty tank. He'd be walking out there, otherwise; she'd rescued him from genuine displaced-refugee status. The wipers smeared the gathering soot in filthy streaks across the windshield. The headlights shown dully on the unlit highway.

Snow crystals under moonlight can have a crystalline reflection, an effect he'd seen in Colorado and British Columbia. The ash, on the other hand, reflected nothing but a deathly white, like lime sprinkled on a corpse in a ditch.

She fell asleep next to him, her hat pulled down tight over her eyes. He thought of Kiatsu; staring out at the road, his eyes stung and moistened. He trusted her to survive, with the children. He drove in the darkness hunched over the wheel, fighting to keep his eyes open, following the looping contours of the dingy road. Few people possessed the wisdom and resilience, he thought, the instincts to survive, of his wife.

They intersected with a larger state highway, and he took a left and headed south toward Santa Fe, thinking "gas station" most of the time. He wondered if Aeva had a gas can in the truck bed, considering that she was planning to go all the way to Mexico. He didn't turn on the radio because he didn't want to wake her, or listen to static and panicked, half-baked newscasts.

For some reason, he simmered at the injustice of all of their plights, which provided an outlet for his angst and frustrations. At best, the radio stations would exploit the disaster, for ratings.

The ash fell fitfully before the lights of the truck's front grill. The engine rattled, the wiper thunked and squeaked, and he only saw a handful of other vehicles pulled haphazardly off to the side of the road.

# #

Soon, the sun rose through the dreary eastern haze with a muted vermillion. Aeva stirred next to him. She passed her hands over her face. She stared through the windshield, then said "yuck" with a faintly spoiled, petulant tone.

He was starved and craved coffee. She turned her

head to look at him, suddenly with a shy glare of suspicion.

"Good morning," he said, coughing and clearing the fur from his throat. For the last hour, passing Santa Fe and following the signs to Albuquerque, he'd been lost in his thoughts, drifting into random dreams, visions, and fantasies.

"We're right outside of Albuquerque," he declared. "Can't be too far from Mexico. I don't know where you want to cross the border. But I'm still planning to get off at Highway 10. I'm grateful for the lift. It was a literal life saver."

She looked back through the windshield, and the shrouded clusters of tall buildings that comprised the skyline of Albuquerque. The surrounding desert appeared vast and featureless in the grainy light.

"I'm going to cross at Ciudad Juarez. A sketchy town, but I know the way through to my destination. You can come with me into Mexico. You might want to do that. Or, I'll drop you off at Las Cruces. That's where Highway 10 is."

"That will work fine. I mean, going onto Highway 10."

"What are you going to do?" she asked skeptically. "Wander along the highway like a lost soul." *That would be accurate,* he thought.

"Crash for 24 hours, then try to find my family. If I don't hear anything soon, then it's on my way to California, and up the coast. At any rate, we need some gas. Maybe there's a place open in the city." He scanned the dark skyline, where many of the lights were out. He pondered if the majority of the population had left, or whether they'd also decided to ride out the distant eruption that dusted their city with ash.

"Even though Albuquerque, at the moment, is not looking promising."

"You know, I'd take you to California myself...but I have...responsibilities. For my parents, and Lucy."

"I understand."

"What are you going to do for food, water, money...it's a changed country out there. The buried land," she intoned melodramatically.

"I have credit cards and some cash. That's not a problem. I'm taking the first gas exit, then we can switch places. I'll get off at Las Cruces."

They passed through a warren of underpasses and exits, urban sprawl that skirted the muted city. The flatter surrounding terrain looked like a sea of sullied white, like the muddy sand that storm surges spill on streets.

"Can you imagine what Denver, Salt Lake City, Missoula look like now?" he said, thinking out loud. "If southern New Mexico is like this."

"As I said, a strange new world." Aeva seemed preoccupied with something.

"I'm taking *this* exit to look for gas," he declared.

"Go for it."

A damaged, off-kilter sign promised Food Gas Lodging. He drove slowly down an exit ramp past people walking briskly, purposefully, but to nowhere.

He took a righthand turn, following a sign that pointed to fuel. Right away they passed a closed Shell station, another shut-down Texaco. He cruised slowly past both of them, hopefully. *We're up the creek without this truck gassed up, he thought. Marooned in Albuquerque.*

The storefronts were dark, the traffic desultory. Bereft pedestrians appeared now and then, isolated on rooftops and overpasses. He drove slowly, until they reached a kind of switched-off "auto mile."

At the end of a sad array of abandoned dealerships, they found a Chevron station with a row of lit-up pumps. The fluorescent oasis had about a half dozen cars and trucks in the parking lot, some dispensing fuel.

He parked the truck in front of one of the available pumps, feeling wildly lucky. "Maybe it takes one of your credit cards," Aeva said.

"Hopefully." They both stepped out of the truck. He noticed the front pane of the Chevron station was shattered. People milled around the shadowy interior. She'd seen the same thing.

"We'll move as quickly as we can," he said, with an edgy tinge to his voice. He watched her go to the back seat, then reach down where the floor mats were. She came up with a moderate-sized black handgun.

He inserted the credit card, feeling spoiled with expectations–all needs and luxuries provided by this wafer of plastic–which were probably obsolete as of about 24 hours ago. He stared at it for a few more seconds, then a loud beep sounded. The screen read Card Rejected. He had three other cards; they all elicited the same response.

He smelled gasoline vapors. He looked up, across the concrete island, to a man busily dispensing fuel into a soiled, scuffed Subaru SUV. The guy flashed a friendly half smile, then said, "Cash only, as of about 30 minutes ago."

"Okay, thanks." He had about $350 in his wallet, but wasn't sure when ATMs would function again. Aeva stood outside the truck, wiping it down with the pistol shoved into her belt, revealing its metallic grip. He told her that he was going inside to buy fifty bucks worth of fuel.

"Annie Oakley," he quipped, with a half-smile.

"What?"

"The pistol."

"A lady needs insurance."

He nodded, walking toward the station office. Its front window had a gaping hole, with shards of splintered glass littering the pavement. He skirted the glass, entered the station.

A man stood behind the front desk and payment monitor. He had shaggy brown hair, a shabby mustache that creeped over his upper lip, and a grease-stained sweatshirt with the hood pulled down over his red-rimmed eyes.

He glared as Brad silently, as he approached the counter.

"Can I pay for gas here?" Garner asked.

"I guess so."

"Okay, I'll take 15 gallons at pump five."

"I'll take the cash first. Give me a 100, to start."

"How do you know how much it is, before you've tabulated it at the pump?"

"Because, smarty-pants, the price has gone up. New conditions. That's free enterprise." He laughed and his face erupted in a cheerless leer. One of the men in the back, who were pulling bottles and cartons off the shelf and stacking them up on the floor, cackled inanely.

"Where's the manager?"

"Gone home. You want the gas or not?" Garner sensed Aeva standing a few paces behind him.

"Turn the pump on, I'll fill the tank and pay afterward."

"Fat chance." The man opened a drawer and began to lift a heavy gray object from it.

"Drop that, numb-nuts," Aeva said from behind Brad, aiming the black pistol at the man's insolent, dim-witted face.

"You don't have a permit for that," he said, trying to weaken the quaver in his voice. "You wouldn't even know how to shoot it. So just leave the cash and..."

There was a loud bang and cordite scent in the air; Garner flinched, his ears ringing clamorously. A punctured and tipped-over quart-oil container on an upper shelf gurgled petroleum onto the floor, pooling at the shocked man's feet.

"I've got eight rounds left; it's a full clip," Aeva declared in a monotone. "Turn on pump five. I'll wait here until it's done."

"What if I don't, curly-q?" The man spat

perfunctorily on the floor.

"I'll put a round into you. New conditions, like you said. You can lie on that floor and bleed out, while we drive away." They heard a sound like a chair scraping across the floor, over by the guy's hapless lackeys. She swiveled the gun over at them.

"You pussies empty your hands and stand against the wall. I have enough rounds for all of yah. Now start that pump!" she yelled. "Five!"

The man reached over and appeared to fiddle with the mechanism. Garner walked outside, telling her over his shoulder, "I'll let you know when it's done."

What a badass she is, he thought to himself. Lo and behold, the pump activated when he squeezed the lever on the nozzle. He filled the whole tank, replaced the fuel dispenser, then scuffed over to the station through the fallen ash. He removed 50 from his wallet.

"This ought to cover it," he said.

"Don't bother," Aeva said, ever the pragmatist. "They'll just pocket it, with the rest of their loot."

"Yeah, but that makes us gasoline thieves."

"Suit yourself," she said. The guy was sitting behind the counter with his booted feet crossed sullenly. The others, lined up along the dairy case in the back, had done as they were told.

Garner walked around the counter, opened the cash register, inserted the cash into the drawer, shut it, then walked out the door, with Aeva behind him. His actions appeared symbolic, even though he hadn't hesitated when leaving the cash.

"Don't move until we drive off," she said. "I have plenty of other clips in the truck. I don't hesitate to shoot people, when things get to this point." Then she turned back towards the truck. "You drive for now," she said, as they left the station and strode across the fractured pavement. "I'll ride shotgun."

"Roger." He got in and started up the truck, half smiling to himself.

"On our way out, let's find an ATM," she said, maintaining the same combative tone. "We'll try out your credit cards again. They must work."

"Why? Do you need some more cash?"

"I need a big chunk of cash, my friend," she said, suggestively tapping the barrel of the gun on the steering wheel. "And you're gonna have to give it to me, no matter what."

His face went blank, then he glanced at her skeptically. She seemed to be on a wicked roll, and now suddenly he stood squarely in her path.

CHAPTER 29: KATY

The ATV rig didn't necessarily mean that someone had already occupied the lodge.

Katy had her hands full with Chris; she'd already lost one companion in the last 24 hours, Kendra. She wasn't inclined to share or negotiate with a squatter, particularly a male.

The lodge was sturdily built with cedar logs, a green metallic roof, and a spacious deck that wrapped three-quarters around the building. A chain hung across steps that led up to the deck, where there was a sliding glass door as a main entranceway. The chain was left over from before the eruption–B.E., before eruption, she thought, after which all life has been radically altered for North America.

B.E. seemed like a dream, right now.

She didn't want to surprise anyone encamped at the lodge. Many people will be armed and protecting their turf. She stepped over the chain, walked to the door, tried it; locked. She knocked. She yelled, "Anyone here?" once, twice, but her imploring voice was met with silence. She thought she'd have to break in; the back door down where the ATV was parked had also been latched tight.

She returned to the Jeep to fetch Chris, but when she got there, the vehicle was empty. She gasped and cursed, her heart rate rising quickly. The passenger door hinged open in the mountain wind.

"Chris, where are you!" she yelled out, her head swiveling from the lodge to the upper slope to the dark forest, a panic rising in her chest. She saw little foot marks on the ground, trailing off into a large scuffed area, then nothing beyond that.

She called out his name again, repeatedly, as she strode to the back of the building. *So this is what it was like for Mom, she thought. Utter instantaneous panic and paranoia.* And Chris wasn't even her son.

She wouldn't sleep until she found him. She imagined herself standing on that beach so many years ago, feeling as abandoned as the last little girl on earth. How strange, she thought, striding around the lodge on the edge of the forest, that dormant feelings of pain, joy, misery, can be so easily dredged up from the mothballs of your past.

A voice jolted her out of self-absorption.

"He's over there, by the trees. The kid...over close to the chairlift." The man's congenial voice came from above her. She looked up; a shaggy head poked from the second-floor window, which proffered a view from a loft space. He pointed, "There. I'll meet you downstairs."

"Thanks!" she said, not taking the time to be shocked or surprised, or to realize that someone had beaten her to the lodge. She trudged through deepening ash over to the edge of the forest. Chris stood with his hands in his pockets, staring into the trees, slowly being buried by this dead skin falling from the sky.

"A reindeer," he said, pointing.

"I know this crap is like dirty snow, but that's no reindeer, honey. That's a mule deer." They watched as the deer gaped at them with its big-eyed, alert expression, then twitched its tail and sprinted away into the trees.

She made another note, for the near future. If they're running out of food, they could possibly take down one of the local herd. She didn't have a gun, but what about this guy? The one up in the window?

She saw the man emerge from the sliding glass door and stand on the deck; leaning on one crutch. A pant-leg was empty and folded over. He had a friendly, tired smile, unkempt brown hair with a knit cap pulled over it, a plaid flannel shirt. She figured he was late twenties, a little older than herself.

"Where did you guys come from?"

"Down below, at the hotel," she said, calling over to him. "Originally, from West Yellowstone."

"Oh shoot, it's just bonkers over there. Well, you might as well come in. My name's Kirby Alvarez."

"I'm Chris Farnsworth!"

"Hey buddy."

"Katy Morgan." Kirby put them instantly at ease. He had a casual, almost convalescent manner. Some people had that gift, she thought, or was it simply that "survival mode" can erect an understandable front of distrust and wariness? And thus, when you meet someone nice, they seem virtuous?

Kirby's laid-back demeanor explained the clutter of the interior, as he held the door for Katy and Chris. The inside was musty, but laden with a cushy sofa covered with various blankets and magazines, an armchair, and the scent of food cooking nearby. The floor had throw rugs and was cluttered with more magazines, cans, plastic bottles, and books.

"You guys are probably hungry, huh?" This isn't what she had expected; she thought they might encounter, well, anyone, standing at the doorway with a shotgun and a scowl.

She palpably relaxed. It was also warm; a fire crackled in a wood stove in the corner.

"Don't laugh–I made some chicken soup."

"We'll have a bit, if there's enough. What d'you think, Chris?"

"Yuh, I'm starved!"

"Okay, champ," he chuckled.

Kirby shuffled over to the kitchen burners, where a pot steamed.

"Have you seen anybody else?" Katy asked, gratefully slumping into a chair.

"I saw a few people pass by from up on the mountain, but only you in the last 12 hours or so." He fiddled with soup bowls that he'd taken down from the shelf. "I worked for the ski area as a caretaker here. There was another guy, Paul Watkins, but he left. Said he had to get back closer to his family in Idaho. Hope he made it."

He ladled the soup as he talked. "Why did you come up here in the first place? I mean, I knew you were escaping. From somewhere."

He came over with soup, unsteadily. Katy accepted the warm bowl in both of her hands, measuring her response.

"We spent one spooky night at the Summit Hotel. There had been a rockslide; it hit the building." Her voice went down a decibel, so Chris couldn't hear. He was off exploring the interior. "Another woman with us was killed in the slide."

"Oh, that's horrible."

"...So we came up here, for a refuge."

"You can stay if you want, as long as you need to." Katy nodded to his offer, not quite sure how much she was going to commit.

"That's very generous, and the soup tastes delicious. Yum..."

"Campbell's," he smirked. "At least it's not pea. I hated when my Mom gave me Campbell's pea."

Kirby gazed out the window, like he noticed or was

anticipating something. "The storm" continued, thick and unabated, staining the glass panes.

"I worked at the Yellowstone Volcano Observatory," Katy said, somewhat animated by the ingested calories. "We don't know how long this is going to last. The eruption could stop this week; or keep generating ash for a year. We know the caldera was full; it's a cataclysmic eruption." She shook her head regretfully, not trying to sugarcoat anything.

"The amount of particlized magma would be measured in cubic miles or kilometers, as if you dug up all the land encompassing a small town in Montana, including a mile down, then spewed it superheated into the air, but hundreds of times." She went on, because it felt good, oddly, given the content, and it had to be expressed.

"The last caldera-forming eruption 630,000 years ago ejected 240 cubic miles of particlized magma. Compare that with Mount St. Helens, which spewed 0.24 cubic miles, or one 1,000th of this eruption. The ash cloud from Yellowstone goes up six miles, sometimes higher. The ash, along with sulfur dioxide, will circle the globe. It will change weather patterns profoundly, for a year or more."

"Wait, how?"

"By making things colder..."

"Oh great, that's just what we need around here. At least we'll get more snow."

"Yeah, but this area will be utterly buried in ash," she shuddered. "I'll stop...this is just too morbid. I'm being a Debbie Downer."

"I'd rather hear the truth, or an approximation thereof." Katy was impressed by that; she felt she could reason with this guy, because they had to get along. This was survival.

"We're really going to have to lay in supplies," she said. "For the long haul."

"What did you do at Yellowstone."

"I was a volcanologist. Am..."

"Wow, so I have one of the experts here. What are the chances of that? I have to admit, I've had an apocalyptic frame of mind lately, so I've been expecting something like this."

She'd realized that, while talking about supplies and their predicament, she'd implied a commitment to this guy and his digs. She wasn't willing to go that far, yet. She still regretted not finding the place unoccupied, despite the soup.

He carried his bowl of soup over gingerly with one hand, then flopped down on the end of the couch. He placed his crutch on the floor. "You're probably wondering what happened to my leg."

"Yuh, I do." Chris was listening. "Did you get it chopped off?"

Kirby laughed softly.

"Actually, yes. Here's the story; the story of Kirby's long but not forgotten leg..."

"Yes, tell us about it," Katy said, tucking her legs under her, while the wood crackled and sparked in the stove

CHAPTER 30: ZEKE

"What do we do now?" Monica asked, watching the helicopter ascend in the distance, its red, flashing rear-rotor lights vanishing in a swirling cloud.

"We get wheels," Zeke said. "We get to Boise. To the West Coast, even better." Tiva was okay for now, he thought. *Damn, I hope the helicopter has safe passage.*

He scowled at his surroundings–the rows of smoldering, charcoal tree stumps, and the greasy collection of burned hulks that were all that remained of cars and trucks. The air smelled like burned engine oil; the ash had spread around like stray, drifting sand dunes, peppered with the charcoal of the scorched forest.

"This place has no future," he commented to the cold amphitheater of rocks and twisted hulks. "We damn sure can't walk all the way out of here."

"That might be the only option," Slater said, his voice sounding dry and pinched. He was antsy, not built for sustained, unpredictable emergencies. He was like Monica that way; he craved control, the way he could control his research and data collection at Yellowstone, until one day the region blew up in his face.

"I'm going over to the car, see if there's anything salvageable, like tools or whatnot."

"Alright."

That didn't seem promising.

The Nissan was roasted, scorched with burn marks, all of its tires melted away from the exposed metal rims.

A few working vehicles roamed through the wreckage on the highway. Slater wanted to wave one down, but the SUV was full of passengers. Its driver stared straight ahead and ignored him.

"I can't believe my Harley is totaled," Zeke said, looking off into denuded hillsides covered with black, toppled-over trees. He didn't want to go near the motorcycle, as if it was the body of a beloved deceased animal he couldn't bear to touch.

"But at least Kiatsu is on her way to a hospital. She'll get some medical care now. We were lucky. 1,500 degrees, shit, it wasn't our time."

"We should find another car," Monica said, as a way to change the topic. "We need to get farther away from here."

"Now you're talking," Zeke said, sounding more chipper, after he'd realized that absolutely no one would console him over a lost Harley. "That home where I found the water and the flag," he added. "We can check it out for more provisions, before we head out and look for a vehicle."

Their predicament reminded him of when he was in Mosul, Iraq 20 years before.

"Our Humvee got disabled by an explosive device. We had to walk half the city of Mosul before we got picked up by a troop truck. Enemy territory, hostiles everywhere. Only three of us. It sounds weird, but I liked it. Everything slowed down. We had our weapons out. People shied away from us. We knew where we were going; it took four hours. We actually bought food from a food stand. Didn't have to kill anyone, never got shot at. It was vivid. Strange how thick your skin is when you're young. Some'd call it courage; I'd call it crazy."

They were walking along the trashed gully next to the highway, looking for Zeke's hole in the chainlink fence. "That time in Mosul was harder than this."

"Really?" replied the skeptical Monica.

"There's the hole." Zeke pointed to it, and they had no particular problem squeezing through. Monica thought it was better that they all were able-bodied at this point. No wounded; no kids.

The winding dirt driveway brought them to the partially demolished structure, about a third of its roof having collapsed into blackened timber. Slater stood on the lawn and yelled to the house, cupping his hands over his mouth. Nothing in response. Since he'd already reconnoitered this place, Zeke went over to the side door next to the garage, and summarily kicked it in.

The moldy, unlit hallway smelled like wet, singed upholstery. Slater clicked on a flashlight; they had found a small kitchen just inside the entrance.

Slater and Zeke continued inside to a main living area, while Monica turned into the kitchen, feeling almost maternal, assuming a role by instinct. The kitchen had a window that looked out upon a pathetic, leaf-strewn pool, with a few tipped-over chairs arrayed around it.

She didn't waste any time; she rummaged through packages on a shelf and began to stack them along a counter: flour, rice, brown sugar, an old bag of pistachio nuts, a crinkled, open bag of Lay's potato chips. She sniffed it, looked inside. *Still edible, no mold, and it's a good source of salt.*

The fridge, without electricity, was nearly empty; the home-dwellers seemed to have left with most of the useful stuff, but she still found a half-consumed bottle of black olives pushed into the back.

She searched through all of the rest of the shelves in less than five minutes, coming up with only stale Graham Crackers and a plastic bottle of Teddy Bear peanut butter, the consistency of mortar.

The two others came into the kitchen; they'd been briefly to the second floor, which they found mostly destroyed by fire.

"The fire seems to have burned itself out," Slater said, "so we can stay overnight?" He shrugged, when the other two didn't answer right away.

"I could use some shut eye," Zeke said finally.

"Me too."

Monica arranged the food on a crusty yellow-formica table. For some reason it made her recall a plump, jolly neighbor she'd grown up with, who made donuts every morning on a flour-covered table like that.

They all stood silently around the food scraps, chewing pistachio nuts and licking peanut butter off of knives and consuming olives out of a bottle with a fork. They opened up a couple of cans of the flat beer from the garage; even Monica had a short glass of it. This made them feel even more sleepy and dopey.

Zeke moved over to the living room, where he made a bed of cushions on a living-room rug that smelled like a smoker's denim coat. He lay his head back.

He thought of Tiva in the chopper, arcing like a hawk over the fires and forests of central Idaho. The birds are used to the fires, he thought. To them, it's only a manifestation of the natural course of the seasons.

The hawks, and the wildfires, existed here long before the white intruders and migrants...

He'd often watched the red-tailed hawks hunt over a desert patch near his home in New Mexico. He imagined their wisdom, the penetrating, intelligent eyes. He'd call out "Hi hawk," and they'd squawk back at him.

Tiva must have the hawk as a spirit animal, he thought. The spirit animal of the Oglala Sioux warrior Red Cloud was a red-tailed hawk, just like his own. Before he shut his eyes, he noticed Monica and Slater making their own beds with scavenged blankets that still seemed surprisingly clean and intact.

"Where did you two spend last night?"

"In the helicopter," Slater said hoarsely. He was about to drift off.

"After being stalked by a grizzly bear," Monica added, mordantly.

Zeke went up on one elbow. "No shit?"

"Yeah, he charged at us from down in the woods. We were getting wood for a fire. I've never been so scared in my life. Sharks and grizzlies…"

"But you lived and worked in Yellowstone. You must have been used to the brown bear."

"I never did get used to the brown bear. You go on a hike, you have to bring bear pepper spray. You wonder if you'd ever be able to get it out on time. Every time you go around a corner on a trail."

"You didn't mind the hikes we took in Montana," Slater said defensively, taking her comments as a personal affront.

"I just never said anything. Thinking about the grizzlies…it was too distracting from what I enjoy about hikes, the scenery, setting your mind free to enjoy nature."

"I was over in Gallatin County once," Zeke mused. "I talked to a couple of locals. One says to me that in the summer, no one, in his or her right mind, I think he meant, went for a walk without a handgun. Then an old-timer told me, 'You think a handgun can stop a charging grizzly, you better keep one in the chamber for yourself.' Yeah, the brown bear is an amazing creature."

"Yellowstone is losing all of its wildlife now," Slater said to the ceiling, with a note of regret. "Except for the birds, who got away. Some of the bison and the wolves left early."

They all seemed to fall asleep at once. Slater had locked the front door with a hanging latch, but the kicked-in door near the garage was still left open. Slater was paranoid, in a way that seemed perfectly natural, so he leaned the top edge of an armchair against the door knob of the door near the kitchen.

Zeke woke up first, when it was still pitch dark in the room. He had no idea what time it was. For a moment, precariously clinging to sleep, he didn't know where he was.

He stood up and moved the barrier chair away from the door, and shuffled outside. The air outdoors was marginally better than inside the house, which still carried the odor of moist, burnt timber.

The cold helped wake him up. He wanted coffee. He imagined places he'd rather be: by the sea at Point Reyes or La Jolla, California; at English Harbor, Antigua, in the West Indies, which he visited during a brief stop on a military vessel; or in the Black Hills of South Dakota and Eastern Montana.

The Sioux believed that their people originally emerged from the vast "wind caves" in the Black Hills, he thought. Zeke was a Ute and a Spaniard, but nonetheless believed the Black Hills harbored powerful spirits. It was strange, what random and magnetic thoughts came to him in the early morning, and he hadn't even had coffee.

He stood on the front lawn. The highway was silent, a graveyard for burned and disabled vehicles. When he was in Antigua, he'd had an affair with a beautiful island woman whom he met on the beach. She was very frank about sex, about wanting it with him that night. "Drink some rum, get hard, and come see me," she'd said, a comment that blew his mind, because it would never have come from any of the other women he had met.

When he first met Amitola, she was sexy, but discrete about it. She was wary of the whole scene of men and drink. Her views of sex and drinking were basically the opposite of this lady's in Antigua. He'd had a brief but delightful affair with the island lady, a swanky evening that began with a good talk and a meal next to the tiki torches, under a warm, bright sky webbed with stars.

He chuckled to himself; the world was full of adventures and unforgettable places and people. When things were more settled, he'd take some peyote, and walk in the desert to set his head straight again.

Craving coffee, he wandered back into the kitchen, where he found an old tin of instant Nescafe. The burners on the stove weren't working; he went outside and set up a small fire to heat water in a pan. He built it under the eaves of the garage, to keep the weak flames out of the ash and the wind.

He gathered some food wrappers, charcoal, and sticks. Nothing was dry or unmixed with ash; it took him too long to get up a fire and heat the water, which he found funny because half the surrounding house had already gone up like a tinderbox.

He thought it might be sun-up already, but the sunlight had been blocked by the erupting volcano. He thought he heard Slater and Monica, quietly chatting.

He walked around to the front again. He saw a couple of flashlights on the highway; a pickup truck slowed to a stop, just beyond the hole in the chainlink fence.

Two men stood in front of the stopped vehicle; their flashlight beams bobbing up and down in the grainy darkness. A man in a trucker's cap stepped down from the driver's side. There were words; an argument ensued, but Zeke couldn't make out the exact exchange.

He thought he might know what was going on; these two highwaymen wanted the truck. Then there was a scuffle, and he heard a shot, the metallic crack shattering the morning, echoing on the side of the house. The driver had gone down. Zeke moved over and crouched behind some bushes.

The men dragged the inert body to the side of the road. It was early; no one else had driven at that time on this path of destruction. Zeke stayed behind the bushes, feeling cold, watching the ash swirl like a fuzzy television signal, drifting in errant sheets through the beams of the idling truck's headlights.

One of the men came over, leaned his elbows on the chainlink fence, and gazed at the house.

Zeke glanced over his shoulder and noticed that he'd

left the lights on in the kitchen. In the dark, they were impossible to miss. He also saw the shadowy form of Monica move around behind the windows.

This was trouble. He ducked down and ran back behind the house.

CHAPTER 31: GARNER

"What are you doing?" he asked. He thought she was mad. Going off the rails. Aeva aimed the barrel of the gun casually in his direction. They were driving south of Albuquerque. She'd abruptly changed her tone in the last 10 minutes, to "unfriendly."

"I'm asking for a favor. Except it's a favor you can't get out of doing."

The truck rattled along the desert road, with pockets of isolated, exurban settlements stretched out on both sides. He stared at her, then returned his gaze to the windshield, clutching the wheel in a moist, tight grip.

"What's the favor?"

She sat silently, breathing evenly, then said: "I need a load of money. For Mexico. We're going to use your credit cards."

"What, to live on?"

"No, for Lucy."

"What *about* Lucy?"

"She's in jail, in Juarez."

"A Mexican jail..."

"Yeah."

"Okay, I get it. You need money for the pay-off."

"Exactly."

He drove quietly for a minute. They weren't very far from Las Cruces, New Mexico.

"How much is it?" he finally said.

She swallowed, then said "One hundred fifty thousand pesos."

"One hundred...fifty...?"

"Thousand..."

"How do you know the amount, did you talk to her?" The road appeared empty, but for them. He'd unintentionally sped up to past 80 mph; then slowed it down, noticing a loud vibration from the back of the truck.

"Nine, ten days ago. I got her one permitted call. She said I have to come to the jail, gave me the address. I could tell a couple of the other men were in the room, the so-called Policia. The Federales. Corrupt, murderous bastards."

He nodded. He wondered if what happened back at the gas station was a rehearsal for what was coming up in Juarez.

"They said 100,000 first, then when we were on the phone, it's suddenly 150,000."

"So it goes, up and up," he said. The Mexican peso wasn't worth a whole lot, in the big picture of things.

"If I'm able to use my credit card, *if* we find a working ATM, I'll only be able to get cash in dollars." He noticed her grimace slightly, then he returned his eyes to the road. He saw a sign for Las Cruces; 15 miles.

"They said 150,000 *pesos*," she said grimly.

"Listen, we'll be lucky to find a machine in the first place. Then, if that works, I have no idea whether it will spit out pesos."

"So you'll do it?" she asked, her voice slightly rising. She tapped the gun barrel nervously on the dashboard.

"You can put that down." He sighed and glanced quickly at her, then back to the road. "Were you really going to shoot me if I didn't?" She didn't answer.

"Do you know how cheap the peso is? It's literally worth a nickel; you can get about 20 for a dollar. So your bad guys sound like small-timers to me. 150,000 is only about 7,500 bucks."

"Quick math..." she mumbled.

"You're lucky they didn't ask for a million, or a million five."

"$7,500 is typically a lot of money," she said. "I couldn't sell the truck for that. I didn't have it in the bank, and we rent a house."

"I know," he said, having forgotten that most people didn't have this much bread to toss around, from executive-suite salaries.

He tapped his fingers on the wheel, then he said, quietly, "We go looking for an ATM, and you'll get your cash. They might take the money and ask for more, or ask for more before they take the money, a higher amount. The situation is completely untrustworthy. Fluid. Shitty."

She sniffed, almost as the start of a crying bout. "I know all that. Maybe I can convert the cash to pesos when I get to Mexico. That's what I'll do. It'll look like more money, a wad of cash."

"That's probably a good idea."

They passed road signs and billboards, mostly advertisements for obsolete subdivisions, doctors who will work on your eyes, new medical treatments, miracles. No signs for town centers, or the possibility of a bank, as yet.

They drove quietly along the road, the truck's rattle becoming faint. For the first time, he noticed the ashfall dwindle to a light coating. It felt like progress.

They took the first Las Cruces exit, heading for the small town's commercial center, *if* it had one. They cruised slowly along a main street; the lights were working, which was a good sign. Many businesses were dark or boarded up, however, as if in response to the sudden onset of an economic depression. They passed an open fuel station, with a cluster of parked cars and a crowd gathered in front of it.

"I'm going to pull over here and ask," Garner said. A chance to run, he thought. *I'll save thousands, but she'll know it if I take my backpack. The lady did pull a gun on me*...the opportunity seemed to vanish as quickly as it came to mind. He needed the ride.

He pulled over to a curb near the restaurant and idled the engine. They had decided that Aeva would drive now.

Garner got out and asked a woman standing on the sidewalk with a poodle dog, where he might find an open ATM. She said there were two she knew of, one outside of a Walgreens, another inside the lobby of a Holiday Inn Express down the road.

He got back into the truck, and they headed for the drug franchise, where they found a line of at least 100 people snaking down the sidewalk from the ATM.

"That'll be milked dry by the time we get to it," Garner said. "Out of cash. Let's try the hotel; look for Independence Street. It intersects the main drag. It might be tough to find any cash. What are you going to do if we come up empty?"

"We rob a bank in Mexico."

"Huh, like the hole-in-the-wall gang..." He laughed.

Aeva didn't crack a smile, staring through the filmy windshield, then gunning it through a yellow light.

"You *are* serious, aren't you?" he said, after she continued to sulk in silence.

"Lucy is about all I have."

Garner looked down at his hands, thinking about his own family, about how they must be clawing desperately for survival. He felt stuck, with her, roped into Aeva's quixotic, single-minded mission. He just wanted to get it over with; get her the money. He noticed that she'd shoved the black pistol back into the side pocket of her jacket.

The hotel, which shared a parking lot with a Denny's, had a "temporarily closed" sign on the front entrance door. They kept driving, to the outskirts of Las Cruces, where they came upon a spacious mall, rising out of the desert flats like a military base. They found a working ATM outside of an open, but mysteriously empty Walmart.

He was only able to pull $3000 out of the machine, using all of his cards; it had a $1,000 withdrawal limit per card. He returned to Aeva, who leaned against the truck in the sunlight, running a hand through her close-cropped, black hair. He almost didn't recognize her, hatless. The beautiful, androgynous stranger.

He handed her a thick stack of 100s, which she wordlessly began to count.

"Thank you," she said, when she was about halfway through the tally. It was as if she was trying to retain a modicum of proper behavior.

"You're not going to apologize?"

"For what?" she said, licking two fingers and continuing to sift through the 100s. There were only 30 of them. She had the cocky tone of a bandit.

"You pulled a gun on me and demanded money. I would have given you the cash, if you'd simply explained yourself."

She shrugged, finishing the count. "You're short."

"They had a cash withdrawal limit. Listen, we're lucky we got any money at all. Society's at a standstill. Three. Two. One. Expect the run on the banks to commence. So they're mostly closed.

"You've got the equivalent of 60 thousand pesos. Those desperadoes will take that."

"I know they'll take it. But will they give me Lucy back?"

"They'll take anything. Tell them that America is in dire straits from the volcano, that there's no cash in the banks. That was all you could scrape up." *That wouldn't be too far from the truth,* he thought.

On their way to the mall, they'd passed the Raw Frontier Diner, with its electric-red, neon sign. Having finished their transaction, they headed for the diner. It was a few miles from a small, out-of-the-way motel called La Casa Grande.

CHAPTER 32: KATY

"Okay, so one day I had two legs," Kirby said. They all sat together in the mountain lodge above the Summit Hotel. "And the next day I had one intact leg. Six months ago, I got side-swiped by a drunk driver in Bozeman. Hit me on the driver's side, running a red light. Never saw him. My leg got crushed from the knee down. I woke up in the hospital. It's true, sometimes you feel no pain, you go into shock, and you're completely out."

"What's shock?" Chris listened intently, as if Kirby was telling a ghost story.

"It's when you're in an accident and you lose blood, your lips turn blue, you get faint, and you black out. Then you have to go to the doctor."

Chris went silent and pensive.

"Anyways," Kirby went on. "They said I developed a sepsis, and that they had to amputate. I said, from my hospital bed, 'Get me a second opinion.' I was thinking about all these things I do with two legs. Then a nurse, her name was Jeanette and she was from Minnesota–a nice, trustworthy lady who'd been a nurse forever–says, 'There is no second opinion. The prognosis with this sepsis you have is not good.'

"So I lay my head back on the pillow, and this resignation flows over me. 'Gut up,' I said to myself. 'Embrace the suck.'"

"You mean, you got up?" Chris said.

"No, that's just an expression," Kirby laughed, "like 'grin and bear it,' or 'make lemonade out of lemons.' Actually, I did 'get up' out of the wheelchair pretty fast. They fitted me for a prosthesis."

Then he read Katy's mind. "I left the prothesis in the bedroom upstairs. I call it Ahab's stump, Ahab for short. It's this strange object leaning against the wall of the bedroom, and I had to give it a name. They can be a pain, literally. Speaking of, I take meds. I'm running out of them, during this emergency. Maybe you can take me down to the pharmacy in Meadow Village, in your Jeep? I only have the ATV."

"You mean, you're filling a prescription?" Katy asked, scraping her bowl. "I don't think they'll be open for that. Don't you think the pharmacy would be shut down?"

"Maybe, but it's worth a try. I'd get into the place anyways." Then he seemed to want to walk back that comment. He breathed a deep sigh. "I need them, you see. I'm almost out." His eyes glazed over with sudden distrust, mounting panic.

"What are the meds?" Katy asked. "Just curious." The question lingered with an air of tension.

"Oxycodone. It does the trick."

"Hmmm, oh. I've heard it's effective but very addictive. Anyways, glad you have a treatment for the pain. Thanks again for the soup; that really hit the spot."

"So we can go down to the Village?"

"When do you need them?"

"To an extent, right away." Then he appeared to backpedal. "I guess I can wait until tomorrow morning."

Katy got up to collect the bowls. "Maybe we can fill up while we're down there," she said over her shoulder. "At every opportunity, get gas."

"Agreed on that!" Kirby said, with a kind of forced bonhomie.

"And food...alright, I'm tuckered. Chris, you can keep playing, but don't go outside. I'm going to sleep on this wonderful couch. I've lost track of time. What time is it?"

"It's two already..." Kirby said. He appeared to have drifted somewhere else, to a more distant, sulky mood. Katy wondered if that was because they weren't going to dash out and retrieve his meds.

"Are the cellphones working?" She lay back on the couch and pulled an old cardigan blanket over herself. "How did you know the time?"

"The clock on the wall," he said. "I set it, when the cells still worked. They don't now, unfortunately. Before it gets dark, I'm going to have to get more wood for the stove."

"Wake me up when you do that," Katy said, in a muffled voice. She heard his voice recede into the hallway, accompanied by the thump of the crutch.

"Will do," he grunted, then added something else that she didn't hear.

# #

She'd fallen asleep and dreamt that she was walking on the water's edge on the coast of Maine, when she came upon her mother, who was supposed to be dead. It was an "angel of mercy or dread" dream. Her mother beckoned Katy to follow her in one direction down the beach, but Katy chose the opposite. She seemed to have chosen life over death, and the dream left her in a positive mood, because it didn't involve a volcanic cataclysm or a lethal rockslide.

She tossed the blanket aside and sat on the edge of the couch. Kirby stood by the door with his coat on.

"He's in the bedroom upstairs," Kirby said, meaning Chris.

"Okay. You're getting wood?"

"Yeah."

"Alright, I'll help."

They opened the door. The ash had blanketed the landscape with a shocking visual effect, a thick, sodden layer smothering the slopes and the woods. It looked like it was sprinkled with pepper. She had expected this;

they were only roughly 70 miles from the epicenter. She felt oddly safe in the lodge, a sturdy, provisioned shelter for now, but this area had no immediate future.

The ash might pile up to a meter thick, she thought, scuffing through about four inches of it underfoot.

She reached down and picked up a handful, like a fine salt that she let sift through her fingers. She was still a scientist; she still had an insatiable desire to probe physical evidence. The stuff felt like it would derive from the surface of Mars or the moon, and she was a visitor, taking a sample.

They walked to a nearby pile of stacked wood and took several trips to restock Kirby's supply, then they cooked a black bean, tomatoes, and peppers casserole and battened down the hatches for the night. Again, he asked Katy if they could head for the Meadow Village pharmacy first thing in the morning.

He was so insistent about it, red in the face and wild-eyed, that she took the Jeep keys and hid them on her person, before she turned in for the night.

It was still dark when they headed out in the morning, a seamless part of an endless evening, like in a Scandinavian winter.

The Meadow Village was only eight miles away, but she had to drive down the acutely steep slope, negotiating rutted switchbacks that were better handled with skis on snow. The fire road was easier to drive up than down.

When she completed the perilous, white-knuckled descent, she thought of Kendra. They passed the spot where she had dragged Kendra's body after the rockslide. Kirby said he had randomly found Kendra's parcel by the side of the trail.

Chris had a survival mechanism; children possessed this by nature. It was an evolutionary imperative, to keep the young alive and resourceful in the event they lose their adults.

Older humans seemed to have built resilience out of their later experiences, she thought, cruising through the hotel's mostly empty parking lot. They only saw one other pedestrian, a lone person wandering through the semblance of a dense snowstorm. Katy was glad; she didn't want the word getting out that a capable refuge existed just a few thousand feet away.

They drove in silence, leaving deep tire marks in the buried roadway, which had quickly become navigable only by using four-wheel drive. That would explain the abandoned vehicles she glimpsed through sheets of wind-driven ash. *Note to self...the natives are going to get desperate. They have to find food, water, shelter, and they've lost their vehicles.*

"The engine sounds like a coffee grinder," Kirby said, a hoarse edge to his voice. He seemed to be on pins and needles.

"That's from putting it in four-wheel drive, but obviously, it's going to need some maintenance." She dropped her voice so Chris wouldn't hear. "If we lose this Jeep to the ash, we're totally screwed."

"Don't you think I know that?" Kirby snapped. His fingers drummed nervously on the plastic frame of the passenger door.

The Jeep fish-tailed down the resort access road, until she noticed the bright headlights of another vehicle coming up behind them. The vehicle slowly overtook them, in a way that irritated her. She gradually steered the Jeep to the righthand side of Route 64.

"This obnoxious driver is chomping on the bit," she said. "The last thing I need is a tailgater in these lousy conditions. I'm going to let them pass me." She slowed down and put on her right directional, gradually cruising to the side of the road.

"Yeah," Kirby said impatiently. "Just don't wait too long." He grimaced and looked out the window.

"Are you in pain *now*?" she said.

"You could say that. I'm out, of the Oxy. I told you that last night." His hand dropped into his lap, where the frantic drumming continued on his good thigh.

"We're almost there. We've only a few more miles."

She finessed the brakes, as the other driver blasted past them on the left. It was a garishly painted pickup truck flying a confederate flag. She got a brief glimpse of the driver, who had a hooded sweatshirt and an unruly black beard. He flashed a hard-eyed glance at her, before he sped past and disappeared into the gloom.

What the hell is his problem? she thought. It's too dangerous to drive fast on this road.

Katy kept a look out for a particular gas station she was familiar with, but when they passed it, it was empty and closed.

She felt her heart sink; she didn't want to return to

the lodge without filling up, without getting more provisions. Every trip was vital. Getting home with only the Oxy was like returning empty-handed.

They passed a parking lot and pulled into the entrance. Kirby pointed out the Walgreens; she parked at the curb next to it, leaving the motor running.

"I guess someone else was chomping on the bit for a scrip," she said, sarcastically. The front door had been padlocked from the inside, but the plate-glass frontage was bashed in, leaving jagged sheets of glass scattered about like broken mirrors.

"Well, nothing to get here," Katy said, shoving the transmission back into first gear. She thought they might try the nearby Marriott, which had a few lights burning. The hotel offered countless scavenging possibilities.

"What do you mean by that?" Kirby asked, staring at the gear shift incredulously.

"The pharmacist is gone. This place is closed, looted."

Kirby's panic was palpable; it showed in his red-rimmed eyes.

"That's bullshit, I can still get the Oxycodone in there. I know what the box looks like. We came all the way here, so just hang on." He struggled with the passenger door, then it flew open. He thrust his right leg out first, to get a purchase on the pavement. They were parked right on the curb, opposite the drug store. He stood with the door open, now leaning on "Ahab."

"Just wait for me. I won't be five minutes."

There was no stopping him, and she thought she might as well search for, at least, bottled water. "Dammit, I can't leave Chris in the car."

"Then both you guys come," he shouted, heading for the shattered entrance. He strode quickly and with only a slight hitch, which impressed her, amidst feeling pissed and frustrated.

She heard an engine cough; the mud-streaked pickup flying the Dixie flag slowly cruised the lot, about half a football field away. She shut off the engine and hurriedly stepped out of the car.

Kirby had already vanished into the shadowy interior of the drug store.

She wondered if the Colorado Highway Patrol would be cruising around these parts; she hadn't seen a single squad car since the eruption. Order had dissolved. "Every man for himself," she figured, had commenced about 24 hours ago.

She could no longer count on Kirby. He was desperate. A lonely vigilance settled over her, like someone who realizes they are the sole survivor of a boat's sinking.

Plenty of food and water, she reminded herself, must still be inside this abandoned, looted Walgreens.

"C'mon Chris," she said, walking briskly around the Jeep to open the back passenger door for him. "It's Halloween time. You can pick out a few goodies. I'm going to find more food and water, while Kirby gets his candy."

"*Kirby* is getting *candy?* Can I have some, too?" Chris

asked in a plaintive voice.

"Sure can. That's the whole point, we're going in here for goodies. Follow me. And we're going to *pay* for anything we take."

They walked up to the entrance, stepping around a glittering pile of splintered glass.

"No one is here," Chris said, disapprovingly. "Someone broke the door and the glass."

"Those are bad people, who broke things and didn't leave money," Katy said, taking his hand. They walked delicately through the debris and inside the dim interior, which was lit only by a few fluorescent bulbs in the back.

Kirby, rummaging through the meds, she thought. She doubted he'd find the Oxy, but he wouldn't leave without them.

When she was partly through the door, she saw the grungy pickup with the limp, weighted down flag. The driver exited it, brandishing a firearm in his right hand. He began walking toward the Walgreens through the storm.

CHAPTER 33: ZEKE

Balls to the walls, they know we're here now.

Zeke hid behind the bushes. The guy still leaned on the fence out by the highway, watching the partially burned house with keen interest. He looked over his shoulder and said something to his partner. They both had just killed someone in cold blood, for a used Dodge pickup.

Through the front window of the home, Zeke could see the indistinct forms of Slater and Monica moving about. These guys just shot a man for his truck, he thought, and they'll shoot us for five cans of beer, potato chips, and a little chump change.

Dammit, my Beretta is inside the house…

The two guys walked along the chainlink fence, searching for the entrance to the driveway. Zeke ducked low and ran around the demolished, left side of the home, past the cluttered pool, to the kicked-in side door. Then he snuck in.

"Slater, Monica!" he hissed, when he got inside. The two stood in the middle of the room. They gave him a surprised look.

"Get out of the window! We got trouble! A couple of thugs shot a guy out on the highway, now they're coming down the driveway. We gotta get out of sight out back before they get here!"

He went over to his makeshift bed and rifled through the small satchel he carried, until he found the pistol. Maybe four rounds left. He needed more ammo. He knew, in the back of his mind, that this was going to happen. He'd have a pistol but no ammo when he needed it. He took the entire satchel and its contents, and the three of them ran to the side door, near the garage.

Zeke saw the flashlight beams on the driveway.

"Shit, too late, turn around!" he whispered, low and nearly inaudible.

"Can't we talk to them?" Monica asked, in a pleading tone.

"Fat chance! They gave that guy out on the highway about five seconds to plead his case."

"We'll tell them we don't have a damn thing, and that'll be the truth."

"Did yuh try to negotiate with that grizzly, too?" he said, injecting some knifey sarcasm. "Let's go up to the second floor!" They ducked back through the unlit living room, as the flashlight beams and gruff voices converged on the garage.

When they'd reached the bottom of the stairs, Zeke said, "You two go first. I'll be right behind you. And take this." He handed the Beretta to Monica.

"The safety's off already. If any of them come to the bottom of the stairs, shoot first, don't ask questions. If they see you, they'll be trying to smile, but it will be a snake's smile. You have about four shots; aim for the chest."

She looked down at the pistol with acute distaste, like it was a severed hand.

"...They just shot a stranger in cold blood back on the highway," Zeke reminded her.

She took the gun silently.

"Why did you give it to her?" Slater asked, somewhat childishly, as though he took it personally.

"Male intuition," Zeke quipped. "Now get your asses up there." If the truth be told, he thought, Monica would hesitate less to pull the trigger than Slater. She had that kind of moxie, he sensed, once it took hold of her.

They better use the gun, too, he thought. Not too many good hiding places up on that burnt-up second floor.

Zeke thought he heard the intruders banging around in the garage, then they entered the back hallway by forcing the broken door open.

Rowdy, wise-guy voices: "Anybody home?"

There was another room, mostly charred, beyond the

stairs, the remains perhaps of a dining room. He pulled his knife out and slipped inside. The hunting knife was a collector's item he'd received as a gift years ago from a tribal member back in New Mexico. He was feted for serving with distinction in Iraq.

The knife looked like something Jim Bridger, the 19th-century mountain man, would have carried. It had a six-inch blade and a sturdy handle that resembled ivory, but actually derived from the shoulder bone of an American Bison. He could never own anything that came from a poached elephant tusk. It was bad enough that the Bison were mindlessly slaughtered on the Great Plains back in Civil War times.

Handing the inexperienced Monica the pistol seemed risky, he thought, crouched down behind an armchair with a large, smelly burn hole. He could hear the guys banging around in the kitchen, grunted remarks, the aluminum snap of beers opening. But Slater and Monica had no protection. He could have simply kept the gun and ambushed these guys and taken them all out, but failing that, Monica and Slater would be toast.

"Come out come out wherever you are!" one of them sneered into the hallway a minute later. He thought there were three of them. They were coming out of the kitchen. They'd probably come in the dining room first, or separate, some heading up the stairs.

Footsteps creaked on the wooden floor. Mumbled comments. "Ain't nothing here but a burnt-up home. We're wasting our time."

"Shut your trap." Heavier footsteps at the bottom of the stairs; a lanky one with greasy black hair, a lousy denim coat, toted a shotgun. "I heard something upstairs. Someone's messing around. Why don't you come on down here and say hello?" he called out with a loud, snide friendliness.

The door to the dining room was not fully closed; peaking around the chair, Zeke could see two of the guys, including the cocky leader in greasy denim. They were the ones standing on the highway, shooting the man in the truck, dragging his body to the side of the road.

The "leader" turned to his partner with a smug smile, then yelled upstairs again, "Now *that's* not being very neighborly, is it?"

He walked slowly, menacingly, up the stairs, followed by the second heavy-set fellow, who had a black beard and was chugging beer out of a can. He didn't have a weapon.

A third emaciated guy wore a wrinkled, unwashed gray track suit, and a red bandanna around his neck. The first man paused on the stairs and said to the third, with disdain, "Gil, you look around downstairs some more, before the whole fuckin' house falls down. Look for silver and jewelry, shit like that."

"Aha!" he said, turning his head back to the steps. Apparently, he'd spotted Monica, or Slater. It was difficult to hide beyond the second-floor landing, Zeke thought, the house was burned so badly.

"So there you are! A little mousy today, are we!"

Monica's voice: "Go away. There's nothing here."

"Well, you're here, darling. Come on down! Don't be scared. Let's be friends." The words all dripped with sarcasm. A pause.

"We're serious, Mac. It's only a burned house. Just leave." That was Slater.

The two men started climbing more of the stairs, heavy creaking steps. "Gil" made his way into the dining room. He walked past the chair where Zeke was crouched down. As he shuffled past, Zeke came up behind him. He laid the blade across Gil's throat.

"You know what this is, right?" he whispered into Gil's ear. "Get down on the floor on your belly, or you'll be breathing out of your neck. Don't make a sound." Gil did what he was told.

Zeke pulled the red bandanna tight around the man's mouth, stuffing some of it inside around the man's teeth as he squirmed. He quickly bound the captive's hands behind his back with a bungee cord he'd previously harvested from the garage.

"Drop that!" he heard from the lead thug on the stairwell, then a deafening shotgun blast.

"Shit!"

Zeke didn't want to have to deal with Gil wriggling free and making noise, so he clobbered him on the back of the head with the smooth bottom of the knife grip, knocking him out cold. Gil's head rested on its side on the wooden floor, his mouth gaping open.

Use the handgun! he thought to himself. *C'mon Monica, shoot the guy!* As if she'd read his mind, as he crept around the corner into the hallway outside the dining room, he heard the hollow metallic pop of two handgun rounds, then another ear-splitting shotgun blast, then two more shots. A body struck the wooden stairs hard. *Now we're out of ammo,* he thought.

The heavy-set guy drinking the beer lay at the bottom of the stairs, moaning, scowling, and pawing at his abdomen. The hallway smelled of cordite, mixed with gritty burned timber.

"I didn't think you had the guts," said the first man, whose name was Fetterman and was from Kansas. He was two thirds of the way up the steps. He cracked the shotgun and started to reload. "Gilroy!" he yelled out, "Where the hell are you? Get your ass out here."

"He's out for the moment," Zeke said.

When Zeke was a boy, growing up on the edge of the Utah desert, he and his friends used to throw knives at trees and the sides of barns. Like all contests, whoever could time the throw and stick the blade in the wood was the best for that day, and Zeke got very good at it.

Fetterman, straddling the stairs, raised the loaded shotgun again, just when Zeke came fully out of the dining room. There was no negotiating with this hostile, Zeke thought. He threw the Jim Bridger knife hard, hitting the man square in the back with a dull thud, followed by the clatter of the shotgun falling to the wooden steps.

The man reached behind his back, from where the knife protruded with its bone handle; then he fell to his knees and landed near his partner's body, where a crinkled beer can leaked the rest of its contents onto a burned rug. Fetterman let out a loud groan, then fell silent.

Zeke walked over to his body to retrieve the knife, while Slater and Monica came back out of their partial hiding space on the second-floor landing. Zeke knelt down and checked the beer-swilling man's carotid artery; he'd expired too, just like the Rainier beverage.

"I think I'm gonna be sick," Monica said.

"We're gonna take that truck out there and head West," Zeke said. It was still early in the morning, and the whole rest of the day lay before them.

CHAPTER 34: KATY

I don't care about that pickup driver, she thought, temporarily blocking it out of her mind. She and Chris were standing just inside the shattered entrance.

"We're going to get some food and water from this place, while we're here," she said, not meaning for it to be out loud. "That guy in the truck, he's probably going to rob the Marriott."

"What?" Chris said, scanning the Walgreens confusedly.

"Never mind. Go over to those food refrigerators, on the right side there. You can grab candy and potato chips, whatever you want, if you see them on the way."

"Right-o," Chris said, and he was on his way. She headed for the back of the drug store, along the walls, where any remaining food and drink were located.

The refrigerators were off, as were the commonly blinding ceiling lights.

She could hear Kirby rummaging around in the back, opening and closing doors and shelves. When she reached the rear wall, she was pleasantly surprised to find usable provisions on the shelves: a quart of "milk substitute," a square of orange, individually wrapped cheese slices, and an eight-pack of hot dogs, none of which, to her trained eye, had yet gone bad. She shoved them all into her canvas bag and moved to the dry-foods section.

No one else was in the store. Yet. She scanned the aisles for Chris; he was taking his time and unwrapping one of the few remaining candy-bar brands, a Mars bar. *It seemed like the looters targeted the cigarettes, candy, and controlled substances,* she thought.

She warily watched the door, feeling lucky to have found a Skippy's Chunk Style peanut butter and an unopened package of Saltines laying on a plundered shelf.

The floor was covered with food crumbs and ripped up packaging, as though an animal had gotten into the aisle.

"Kirby!" she called out, toward the back. She kept a suspicious eye on the smashed front entrance. Still no one.

"What?"

"We have to go soon. Like now."

"Alright alright, hold your horses."

"Chris," she said. He looked up, slowly chewing. He

was happy. "Don't go anywhere. I'll be right back." On the way to the back room where they kept the meds, she copped two warm bottles of energy drinks off a shelf–Gatorade and Heed–and a six-pack of Red Bull. She wasn't a fan of the latter, not eating much processed food by creed, but *beggars can't be choosers.*

She found Kirby sitting on a stool with an open box and pill container. He looked at her without much recognition, then washed some pills down with a pilfered Diet Pepsi. He then sat quietly, staring at a row of narrow, pull-out medicine-storage containers. Many of the latter lay on the floor amongst hastily torn cardboard boxes.

The flock of looters had been through here, she thought. Only the first wave.

"Are you okay?"

"I am now."

"Did you find Oxycodone?"

"Generic, extended release tablets. I think it will do the job." He cleared his throat. He appeared to be breathing heavier, awaiting the result with a certain savoriness.

"Katy!" That was Chris' voice.

"Oh shit, I just left him alone out there." She felt jolted by the same feelings that were evoked when she couldn't find him on the mountain.

Still clutching her harvest, she jogged through the door and into the aisles, to the front of the store. She found Chris standing with the bearded man in the hooded sweatshirt. He gave her a neutral smile from a distance.

She noticed that he had hidden his weapon.

She stopped and veered toward the entrance door. "C'mon Chris, we're done here."

"Oh, I was just asking Chris whether he wanted some water." Up close, the twenty-something man had a flat, harmless demeanor. Her present state of mind, however, assumed a threat until proven otherwise, and the suspiciously cruising, flag-waving pickup hadn't left the best impression. He added: "I know where to find some here. Do you need some water?"

"No. We have some food items, and we're going to leave some cash and go. Come on, Chris."

"I want some water!" Chris complained.

"You don't have to worry. I just wanted to make sure you guys were okay. I'm with the Gallatin County Sheriff's Department. I was doing a sweep, before I left myself."

"You don't look like a policeman."

He dug his wallet out of a back pocket, then removed an I.D. "I'm plainclothes and yes, I'm looking a little scruffy these days."

"Let me see that." She took it, hastily scanned the I.D., handed it back. "That's all fine and dandy, but we have to go."

He smiled warmly for once, then chuckled.

"What's so funny?" Katy asked.

"It's just that, you're the first normal people I've encountered during the last 48 hours. It's been mostly, you know..." He dropped the subject; she got the impression he didn't want to scare her. "Don't go. Let me get you some water. Do you have a place to stay these days?"

"We have to go. You have a gun. I saw it."

He put up a hand apologetically.

"That's my service pistol."

"Cool!" Chris said. "Can I see it?"

"I guess so."

"*Really*?" Katy said, exasperated. She was also getting thirsty and exhausted. "What about that flag you're flying, the southern Dixie flag? Why would a policeman have that on their truck?"

"Oh that," he said, somewhat sheepishly. "That's my grandfather's flag, and I had to leave my house in a big rush. I couldn't bear to leave it for the fires in the neighborhood. It's actually not Dixie, but a thirteen-colonies flag. An antique. I'm Casey Johansen, by the way."

All very fascinating, but not quite convincing, she thought.

Kirby came out of the back, walking quickly. He ignored Johansen in a studied way. "Are we going now?"

Johansen swallowed and dropped some of the friendliness. "Alvarez," he said.

Kirby didn't say anything, but stood impatiently clutching packages to his chest.

"You two *know* each other?" Katy said.

"You could say that," Johansen answered, after a tense pause. "You're just going to take that product, Alvarez?"

"Oh Jesus," Katy said, now fully exasperated. "You're still policing around the edges, with all this going on? We're paying for everything we leave with, and if I don't have the cash, we'll leave a promissory note. I'm not his keeper or apologist," she added, with a note of harshness. "But he needed some painkillers, for his injury."

Johansen tapped lightly and nervously on his thigh, as though itching to remove his gun and make an arrest. He didn't like the *de facto* stripping of his authority, by the state of emergency, and the unraveling of things.

But he gave way to the willful Katy.

"Alright, this time. But don't loot any more places," he said to Kirby directly. "Just go home, wherever that is."

"Us too, that's where we're headed," Katy said. "You mentioned some water?"

"Yeah, it's over here."

They walked quickly to another peripheral wall of the store, where they found six-packs of bottled water encased in shrink wrap. She felt greedy. Johansen showed her to stacked water hidden behind food crates and cardboard boxes.

"Did you hide these?" she asked him.

"Let's just say I didn't unbury them."

"Don't you feel like a hoarder? I do."

"The riffraff would have stripped this place by yesterday," he said, stuffing a few sixes in the crook of his left arm. "I was helping save water for the good people."

"'The good people,'" she repeated, facetiously. She picked up two six packs for herself. Chris had to drink; she did, too. She turned to Johansen.

"You mean, 'the good people' like you? It seems like you could make a snap judgement about someone, and get it wrong."

"From what I've seen, the difference between those inclined to loot and commit violence, and those just trying to survive, are graphic. I would think martial law is coming, with the volcano killing people and emptying all these cities and towns. That sets the hornets loose."

"Now martial law, that'll certainly improve our lot," she quipped. They walked back down the aisle and the line of idle cash registers, where people formerly lined up to buy toothpaste, razor blades, Tylenol, and slurpies.

They reached the pile of shattered glass at the entrance.

Johansen turned his head to her.

"Your friend, or should I say, temporary companion, has a record a mile high. DUIs, drug violations, drunk-and-disorderlies, petty burglaries. That accident he got in, you know, he was fleeing an arrest for a breaking-and-entering."

"Really? It appears to me he's recovering from some blows. Aren't we all?"

The ash had blown in and buried the sheets of broken glass. Chris stood alone on the sidewalk, calmly chewing on a Mars Bar. Kirby was nowhere to be seen, and when she looked to the curb, the Jeep was gone, too.

"Where's Kirby?"

"He drove off in the Jeep," Chris murmured, disinterested and rendered lushly comatose by the chocolate.

"Oh, *shit,*" Katy swore. "I gave him the keys to get into the Jeep for a second, and he took off. Did he say where he was going?"

"He just said, Bye kid," Chris answered.

"That was my Jeep! Shows you where trust will get you! Thank god I brought my backpack in."

"Look at that," Johansen said, with a mixture of alarm and fear. "What *is* that?"

A black, swirling cloud from the southeast covered the peaks and poured down into the meadow, as if propelled from behind by hurricane winds.

It was coming from the direction of Yellowstone, 70 miles away. As the exploding caldera continued to spread ash thousands of miles across a continent, Katy thought, it also regurgitated massive levels of magma fragments and gases into the atmosphere below, creating uninhabitable and unimaginable confluences of toxic weather systems, leaving a swath of local death and destruction.

"Let's go!" she screamed. "That's poison and we won't survive it!" She grabbed Chris' hand, and they sprinted with Johansen towards his pickup, and the semi-abandoned Marriott.

CHAPTER 35: KIATSU

Kiatsu didn't remember much of the helicopter ride, only that she had been transported, as if by magic to somewhere, where she was then ferried into a hospital. The unbearable pain had subsided; whatever Tiva had given her induced a swoon that was more dream, a flock of competing visions, than reality. As soon as she had realized that her children were also aboard, she let herself float into a black unconsciousness, wondering if this was her path to death.

Papa Saito, her dad, dominated these narcotic dreams. He was standing in the sun in his backyard in Idaho, in a Japanese soldier's uniform. He was carrying a carbine, smiling proudly as if for a camera. He looked too young for the outfit; he seemed to be a child soldier, naively making himself taller and more manly than he was.

At one point during the war, in 1944, he told her once, the Japanese military had still held onto a far larger landmass–the Philippines, Vietnam, Singapore, Burma, Papa New Guinea, vast swaths of conquered territory in China–than Hitler had occupied himself. They couldn't imagine defeat.

When he told her that, a small, dapper, driven Asian man who had thrived amidst the massive industrial machine that had devastated his people and atomic-bombed his own home city, the leap he had made in his life, from bombed and near dead, to a business leader among his conquerors, seemed unbelievable, too grand to be true.

Had he now survived Mother Nature's onslaught, an explosion several magnitudes greater than Nagasaki?

She opened her eyes fleetingly, as she drifted in and out of consciousness. Something had jolted her awake; was it the aircraft settling on the ground? She thought of her children, Jake and Abby; they would be taken care of, she was sure of it. The helicopter has landed somewhere. Tiva is competent, and there would be capable adults around; the ones who are still left when society is devastated, young soldiers and medics.

She hoped, prayed, her children wouldn't despair upon her death, should it occur.

She heard urgent, relieved voices, everyone being happy that they'd safely landed. A minute later, she felt herself lifted out of the aircraft and into a cold wind. They placed her on another bed with wheels on it; she heard muffled voices. Her body felt like a detached entity, separate from her mind; then fuzzy, prickly, with the pain creeping back, like an old psychic wound.

Someone threw a blanket over her, including her face. T*hey don't think I'm dead already, do they? Are they covering my body, out of respect? How horrible, to be thought dead, when you're not.* She tried to make sounds, but they came out like grunts and squeaks. Then she heard Tiva talking to her, and that relieved her anxiety about being prematurely classified as a corpse, which must happen more than one thinks.

Dying is easy to do, physically, she thought. It's handling the regrets, the unfinished tasks and words unspoken to loved ones. She felt so small and burned, the life leaking out of her. She wanted to be able to laugh, weep, once more, to have someone hold her hand.

Wheels clattered beneath her. She thought of all these people, 80 years ago in Nagasaki, so burned they were unrecognizable as humans. They could only go down to the river; they had no one to take care of them. Perhaps, in that context, she was lucky.

Wherever she was going, if there was an afterlife, she wondered whether she would see Papa Saito. Was he there already, a man in his 90s, finally killed by a volcano; so dramatic, when he deserved a calmer, more dignified death? She thought again about the saying among Japanese people, "Duty is heavy as a mountain, but death is lighter than a feather."

She felt warmth; she was inside a room, the ambient

light weakly permeating the surface of the blanket. She heard a child's voice, that was Abby, and she tried to turn her head toward the girl, but felt even too weak for that maneuver, so brittle and tender. Then it was only the darkness and floating colors behind her eyelids, and her chest still moving up and down, like a bird that has struck a window but still lies alive on the grass.

CHAPTER 36: GARNER

The Raw Frontier Diner had retained the reliable orderliness of the past, before the volcano. Only a total of an inch or two of ash had fallen outside. The storm had let up. Garner and Aeva sat at the counter together, as if by habit.

Half the other booths were occupied. The diner had only one waitress, an attractive brunette lady with a denim skirt, and a light-blue shirt with red, Western-style embroidery. Her name was Julie. She moved about efficiently, smiling, taking orders, wiping down tables and counters.

Brad had black coffee, eggs over easy, crispy bacon, wheat toast, and hash browns. Aeva had a large, dripping cheeseburger and french fries, with a lemon tea.

They were completely absorbed in the meal, not saying much. Garner's cellphone still didn't have service. With Aeva heading off to Mexico in pursuit of her hostage girlfriend, Brad's next mission was to find wheels. No, he thought, urging himself on, it was to connect with his family members, and find out if they were okay, and where they were.

A dog wandered out of the kitchen, sniffing the air for anything of interest, slowly wagging its tail. It was long-haired, black and white, with floppy ears that perked up if you made eye contact or greeted her.

Now this was something that Garner was still in the mood for, a good dog pet. The dog settled down on the floor and rested its chin on its paws. Garner got up and wandered over; the dog noted his approach merely by raising one eyelid.

He knelt down and stroked the top of her head and along her back. The dog regarded him with a warm patience. "Good girl," he said. He felt himself relax. "What's your name?"

"Tanya," answered a gruff voice in the back. A line cook busily arranged plates on a counter. Each plate was marked by a ticket. He had a papery hat pulled down over scraggly, thinning gray hair. He wore a white, yellowed T-shirt. The diner was pervaded by a shared desire to bring out tasteful food quickly. The air of busyness fostered a sense of normalcy.

"Tanya," Garner said, breathing easier. "We had a dog at home, part boxer. Named Tony." He kept petting her, and as he did, his heart rate slowed down.

He felt a physical ease that had escaped him up till then.

When he was finished, he stood up and rejoined Aeva, who was almost done with her food.

She wiped her face with a napkin."So what are you going to do now? Come with me to Mexico?" Her clipped tone suggested he was her sidekick, Butch's Sundance.

In and around swabbing yoke with a piece of toast: "No, thanks. I think I'm going to have you drop me off at that motel down the road. I'll get collected, hopefully call my wife, and hit the road for California."

"You have no car. That motel, La Casa Grande, it looks like the end of the road."

"I can get a car…ma'am." He signaled the waitress. "What do we owe you? That was delicious. Really hit the spot."

She looked over her shoulder at him with a half smile. She was pretty, he thought. *Very.*

She cleared another customer's plates, then strolled past him, on the way to the kitchen.

"My name's Julie. Ten dollars will cover it."

"That's all?" In his mind, with everything that was happening, the diner deserved a bonus. He tucked a twenty beneath his coffee cup, then wiped his hands with the napkin. He stood up with Aeva, then he went over and knelt down and stroked Tanya for another minute. He watched Julie walking around the diner.

Aeva held the entrance door for him, acting impatient. Before he left the diner, he said "Bye Julie, thanks." She was clearing their own plates.

"See you later," she said, with the faintest hint of hopefulness, he thought. He assumed she was "looking for normal" too, as in nice customers that return day after day. He planned to, as long as he lingered in this area.

Twenty minutes later he was standing in the parking lot of La Casa Grande next to Aeva's pickup truck. The driver window was open, and Aeva prepared to start it up.

"Well, I've got to go," she said. *When she's not wielding a pistol and getting ready to kick some ass, he thought, she could be quite companionable.* Given the fix they were both in, they'd both needed a slow, almost laconic and classic breakfast of delightful fixings from the griddle.

On the way to La Casa Grande they'd stopped at an open convenience store. Its glass entrance had not been kicked in and looted, and behind the counter was a skittish but friendly teenaged boy.

Garner picked up some survival food for the motel, which seemed mostly empty and forlorn in the desert: quart of full-fat milk, jar of Teddy peanut butter (smooth style), loaf of non-moldy white bread, fistful of beef jerky, two apples, a banana (the only fruit left), and a pint from behind the counter. Jack Daniels.

He paid cash, and left with the stuff in a plastic bag. He'd already been inside the small motel lobby, where a quiet, faintly suspicious proprietor with a gray ponytail gave him a key to a room, four parking spaces down from the blinking, green neon cactus.

"So I guess this is it," Aeva said.

"Again, you were a life-saver picking me up, but things did get a little crazy for a time there."

"Thanks for the cash. I'll pay you back."

"No worries," he said, reasoning, *we'll never see each other again.* "I hope you find your friend Lucy, and it all goes well."

"I hope you find your family. Jeez, we both have tough but admirable missions."

He reached his hand in to shake her hand. "C'mere you fool," she said. When he leaned down, she pulled his face forward and kissed him on the right cheek.

"I'm gonna give 'em hell," she said.

"I know you will."

When she drove away, she was smiling, and he stood in the parking lot carrying his backpack and his food, watching the truck drive south on the long, flat road, until he couldn't see the back of the pickup any longer.

CHAPTER 37: ZEKE

Monica stepped over the downed men on the stairs, the air thick with bitter smoke and cordite.

Zeke yanked the lifeless bodies by their boots down to the bottom of the steps, then he rifled the pockets of Fetterman, who'd murdered the truck driver and fallen victim to his own brand of frontier justice.

Monica grimaced, holding onto her stomach, as she eased past the two prone men, one of which she'd shot herself.

She pondered if she'd ever stop reminding herself of that fact, or maybe she'd block it out and learn to live with it. She'd done what she had to do. She didn't think she'd have to go into the backyard and retch; she just wanted out of there.

Let's just go with Zeke's plan, and get the hell out of

here.

"What are we going to with him?" Slater asked, nodding his head to the still bound man in the adjacent room, who squirmed around and gaped at them wild-eyed. He'd slowly regained consciousness, groaning and rolling over onto his back.

"We're gonna leave him," Zeke said. "He'll learn to stand up after a while, after much trial and error. I'm not going to lose any sleep over that lowlife."

They loaded up the scraps and leftovers from the kitchen, which the Fetterman gang had ransacked like rabid raccoons. They made their way up the driveway and back to the highway. The idle, muddy Dodge Ram still appeared sturdy, drivable, of a recent vintage.

"I can start driving," Zeke said, jingling the ignition keys in his hand. "We'll take turns."

Slater stood pensively beside the passenger's door, the ash falling lightly. It reminded Monica of shaking the down feathers from one of her old sleeping bags, the weightlessness of the dust, the way it took forever to flutter to the ground.

She hugged herself in the cold wind. The owner of the truck lay curled up and dead in the cruel shadows of the scrubby roadside.

"What about the man?" Monica said, speaking more to the leaden sky. "I don't feel good about just leaving him there." She coughed, a stray emotion rising into her throat, but her chest felt heavy, congested.

"I don't either," Slater said. "We're taking his truck. We can at least find his identity, try to alert his relatives.

Sometime."

Zeke scratched his chin. He'd been ready to leave the body; the circumstances called for that. They had no burial detail, no shovels.

"The ground's too hard to bury him, and we really have to get moving."

He thought of Tiva again, hoping she'd at least crossed the Oregon border, and found refuge somewhere safe.

It didn't make sense to toss the body into the truck-cargo bed, he thought, swaddled in a sheet. They'd simply be transporting a decomposing corpse. They ended up wrapping him up head to toe in a quilt inside the house, like a sailor buried at sea, and left the body on a couch. They put a note and his wallet on top of his torso.

Gil was still on the floor; eyes closed, he'd seemed to have passed back out.

It was late morning, the light grainy and indistinct. Ash fell in dreary curtains that drifted across the highway. Zeke started the engine, and the truck lurched forward through dense, unevenly arranged soot piles. Monica sat next to him, hands in her lap, the dirty canvas bag containing harvested food at her feet. She gazed blankly out the window, as they left the ruinous scene behind them.

It felt nice to move, she thought, but seeing the sun and the ocean would be better.

Zeke stared out the windshield silently. The highway was empty and obscured. He seemed thoughtful, pensive. The lack of full sunlight on Monica's face, or radiating upon her back, felt, to her, like chronic starvation.

"Is the killing over now?" she asked, quietly.

Zeke looked at her quizzically, then seemed to catch her drift.

"Yes, for now. We're on our own." Slater leaned forward from the back seat.

"How much gas do we have?"

Zeke glanced at the gauge. "Two thirds..."

"A friend of mine had a Dodge like this." For a moment, Slater wondered whether this friend, a fellow researcher at the University of Montana in Missoula, had escaped; was actually alive. He was in no mood to run the numbers on casualty counts from the volcano, but the calculations appeared to form in his mind, as if against his will.

"His truck had a 26-gallon tank, so we have about 16 gallons left. Lucky to get 15 miles per gallon, so we might be able to go 240 miles. That barely gets us past the Oregon border. So we'll have to fill up somewhere along the way."

"What are you, a human calculator?" Zeke said.

"Some have claimed that."

Slater had a mathematical mind, which he couldn't always switch off. He thought of the combined populations of Montana and Wyoming, about 1.7 million people. Even a 10 percent death rate from a variety of lethal volcanic effects, including loss of hospitals and food distribution, would mean a conservative estimate of 170,000 casualties, and that wasn't including Idaho or Utah residents.

Ten percent was even optimistic at this point. It depended on how everything played out over the next few weeks, he thought, pressing his forehead against the window. He pondered the pine forest skirting the road, the branches heavily weighed down by nests of ash, many of the trunks, blackened by fire, forlornly toppled over by the roadside.

Monica, in the front passenger seat, put her hand over her mouth and coughed strenuously.

"Are you okay?" Slater asked. She sounded dry, raspy. He fetched one of the remaining water bottles for her. She took the bottle, cracked the plastic cap, then tipped it up, washing the clear water over her parched throat.

When she'd finished drinking, she said, breathlessly, "I've had this since yesterday." She swallowed hard. "I'm not shocked; I've been breathing in that wood smoke, all the Goddamned ash..."

"Is it in your chest?"

"Yeah."

"Not good, we'll keep an eye on that," Slater said, glancing at her warily. "When we're outside, try to keep your mouth covered with that buff."

In 30 minutes, Zeke pulled the truck over to the side of the road. They'd decided to eat, stretch their limbs, check their cellphones. They had to discuss a plan, a common destination.

Zeke shut off the engine, got out, stood by the side

of the road with his underused Samsung. The "oblong." He pressed the power button, then lifted his face to the sky, to the faint, pale sunshine. The logo on the phone came to life, blossoming like the cheap print of a Japanese sunrise. He had a connection.

"Fancy that," he muttered, standing on the hard ground where the road descended into a trash-strewn gully.

He saw the ruts made by their tires, tracking from the east. Evidence of any vehicles traveling from the west had long been covered up by the drifting debris. The blanketed landscape had become a hilly, sandy barrens, more resembling North Africa, or the moon, than southern Idaho.

When he kicked at it, the ash annealed into chunks like moist, stale flour.

He had messages; he tapped around the screen inexpertly. Slowly, they loaded. He looked at the horizon; buttes and pockets of surviving forests. Only a few isolated homesteads and farms appeared. The countryside was silent.

"Tiva's in Boise," he said, eyes brightening and watering with emotion. "They're going onto Portland. Kiatsu is stable. They're all safe. The kids..."

"Sweet," Slater said. "That's so good to hear. Good news, for once." Slater felt a faint sense of accomplishment, but it wasn't enough to assuage his guilt. He'd sat at the center of a cataclysm, as the lead scientist. Thousands died. *Get over it,* he told himself.

Beating yourself up ceaselessly will get no one, nowhere.

"Tiva is okay now," Zeke repeated to himself, as if sifting options, calculating odds. "I've got to find Amitola now." His eyes were fastened on the southern horizon, where the sun hardly permeated clouds that were like a brownish gray film.

He shoved the phone back in his satchel and began to pace.

"Go south, not west. I've got to check on my wife. I've heard nothing from her." Silence from the other two, who stood across the hood of the car.

"You mean, you're going to split from us?" Monica said, then started spasmodically coughing again. A lilt in her voice made the words seem like a childish plea.

"We need to get you looked after," Slater said. "An X-ray in Boise, if we can."

Zeke looked down and kicked at the ash again. "At the next town, I'm going to take the southern road, into Nevada. You can come, but if not, I'll give you guys the truck."

"I don't want you to go," Monica said. "We're a team."

"I have to, if I can't reach Amitola on the Samsung."

"How are you going to travel?" Slater asked, incredulously. "Fly?"

"I wish I could. I'm gonna find me a motorcycle in that town up ahead." It was a tough decision, with Monica implying that he was abandoning them. But obligation and devotion pulled at him. He reached into his satchel and found the plastic bag that contained his pipe and peyote, just to make sure they were still there.

The dusty, arid plains stretched for miles to the beckoning southern horizon. New Mexico was somewhere southeast of there, like a distant, hazy place he could only travel to in his dreams.

CHAPTER 38: KATY

They sprinted through the Marriott hotel's front door, which had been pried open by intruders.

Casey held the door open wider, then tried to slam it shut as Katy dragged Chris through the opening.

The swirling cloud, freighted with lethal fragments of minute magma, smashed into the building's glass windows, with the rapping sound of grapeshot. The glass panes shuddered under the force; cracks ramified across their surfaces.

The scene outside vanished into black turbulence, which had turned noon into violent, stormy midnight.

"We have to go farther into the hotel! Those clouds contain poisonous gases!" Katy yelled. She couldn't stifle the scientist, talking quickly, frenetically; not even now. "Hydrogen sulfide, carbon monoxide, hydrogen fluoride, intense CO_2 levels. It'll suck the oxygen from out of the air."

"Are we gonna die?" Chris cried out.

"No, of course not!" she answered, vaguely. The lobby had begun to fill with sickly brown vapor.

"Let's go! The stairs!" Johansen screamed. "The upper floors! We'll find some rooms that are more hermetically sealed!" *I hope,* he thought.

They sprinted past the check-in desk and a set of elevators to a stairwell, labeled with a red exit sign. The toxic, particlized vapor had choked the hotel foyer; it appeared to be chasing them as it seeped along the lower-floor spaces.

They entered the stairwell, Johansen picking up and tossing Chris over his shoulder like a sack of sand. Katy sprinted up the stairs ahead; Casey plodded with the boy. Katy could see the poisonous effluent seeping from beneath the closed exit door, as though it was pumped into the stairwell from a hose.

They made one flight, turning into the next, breathing heavily, sweat pouring down their red faces.

"To the top floor!" Casey yelled hoarsely.

"Put Chris down!" Katy yelled behind her, watching the thick smoke gather behind them. Her mind worked over the outcome; trapped in an enclosed space, they'd be asphyxiated in less than a minute, especially Chris. They would die on the floor. Three anonymous bodies, undiscovered for days. Months.

"He can run faster!"

"Let me down!" Chris squealed. Casey set him down

on the next landing. "Run!" Katy screamed. Chris put his head down with a look of game determination, then ran up the flight of stairs with his little arms pumping. He went fast, Katy led the way, a sweating and huffing Johansen plodding right behind them.

Katy smelled the hydrogen-sulfide stink. Up past the next landing, to the next set of stairs, another landing. Fourth floor. The air was thick, her eyes stung. "Keep going!" *This place maybe has eight floors?* she thought. Nose still full of the god-awful odor of death.

Chris began to slow, tire. She seized his hand. Her throat was tight, the demands coming out like raspy shrieks. "Keep going," she cried, through that inflamed throat. "You can do it!"

Pulling at his arm; Chris crying, tears coursing down a soot-stained face. "Casey!" she yelled. He wasn't behind them, then he appeared. Sixth-floor landing. They make the seventh. A blank plastic wall; a wooden door. They'd reached the top floor. *That smell, that sour, eggs-rotten smell.* When she looked down at Chris, the brown vapor had risen to his neck, her waste.

"Go!" Casey barked hoarsely from behind.

Chris started to cough; she sensed a wave of dizziness. She opened the last door; the toxic vapor poured into the new space with them, like brown water, as she dragged Chris inside. No Casey, no Casey. He wasn't with them; he hadn't made it. After a long 15 seconds, she slammed the door shut.

CHAPTER 39: SLATER

"Get me to the hospital," she whispered weakly, curled up on the passenger side of the front seat, her head leaning against the open palm of her hand.

"That's where I'm headed," Slater yelled back, jamming the truck's accelerator to the floor.

Monica's breathing was labored; a wheeze arrived with each exhalation. They'd been on the road for an hour since Zeke left; and during that time she'd declined. She fought for her breaths. She was terrified, frustrated. She'd been able to avoid injury and sickness, *throughout the entire escape, the volcano, the grizzly, the human predators...*She'd been able to persevere.

Maybe it's something that will pass; maybe I should just calm down. The stress is making it worse.

She took a deep breath again, launching another

spasm of weary coughing.

She closed her eyes, trying to visualize someplace sunny, where the ash hadn't buried everything, where the magma hadn't eternally blocked out the sun. A coast, a beach, curling waves, a sunset, they just had to keep driving; she just had to clear this congestion, this slow-motion suffocation.

They knew, from making a call back on the road, that Boise had a functioning ER.

Slater could see the skyline, partly obscured by a cloud that was like a huge gray disk. He sped up to 60 mph, as fast as the old Dodge could go, tires grinding along the gritty, partly buried highway.

Drivers exited Boise in droves from the opposite direction, a slow, creeping evacuation. Volcanic ash still mounted in the city, drifting against the telephone poles and the parking meters and the boarded-up, graffiti-marred storefronts.

Boise, Idaho was located within the geographic zone that would receive up to 300 mm, or more. That translated to 30 cm, or about one foot. *Ash piled that high will shut down every machine, every motor, every turbine; it will collapse every roof, and civilization with it.*

The citizens seemed to realize that, he thought; this wasn't hype. They were heading west. His Dodge Ram was the sole vehicle heading *into* the city, it seemed. He hoped the hospital continued to function, that it wasn't every man for himself.

He had to pull over to consult a paper map he'd found in the truck's glove compartment. He had to gather his thoughts; all this had happened so quickly. He didn't know exactly where the hospital was.

What are we doing? she said.

"I just need to pull over for a second."

He thought she needed steroids, a bronchodilator, such as for those suffering from an asthmatic attack. This would be available at the ER; he might even find one at a CVS pharmacy.

His cellphone wasn't working, because they'd lost service again...

He sensed a bottomless exhaustion, compounded by the extended ordeal; the sweat trickled down his rib cage, a tight throb centered on his temples.

Outside the windshield, past the rhythmic thunk of the wipers, sat the deserted, dejected city, offering scant salvation. Still midday, he had his high-beams on. The floating curtains of airborne particles reflected back at him dully.

He swerved awkwardly into the parking lot in front of a defunct small-business center: a flower shop, tattoo parlor, tanning-bed emporium, auto-parts store. A few unmanned vehicles were parked haphazardly. He left the engine running, got out, walked to the other side of the car, removed the map, unfolded it, conscious of the clock ticking.

Only minutes left to find help for Monica.

He fumbled with his glasses; he ran his finger along the edge highway they'd entered Boise on. Monica had fallen *very* silent. He finally located the hospital. He had to drive into the city's downtown district, *and* floor it.

No time, no time to waste.

Paranoia set in; he feared he'd find the hospital but the doors would be locked, the clinic abandoned. *Don't fear,* he thought. Fear paralyzes. The hospital will be their main destination, *but if I see a CVS or Walgreens first... no! Aim for the hospital.* He had no expertise in first-aid, per se, beyond a few first-responder courses he took on a whim in college.

He missed Zeke. He had the sinking sensation that Zeke would have a better plan. He could execute it with more precision than Slater could.

Monica gazed at him lifelessly, conveying a look of pure dependence and need. *I love her,* he repeated to himself, *I have to save her. Save Monica, that's my endgame. That's the purpose; my destiny.*

Glasses still clinging to the end of his nose, Slater folded up the map, shoved it in the glove compartment, shut the passenger door. He walked back around the front of the car to get back in.

He saw a man and a woman emerge from the auto-parts franchise, arms full of boxes; looted goods. The guy had a hooded sweatshirt on, boots with floppy laces, a mohawk-style haircut, with a tattoo on the bald parts. The female had vividly dyed hair; silver-metal studs decorating faux black-leather coat and pants. They walked quickly toward Slater's truck.

He figured he could beat them out of the parking lot; he shut the door behind him, jerked the truck's ignition into Drive.

The two twenty-somethings had reached the truck;

the lady hurled the boxes into the cargo bed as Slater ground through the caky gravel of the lot. The guy slammed his hand on the hood of the vehicle, yelling indistinct curses at Slater, who floored the accelerator as both of the looters seized the sides of the truck's cargo area and vaulted themselves into the back.

What is happening? Monica whispered.

"We're being car-jacked. Or, I should say, an attempted car jack." He swerved back on the highway. A glance to the rearview mirror; a thump on a window back there, blurry movements. "I always read about car jacks. Always wondered what one would be like."

How can you make such a casual comment when it's happening? Monica said, leaning her head back on the hard cushion of the passenger door.

Slater looked into the rearview mirror, a menacing glare and more uninterpretable curses. *I still have Zeke's pistol; it has two bullets left.*

He picked up speed. It looked like the crazy lady was trying to climb onto the roof. They're hopped up on some kind of drug cocktail, he thought. This gives me an advantage–I can exploit their compulsions.

He increased his speed, reaching the main drag through the city. The hospital would emerge soon, maybe 10 blocks. *They can't go anywhere...* then he heard a loud jolt and crack as one of the crazies went at the rear window with a tire iron.

Shit, I have to pivot. New tactics are in order. Thunk! A crack ramified across the back window; it was about to give way.

He pulled into the lot of an abandoned gas station. It had a raised concrete island where the gas pumps were. He threw the ignition into Reverse, stepped on the accelerator, and slammed the back of the truck into the concrete island.

The collision force threw his two unwanted passengers to the floor of the truck bed. He pulled forward, back into Reverse; smashed the rear of the truck again, into the concrete. Both passengers were on the floor of the cargo bed, mad as hornets. Both scrambled to their feet, surrounded by the disarray of their scattered loot.

The job wasn't finished. Slater pulled forward, then back into Reverse, smashed the rear of the vehicle again; rendering not much left of the rear bumper or fender panel of the Dodge. Both car jackers went flying into the badly dented, hinged rear door.

Slater thought the feral guy with the fucked-up head was beyond beside himself with volcanic anger. He gave him a moment as the guy, screaming his red face off and holding his leg, leapt off the rear of the truck.

Mohawk sprint-limped toward the driver's side to get at Slater, who jammed it into Drive again, accelerated, and left the guy cursing and waving like a lunatic in the empty parking lot, with only the female in the purple and green hair still in the truck's cargo bed.

She had a pistol out now and she pointed it at them through the cracked window. *Why didn't they use that before? Because they didn't want him to crash the truck?*

"Duck!" he yelled to Monica. He seized their own

handgun off the floor of the truck, still driving with one hand. He heard the bark of the gun behind them and the glass exploded like a shattered illusion.

He slammed on the brakes of the truck, in the middle of the empty highway. Left the engine on; put it in Park. He stepped out into the ash, gun clutched in his right hand. The lady raised her gun and both weapons discharged at the same time.

He had one round, it turned out; it hit the lady in the clavicle, just below a silver-studded faux-leather neck band. She got off two rounds; he'd felt one tear into his right ribcage, about 10 inches beneath his armpit.

She lay spread-eagled in the back of the Dodge. Slater bent over forward, sidestepped back to the open driver's door, with the engine still running, groaned, slid back in. Slammed the door.

Monica, pale white face with tears running down her cheeks, stared at him. *You're hurt!*

"So are you. ER, next stop..." The rosy wetness on his side bloomed like a flower. The truck jerked forward, speeding back up into the middle of the vacant highway.

For once, Slater knew where he was going. He knew his destination.

CHAPTER 40: AEVA

Ciudad Juarez, Mexico, across the Rio Grande from El Paso, Texas, Late October, 2025.

The pickup cruised slowly along a dusty, crowded street. The inhabitants were used to this, a vehicle with an air of mystery. They walked along the cracked sidewalks with deadpan faces, or paused in groups for animated conversations. Sometimes gunfire broke out around these slowly driven pickups; the street existed along the edge of vast squatter camps, a poverty-infested dead-end for Mexicans who didn't make it across the Rio yet.

Vast numbers of loose children, from large families, who, playing in the streets, couldn't imagine the stagnancy of their future.

Often, gunfire *didn't* break-out; it wasn't always a

cartel member. Perhaps, only a vegetable grower delivering his goods, or a truck full of maquiladora workers. The boulevard, not in a nice part of town, went on forever, with its square warehouse-style structures and ramshackle hovels, endless square miles of crumbling, hastily built habitations and neighborhoods, until a row of dry, brown-sculpted mountains appeared, fuzzy with an orange haze.

The lady driving the truck had been given an address. It was a miracle that she found this neighborhood; she thought she had the right place. She parked in front of a bodega. It had the name the man on the phone had given her. Bodega de Coloso. The sign just said Coloso. It had whole chickens on skewers in the display window; incongruously, various cartons of cigarettes were displayed next to the fowl.

She figured it was because this was no grocery store. It was a front for corrupt Policia and kidnappers and cartel bangers, or whatever. She was under no illusions. Some poor people, no doubt, bought a little Mexican food there.

She was nervous, but seized with an uncharacteristic sense of laser focus, which boosted her morale. She took it to be courage.

She had a wad of cash, Mexican pesos, in the inside pocket of her black coat. She knew she'd be searched upon entering Coloso. People wandered along the sidewalk in front of the bodega, women with the broad-cheeked, good-natured Mayan features, wearing clean peasant dresses. She watched them for a minute, before she opened the driver's door and stepped out onto the street. They paid her no mind; a gringa with some business in the neighborhood.

No ash fell here. The air was warm, muggy compared with New Mexico. Full sunlight blazed above the mountains.

She had baggy trousers on, and along her calf she'd duct-taped the pistol. She'd practiced removing it several times. She had cowboy boots on, fashionable ones, she thought. She wondered about people, Americans like her, who would come to Juarez as tourists. They had an optimism, and a suspension of disbelief, which she did not possess.

In reality, she felt like she was in enemy territory.

It was dark inside the bodega. When she opened the door, a bell jingled. The smell inside was not of cooking chickens; more of a stale, cigarette odor. Cheap liquor and sweat.

The smoky smell made her think of a former plan to arrive wasted on good weed, in order to give herself courage, but she'd quickly dismissed that as a bad idea. She needed her wits about her, her reflexes. Her anger.

An older Mexican lady stood behind a wooden counter containing various articles Aeva wouldn't be interested in buying, mostly candy, plastic animals, and playing cards with funny designs on them. Cans and boxes lined the walls; beans, flour, pasta, cereal. In the darkness, in the back, two men sat at a table. Not feeling welcome, she remained in the front of the store.

"I'm here to see Franco," she said.

The two men sat in their chairs lazily. They were drinking tequila. One of them was smoking; the vapors lingered up by the ceiling, wafting up from an ashtray.

"Who's here to see Franco?"

"Dillon. Aeva Dillon."

"And who gives a shit?" the other one said, then reached down and gulped the short glass of tequila.

"Franco does. He wants my money." The first man got up and went into the back. There was a curtain of beads. He pushed it aside and went into the next low-lit room, said something.

Aeva swallowed hard; she sensed that focus that had pervaded her recently.

The third man, Franco, came out. He was oddly, unexpectedly cherubic, short, with a black, greased handlebar mustache and a pleasant smile.

"So you're Aeva? I'm pleased to meet you." He sized her up and down. "I like your boots. I really like your western boots. Like an American cowgirl, huh? Do you like horses? We have lots of herds in Juarez, lots of thoroughbreds. You'd be interested."

"Where's Lucy? I have your money."

"Show me the money." Franco's smile vanished with a cruel quickness.

"Show me Lucy. Let me see Lucy first. Bring her in here."

"Now now!" Franco said. "Don't make demands. Do you want a drink first?"

"Let me see Lucy."

"A business lady, I see. I like that. No foolishness.

No wastes of time." He nodded at the second man, who stood up and turned to face her. He started to move.

She put her hand up. "Wait a second, wait a second. I'll give you the money. Just bring Lucy out. We had a deal." She reached into her coat and removed the wad of pesos. The amount was roughly one half of what they had asked for on the phone. She walked over to the counter the pleasant woman had walked away from, and stacked the money there, next to a half empty bottle of mescal.

"Where's the rest of it?"

"In the truck. That's most of it."

"Alright. Why don't I just kill you now, and Lucy?"

"Because the Americans know I'm here. I gave them the address. The Americans at the border."

Franco laughed at what he thought was a good joke. "Okay." Franco waved at the back room. The other man walked through the beads, into the back room, and emerged a minute later with Lucy, who had long black hair, a gray sweatshirt, and a stretch of black industrial tape fastened across her mouth. The man with her reached over and ripped the tape off, and Lucy shouted, "You motherfucker!"

Aeva reached down, lifted her trousers, ripped the pistol off her calf, raised the handgun, and shot Franco in the face. He went straight back like pushing a piece of plywood standing on one end. She then shot the tequila-drinking guy once, twice, three times before he could produce and discharge his own handgun.

Lucy slapped hard and kicked at the groin of the

man who'd ripped the tape off her face, and when he grabbed her by the neck, Aeva stepped forward with a hunting knife that had a hard black handle and jammed it into the side of his neck. His eyes went as wide as saucers, and his neck spouted a fountain of dark blood onto the spotless floor. The floor the peasant woman had just swept.

"Let's go!" Aave grabbed Lucy's hand, and they ran. On her way out the door, Aeva snatched the wad of cash off the counter.

The nice older woman in the dress squatted behind the counter with both hands pressed to her ears.

# #

Garner sat in the sun on a small stool he'd moved out there. He was in front of La Casa Grande, in the parking lot's warm sunlight. He read the local newspaper, the *Las Cruces Sun-News*, which he was grateful they were still publishing and distributing. He liked to read and drink coffee in the morning. It was a cherished, reestablished habit.

He read a story that had been reproduced from the Associated Press. It was about a shooting in Juarez, which involved a kidnapping. A woman, thought to be an American, had killed three men, reportedly members of a local narcotics and kidnapping syndicate. She'd then fled with another woman in a pickup truck. She was still "at large," but was thought to have crossed the border back into El Paso.

"Hot damn," Garner whispered to himself, "I know that was her. That was Aeva." He let the paper fall back into his lap. "She knew what she wanted to do." The paper drifted to his feet, where it was mussed up and crinkled in the breeze. He bent forward and picked up the newspaper and the paper cup of coffee and sipped it, reading the short article again, sitting back in the chair in the sunlight. Smiling. He didn't care about the money he had given her. It seemed to have gone to a good cause.

"You remarkable, unsinkable badass!" he remarked to no one, but the quiet desert.

CHAPTER 41: KATY

Katy drove the pickup north towards Bozeman, Montana. She hadn't bothered to remove the flag, the antique that resembled a Dixie logo.

Everything about the truck was still as Casey Johansen had left it; empty cans of Red Bull, a toolbox, a tarp, a half-full cardboard container of 9 mm ammo, crinkled up trash on the floor, from buying food on the run.

The amalgam of smells even evoked "guy truck" in her mind–chewing tobacco and sugary food; cheap beer and Lucky Strikes. His presence in the truck interior, where Chris sat in the back, was heavy, but as Katy kept reminding herself–Casey was dead.

She'd found him unresponsive in the Marriott stairwell. She did a little CPR, but he was gone. She'd shut the door leading to the seventh floor just before she passed out herself, thinking it was the only way to save Chris, which it was, because here the both of them were alive, but Casey hadn't made it.

She'd searched through Casey's pockets for the truck-ignition fob, found it, retreated to the upper floor. She and Chris didn't emerge from the hotel until the poisonous weather front had bled past, and the air appeared diluted by cleaner air, and marginally refreshed, because the ash was still heavy.

Catastrophic volcanic eruptions usually kill you if you're in close proximity, and quickly, but somehow they'd survived. *Somehow*–she wasn't going to fret over it. It just was. She figured her fitness had saved her, and Chris' youth. And divine intervention, whatever form that took.

They traveled slowly along the road north, but still had about 100 miles worth of gas. They were going to Bozeman, then heading northwest.

She'd quickly dismissed a return to the lodge above Big Sky, because the eruption hadn't abated, and the place was still too close to ground zero. It had no future; Yellowstone could still be spewing magma next month.

She hadn't showered in days, not since she'd fled the office with Monica and Slater. She must look frightful, as grungy as she feels. Scraggly hair, red eyes, dirt caked on her face, arms, hands. She hadn't even looked in a mirror. She didn't have a change of clothes. If they passed a Salvation Army, she would be a likely customer. Maybe they'd have to turn into Salvation Army looters.

She'd lost about eight pounds she didn't have, from running and stress. Her body and mind were in first gear, the truck in second, and they couldn't go much more than 20 mph through this slop.

They reached Bozeman; she'd pick up Route 90 northwest at Belgrade. They weren't stopping; they weren't going to get involved with anyone else. This was beginning to feel like her romantic life.

They were all dead, all the others. Again, it was just her and Chris, in their little lifeboat, castaway in a sea of ash. They passed the road to Bozeman Airport, cluttered with abandoned vehicles parked at skewed angles, their drivers having perhaps never made the last flight out. They crept past a boarded-up grocery store; *not stopping,* she thought, *not now.* Beyond that, a cavernous, dead mall that had apparently expired before the eruption.

Nothing to loot.

They still had the food and bottled water from the Walgreens. Junk food, which they both nibbled on. Chris stared out the window, in a dazed shock. They crossed a set of railroad tracks into Belgrade; she wished the trains were still running. That had promise. She saw a sign for 90.

If they ran out of water and gas, and got stuck out here, a previously civilized Great Plains region with all the power turned off, and the people gone or dead, then they were fucked. Harsh reality set in, eroding her morale.

"Where's that guy?" Chris asked. "Who talked to me in the store? Who knew where the water was?"

"He's back at the hotel."

"Is he dead?"

"The brown cloud got him. Yes."

"The lady's dead who found me at the lake."

"...Yes."

"My parents are dead."

"We don't know that." She looked at him in the rearview mirror, his eyes wet and his face all smeary. *The things we put our children through.*

"Kirby, he drove right into that thing. I saw him. That poison brown cloud. *He's* probably dead!"

"He shouldn't have taken my Jeep."

"Everyone dies! You're going to die! I know it! Then I'll be all alone! No one to take care of me." He put his hands on his face and began to quietly weep.

"No, I'm not going to die. Listen to me. We've made it this far. There's some reason that we keep escaping–keep making it. God keeps sparing us. Here I am a scientist, talking about divine intervention. I will *not* leave you alone! We're going to get through this together, you hear me, Dammit!"

She sobbed herself, out of weariness, hunger, loneliness. She wiped the streaming tears away with a loose sleeve. She took an exit for 90 north, grinding through the debris of the entrance ramp, and onto the highway.

She hadn't the energy to go food harvesting again, when they'd passed through Bozeman. Another 30 minutes went by; she didn't explicitly keep track of time. Day was like night. Strange lightning storms coursed across the swirling black sky. She couldn't see the Northern Rocky mountains anymore. The stars were smothered and gone. The sun was like an old light bulb quietly dying.

She cast a wary gaze to the gas gauge; only a quarter tank left.

She felt herself plunging into resignation, the first stage of giving up. *Have a plan,* she reminded herself. If that fails, then form another one. *Always have a plan. Always always.* The adrenaline had worn off; she was exhausted. No coffee to keep her eyes open.

Katy saw a family of deer running across a vacant lot, or a golf course, then they saw a pack of three gray wild dogs in pursuit. They could have been coyotes; she thought they were house dogs, merely surviving.

"Don't look at that," she said.

"What?"

"Nothing."

'Those lights," Chris said, staring out the window. "What are those lights?"

Above them, to the north, a cluster of lights made its way through the murky pall. One red light blinked.

"It's a UAP," she quipped sardonically. "Unidentified Aerial Phenomena. I'll take a ride from anyone." She slowed down, watching its progress, faintly hopeful.

The fog and the debris swirled around and obscured its shape, but her eyes weren't tricking her. It appeared to be descending. Somewhere between the golf course where they'd seen the deer, and the airport.

She stopped, pulled a U-turn, went the wrong way down the highway, keeping an eye on the red light.

"What is it?" Chris cried, now watching with fascination. Tires plunging through ash piles, engine complaining, truck accelerating.

"I think it's a red tail light. I think it's a helicopter." The craft descended, with its bulky fuselage, probably military related, Coast Guard or U.S. Army.

It settled into the field, off the highway, barely visible, ash swirling around. Two football fields away. She pulled the truck partway off the road; she thought she saw turbines, turning, turning, slicing the thick, palpably coarse air.

"Get ready to go!" she yelled at Chris. The craft was a bulky, seaweed-colored blur, but the way it settled to the ground, red signal lights pulsating, conveyed to her–definite helicopter.

She stopped the truck. The driver's door flew open; Katy hit the ground. She ran around to the other side of the truck, let Chris down. A field of sickly beige ash lay before them, clouds of soot driven into the air in the distance by huge, cranking rotor blades.

She took him by the hand; they ran. She waved as they ran, the aircraft still only a blurry, murky object. No soldiers, that she could see, stepping out from it.

They ran; she thought she heard the engine, growing louder. They ran, faster. Tears coming down both their faces. The only other noise, the wind. They ran, Chris breathing heavily, black uncut hair flopping up and down, the little legs not faltering.

On the other edge of the field, the left periphery of her vision, the pack of gray dogs, still silhouettes in the distance.

They started moving.

They started moving towards her and Chris.

Katy shot a look over her shoulder, watching the running dogs; then she stepped into something, a hole in the hummocky field, and she felt her ankle go, a tendon snap behind her heel.

Oh shit!!

She pitched forward into the ash, crying out in angry pain, sharp jolts throbbing from the ripped heel. The dogs were coming, coming, not stopping.

Chris: "What's wrong?"

"I'm hurt. God dammit!' she yelled, as she put weight on the flummoxed foot. It couldn't take any; her foot crumbled.

The helicopter was still there, rotors turning. Still no soldiers. Seventy-five yards away. Katy on her knees. She looked again, tears streaming down, the dogs were coming for them, 50 yards away. Closing.

"Run, Chris, run! I'll be right behind you!"

"But..."

"Run! Run for the helicopter! I'm coming, just limping. Run as fast as you can!" She pointed to the helicopter. "Those men will help us! That's the way home. Go!"

Chris looked at her again, torn between staying with his only companion, or running, then he turned, sprinted, little legs chugging short strides, black hair flopping, mussed by the wind. Towards the helicopter; rotor blades churning, splitting the air with greasy shrieks.

Katy in the pushup position heaved herself to her one good leg, turned, faced the dogs.

CHAPTER 42: ZEKE

Zeke Sanchez rode a motorcycle south into the Nevadan desert, as far as he could go without stopping. It was a Kawasaki KLR 650.

He hadn't found a Harley to ride south on. That would have been too good to be true. Slater left him off at the next large town they'd reached, going west, then he asked around for vehicle dealerships.

For a couple of hours he wandered around aimlessly, all but feeling like an idiot, until he hit pay-dirt.

Obviously, nothing was open. The town was mostly shutdown and evacuated. The downtown was quite bustling, however, as people cleared the shelves of the local shops before they closed, and prepared to head west.

Zeke had a lot of cash leftover from his peyote deal

in Nevada. This bread had survived their ordeal, and he used the cash to talk a man out of the Kawasaki.

Its former owner was dead, and the seller already had a bike, so they made a deal, and off Zeke went.

With a full tank, just short of six gallons, he figured he could drive the KLR 650 about 280 miles without a fill-up, but he would only stop for gas, being impatient to connect with his wife Amitola.

The road was terrible, almost non-navigable at first, but it got better the faster he drove south, a sky-blue buff pulled over his face, a pair of glare-resistant glasses with leather on the sides. He didn't wear a helmet. He still had the beaded band around his forehead.

The wind tended to blow the ash into wavy sand-dune formations; the bike's tires could still gain a purchase on the highway's clear, leftover concrete. He skirted damaged parts of the road by taking the sturdy bike off-road into the desert.

He drove four hours in a row. It felt great again to have the wind in his hair, the open desert on both sides, dim views of dark-green, distant mountains, the pale sun still fighting through the pall.

The sun had just started to go down, the sky flaring pink off his right shoulder. He neared the Nevada-Utah border; he didn't want this road trip to end, but the bike needed fuel and he hadn't planned on riding much at night.

Then a coyote chased a large jackrabbit into the highway, right in the path of his bike, going 50 mph over a sketchy surface. He steered away from the coyote and the rabbit and went briefly airborne, off the highway, landing on the back tire first, then sliding and cursing into the gravel and desert scrub, where the bike, still loudly rattling, came to rest in a cloud of dust.

The bike lay about 40 feet from him, one of its tires rotating in a warm wind that swept and drifted the sand. He was banged up; he lay on his back, his left leg killing him. He didn't move for several minutes.

He looked at the sky; it was clearing. He could still see patches of burnished blue. His right shoulder hurt like hell, too, but he concluded that it wasn't broken after moving it about a bit. His left leg had a bad pain. He didn't think he'd broken it.

He thought he mostly had bruises and scrapes; luckily, he hadn't smashed his head. Yet, his whole body seemed to throb.

The coyote and the rabbit were gone. The highway, empty. He was alone in a remote desert area. Finally, he stood up unsteadily, trying the left knee, which he determined, with some bending and testing, was badly smashed, but not torn up. He scraped and shuffled over to the bike, finally shutting off its engine.

His body radiated pain, head to toe, in a way that was difficult to pin-point. *Shit.*

In the near distance was a jumble of rocks of a reddish hue, a feature that was common to the desert southwest. The light was already grainy with the beginning of the sunset; he would have to spend the night over there, he thought glumly.

He walked over and checked on the bike again,

which appeared to have emerged from the accident about as well as he had. He smelled oil and gasoline; a pool of petroleum stained the gritty floor of the desert.

Because of his knee and shoulder, he couldn't push the 650 upright, so he gathered the essential belongings, which did not include water. He looked north, then south on the highway. The purity of the view, a divine void of arid, sunset emptiness that would have moved him on past trips, now seemed threatening. For once, *he* needed help.

He began the shuffle toward the rocks. His whole body hurt; he felt like Ahab the peg leg, scanning the desert for a stick or fence post that would help him walk on the injured left leg. The pain was taking his mind off more important things. He began to wonder, again, if he'd fractured anything, or had internal bleeding.

A ringing in his left ear reminded him of that IED explosion back in Mosul, Iraq. He was a much younger man; he'd thought he could survive anything. Youth in men provided a built-in physical confidence, aging eroded it.

Shit brother, quit whining and feeling sorry for yourself. Embrace the suck.

Unfortunately, the last week had inflicted a lot of suck.

He reached the ochre rocks as the sun was beginning to dip into the mountains. The desert got cold quickly, but he was at home in it. He found a concave element amidst the boulders; it passed for a shelter. In fact, the area might have been home to Ancients a millennia ago.

It took him 40 minutes to light a fire. *He hadn't called Amitola–maybe the damn cellphone works and I can call Tiva and ask her for emergency medical advice.*

He got out the phone. No service. The battery had maybe 20 percent life left, so he shut it off. He struggled to sustain the weak, flickering flames, which he needed for warmth. There wasn't much stuff to burn. He switched himself into survival mode, but again…there was the throbbing, persistent pain. He would have to do something about that.

He lay his coat out on the dirt floor, close to the fire, which crackled and threw embers into the gauzy, darkening sky. The red rocks became dark red, blending into night. The licking flames cast wavering shadows upon the rock wall.

When he couldn't sleep, he sat up beside the fire, threw a few sticks onto it, and sang a few songs his grandmother had taught him. She was a mixture of Ute and Sioux, he was told.

She said they weren't war songs, but Sun Dance songs, which derived from Sioux and other Plains Indians. The Sun Dance was a grueling, brutal, extended spiritual ritual that Indians performed for centuries. The northern Utes, Zeke's people, had a Sun Dance tradition, although he was also Spanish by origin.

The songs also derived from the Ghost Dance.

The songs made him feel calmer. His voice carried with a certain stridency in the silent desert. He tapped a stick on the rock to provide a tempo. He rolled some weed and smoked it, tended to the fire, then he slept some.

He woke up with a sore neck, the fire smoldering and cold. He'd heard coyotes yipping and calling, to a moon they were trying to summon, from behind its lingering curtain of ash.

He got up unsteadily, using a protruding rock to pull himself up on sore legs, as though he was climbing it.

I'd be in a clinic if I wasn't stuck here, on painkillers, a "motorcycle accident victim" listed in that week's police log. In the distance, a string of black smoke curled into the sky. That was the first sign of other people he'd seen in a day, if it wasn't a stray wildfire. Which he didn't think it was.

The sun hadn't risen all the way, the highway was empty and windswept. He spotted the lonely form of his toppled-over KLR 650, like a piece of junk by the side of the road. He felt more like a cripple, however, than a guy who could saunter over and tip that bike back on its wheels.

He turned on and checked his cellphone again, which he hadn't looked at all night. Surprisingly, it had service, even though the phone's battery was about to go dead.

He had a message from Amitola. That gave him a reflexive smile, a warmth inside, which had been lacking since the motorcycle crash. She asked where he was. She was in Albuquerque, with her sister. He slowly began to type out an answer; he was terrible at typing text messages, but for once he appreciated the utility of texting.

He told her he was hurt, not too bad (bit of a fib there), and that he was going to get checked out then head south. Could they meet in Flagstaff, Arizona, or perhaps north of there, as he still had a lot of Utah to cover?

He put the phone away; it seemed unrealistic, as in, not a real solution. He wondered if, where the rubber met the road, you can't depend on the phone for salvation. You have to save yourself; *no one is coming to rescue you.* Amitola, however, being loyal and big-hearted, despite their marital problems, would come north as far as he asked her to.

Zeke went searching for water. He poked around the north-facing part of the rocky outcropping, where water from rainfall would be more likely to collect in bowls or depressions in the rock, because it received far less direct sunlight. He found three small such reservoirs in the rocks. Water.

They were murky and gritty but better than nothing. He fashioned a makeshift straw out of a reedy stick, and sucked all the little pools of water down. It might not have amounted to two-thirds of a liter of water, but it was highly reviving. He felt less stupid and unprepared about not bringing enough water on his motorcycle.

He scanned the horizon for several minutes, looking for reflections. The highway was still empty, the pain in his knee and shoulder, worse.

Military nurses would ask you for a pain scale: this was eight, approaching nine.

He estimated the roped smoke to be five to 10 miles

away.

If he sat by his motorcycle, he may not see another driver on this desert road for the entire day. He may also succumb to his injuries; become a corpse, he thought, before his time. Therefore, he planned to walk west towards the rising smoke, if he didn't find anyone first.

He fished around in his pocket and removed the zip-locked bag containing the remaining peyote. It came in a powdery form that was not unlike the ash that had settled over the North American landscape, but finer in granularity. Then he removed the pipe, which was a clever wood carving depicting an Indian with his arms crossed over his chest. He filled the pipe's bowl with a pinch of powder, held a quivering match flame over it, brought the pipe to his mouth, and inhaled.

Zeke continued to limp across the desert. He didn't expect to feel much pain for the next few hours. He lifted his face to the sky, where he spotted a red-tailed hawk etched in black, riding the thermals above where he had spent the night.

# #

Bent over forward with nausea, he lifted his head again, and the pellucid tropical waters flowed over him on both sides. Sunlit and aquamarine, he could see right down to the bottom, which was dense with colorful marine life.

He was in an open canoe, paddling. Paddling and paddling. He had no clothes on, and his body was covered in Kon-tiki tattoos, all depictions of beautiful women he had known in his life.

The sky was dense with seabirds; delicate white ones that would land on the prow and watch him tenderly. He could smell their perfume, and imagined they were the spirits of goddesses and the women he'd known.

He thought he approached one of the smaller Hawaiian islands, which he'd dreamt about in Iraq, fantasizing about taking leave in Kauai or Lanai. When he looked down, he saw a knife sticking out of his left knee, but he felt no pain. He kept paddling hard, moving forward through waters, laughing and smiling; his spirit was full of this happiness.

The trip was long, hard to say how long. His shoulder also had a projectile protruding from it; this resembled a hairpin, but he felt no pain, only happiness.

He was paddling toward Amitola, towards this island, but her hands appeared on the canoe's gunwale, and she pulled herself out of the water, in all of her nude glory, a sun tan, long black wet hair falling over her breasts, which filled him with lust and happiness. She sat in the front of the canoe with the white birds, which fluttered gently around her.

The canoe beached on the shore of the island, where there was a large, flaming bonfire. Bearded men, lean shirtless men, came to greet them. When he stepped out of the boat, he was having trouble, real problems, walking on the sand.

The flames of the bonfire were tall, and the embers dispersed into the sky, where they became stars. One of the smiling, bearded men said, taking him by the waist and good shoulder, "Holy crap brother, how long have *you* been walking in the desert? You don't look too good, but you're alright now!"

CHAPTER 43: KATY

The pistol's discharge crackled in the foggy air, dispersing two of the gray dogs, which ran in the opposite direction across the field.

A uniformed man jogged over from the lumbering Chinook military aircraft. One of the dogs had reached Katy; she raised her fisted hand, then let it down. The mangy mutt, incongruously, licked her hand, then turned and ran off.

The man wore a bluish black uniform and a helmet and goggles. He'd fired off a flare gun to disperse the approaching dogs. Katy watched as another corpsman many yards away, yanked Chris into the aircraft.

The last dog ran off to join its feral companions, as the man trudged over to her through the ash.

"Can you take one more?" she said. "I think I tore

my achilles."

"Well, I think so, but I better ask my superiors." He had a British accent. He stopped, looked at her, then smiled.

"My God, I thought you were serious," she gasped.

"If we wait any longer, they will leave without us. The conditions, in case you haven't noticed, aren't ideal for flying. I'm going to have to pick you up and carry you. Do you mind?"

"No, please do."

She collapsed into his arms; he seemed sturdy and strong, she felt small and incredibly light, as he hoisted her through the ash. "What's your name, by the way? I'm Katy Morgan."

"Roy Hinson. Pleased to make your acquaintance, Katy. How did you and the lad get into this mess?"

"It's a long story. Isn't everybody in a mess?"

"True that."

"You have water in the chopper? We've been on the run, you see..."

"We've got water, and we've got hot water for hot chocolate. And we've got food, if you like MREs..."

"I'll take anything, right now. I'm starving and..." They had almost reached the Chinook, which had twin engines and two sets of loudly cranking rotors that kicked up a noxious fog of dust. They ducked, covered their faces, and Roy carefully handed her to two other corpsmen, one a female.

Katy was overcome by dizziness and thirst as they hoisted her aboard; she realized it was the stress of the ordeal, not her injury.

They laid her on a pad next to Chris, and handed her a blanket. They gave her a plastic water bottle and an MRE. A medic was going to look her over. She cracked the bottle open and guzzled it greedily, almost with an air of desperation.

The last 48 hours unwound in her mind: leaving her colleagues, finding Chris, Kendra's body, Kirby nicking her Jeep just before the pyroclastic weather front. She tried to put it behind her, like a nightmare; she felt relief, and a basic, crude appreciation of life.

She pulled the blanket tighter around herself, her eyes watering up. She was simply grateful for heart beats, and for having brought Chris through. Failing that, she never would have forgiven herself. She looked at him wearily; he sat calmly eating a protein bar as the Army lady tore open an MRE for him.

"Chris, are you good?" Katy asked, as she still felt responsible for him, even though he was at the moment less disabled than herself.

"This tastes good," he said, and smiled. "Where's the bathroom on this monster helicopter?"

"We'll ask," Katy said, forcing a smile around her pain. "Isn't it amazing?"

"What?"

"That we made it?"

He shrugged. "I guess so. A lot of people didn't. All those people we know who are dead." He seemed more resilient than she. *The wisdom of the babes.*

Roy stepped up into the aircraft and latched the door

behind him. At least another 20 bedraggled passengers huddled in blankets, beneath a row of yellow lamps in the Chinook's cargo hold.

Katy felt, in that one instant, 100 percent safe, for the first time since they watched the giant explosions outside the window of the Yellowstone Volcano Observatory.

A shudder went through the cabin and the fuselage, as the Chinook prepared to lift off. Through a portal, Katy could see the field next to which she'd left their pickup truck, then as they rose, desolate squares of buried and abandoned neighborhoods and woods, giving way to distant, dim views of the mountains.

"You have a British accent," she said to Roy, hovering nearby.

"We actually came down from Canada," he said, amiably. "We're a joint ANZAC group, you know. Britain, Canada, Australia, New Zealand. People are getting picked up and rescued all over the place. Mostly U.S. Army, National Guard, but we're helping out. Ever been to England?" He was chatty, by nature, a personality designed to put traumatized people at ease.

"Once, Scotland actually, to spend a semester at St. Andrews. I loved it. Where are we going?"

"The West Coast, Washington, a military base. Everybody will be given warm beds, meals, a way to reach their loved ones. They're bringing refugees in by the thousands."

"You don't seem too concerned by everything."

"This is what I've been trained for."

Thirty minutes went by, as they fitted her with a temporary brace, provided her with crutches, a round of pain-killers, hot chocolate.

She didn't know when or if ever she'd see Montana again. Her good leg was also stiffening up and cramping. She asked Roy to help her to her feet; then she leaned on one crutch and worked her way to a porthole-style window.

The view more resembled the surface of the moon, blanketed in dust, pocked with charred forests and burn marks that appeared like craters, than the southwestern Montana landscape of old. They flew over a wilderness area, with a highway passing through it. They didn't appear to be more than 1,000 feet above the ground. She turned back to Roy, who sat off the side eating a "meals ready to eat."

"Why are we flying so low?"

"We're refueling, or picking up more passengers, or both." She looked back out the window. On the edge of a forest, in the prairie not far from the highway, she saw a pack of wolves feeding on what appeared to be an elk.

The snow all around the dead prey was stained with blood. Her hand went to her mouth, her eyes narrowing. She saw several cars off the highway a few hundred yards further, some lying on their sides.

The wolves had dragged the remains of humans out of the wreckage, and were feeding on them. The abundance of relief she'd felt, gave way to fear, a kind of dread, again. She was safe, she hadn't felt safer since this all began, but she couldn't dispel from her mind the reality that the Yellowstone region and the northwest, remained a killing land.

CHAPTER 44: MONICA

Slater had almost driven the truck into the emergency room. The hood of the pickup came to a stop just short of the entrance door. Two remaining ER staff came outside, two men wearing protective equipment and surgical masks.

Slater struggled to open the driver's door, then stood up, holding onto his side: "She can't breathe–she's got ash in the lungs. Help her! Please!"

He heard one of the guys say, "Alright, alright." So that worked; they ignored him. One of them went inside, emerging moments later with a wheelchair. They came over to the passenger side and together worked her into the chair.

She murmured, with a tubercular rattle, *help, him,* but they ignored her and wheeled her inside, one of them yelling over his shoulder at Slater, who'd slumped back down into the driver's seat, "Get that vehicle away from the entrance!"

Monica strained to look back over her shoulder. She saw Max's head resting on the steering wheel. She noted that his eyes were still open.

That's the last she saw of him.

She shared a room with other patients; when her eyes were open, the room appeared to be organized as a triage, on the edge of chaos. When she closed her eyes, she imagined herself someplace else, far away from the devastation and the fear. They'd spent five days together in Baja California once, so that's where she projected her mind. She felt her own chest straining, expanding up and down, as if it was a wheezing bag someone had put on top of her body.

They seemed to take forever to get to her; she understood this trauma center was close to the breaking point. They were straight out. But she also realized that she was dying, and too weak to cry out. No one's hand to hold.

Can you be dying, yet in better shape than most of the people in the room? When were they going to bring Max in, and lay him beside her?

A soft-spoken, no-nonsense physician finally came to her side. He moved quickly and conveyed little emotion, as if Monica existed on an assembly line. He placed a hand on her shoulder, and said they were giving her corticosteroids and an inhaler. To reduce the inflammation in her lungs. He mentioned that she was lucky, because they would soon run out of supplies, but that she was going to get enough of the treatments.

The atmosphere in the clinic was like when a missile strikes a residential building in a crowded city; hospitals are overwhelmed with gravely injured citizens. They were laid down in rows in the hallways, some of them already dead. Yes, she was fortunate; she had a small bed with a pillow.

He gave her a sedative in pill form, said "Good luck," as though they were through with her, then he rushed away. Her breathing had improved with the inhaler and steroids, but she still felt like she was underwater and sucking air through a straw.

She closed her eyes, began to drift off. The clipped remarks of doctors and nurses, the cries and the moans of the ill and injured, all blended together, and became the background noise of a surreal dream.

Tears trickled down both of her cheekbones; her lower lip quivered. Before she conked out into delirium, she reminded herself, she was in Boise, Idaho, which was still too close to Yellowstone's massive eruption, and she still had no rational way to escape to the coast. If she lived.

She gave in to her affliction, ceasing to endlessly speculate over her fate. Her life was in their hands. She wondered whether she'd ever get her lungs back, or see Slater again.

People came back to her, to replenish her meds, food, and water. It was difficult to count the hours, the days, or distinguish between night and day. They moved her around, one time, for a while, into the hallway outside her room. They didn't have time to spend more than a few minutes with her. She knew her breathing had improved; her lungs gradually cleared. She got the impression that steroids worked. They were like a fountain of life; she craved them more than food, even more than water.

Monica was simply a passive receptacle for meds and barebones medical care; the nurses, excepting one or two during brief moments, had no juice left to treat her as other than barely alive meat, then, as meat that was recovering.

She said to one of the female nurses, *I want you to check my abdomen.* And when the nurse ignored her, she said, *I might be pregnant.* The lady stopped and stared at her meaningfully, then she went to work, checking Monica's abdomen and cervix.

You are, as far as I know, the nurse said.

Is it still alive? The nurse looked at her kindly, with a veil of pity.

I'll check... She left and came back with a handheld probe which could detect a signal, heartbeats. It was amazing they still had this device working, given that people were still stretched out in the hallways, being moved around, and saved or lost.

Monica got an intensified impression of the heroics inside of hospitals, and she felt lucky and almost guiltily privileged. They could have just let both of them die, in this Boise hospital, by choosing other people to live.

It's still alive, healthy, the nurse said, pausing for a

moment wearily, then smiling. She folded up and gathered away her device, then was quickly gone. Monica was strangely detached before, but now that she knew, she was nervous, elated, and felt a swarm of strong emotions as she lay there.

She wanted to get moving.

We're moving you soon to another location, one of the other nurses said that afternoon.

Where?

Everybody's leaving in buses.

Finally, they wheeled her out of the room, into the hallway, down to a stairwell. Two men hoisted her down the stairs to another hallway, and out the exit to open air. She felt pathetic, pitiable, weak; Monica couldn't believe the manpower her condition required, how much it cost to keep her alive. To keep *them.* She was then hoisted into a bus.

After several minutes, the bus began to move. She sat up, looked out the window at the still functioning city, fascinated by small things, like a child. She craved the recovery of her stronger self, the one that ran through the wilderness, pursued by a wild predator; the one that shot a felon. The one that had, so far, sustained a baby, and survived, up until the air became unbreathable.

Most of the passengers were ambulatory patients, but a few were hospital personnel, the ones that could be spared. Monica no longer only spoke in whispers; she asked one of them, a man making his way up the aisle, where they were going.

We're going to Eugene, Oregon. We'll be there at

the end of the day. There seems to be longterm plans to ferry people to California. Or someplace south, less hard-hit by the ash. The officials are putting together large refugee camps.

Do you know where my friend Max Slater is? He came in with me, suffering from a gunshot wound. She had asked everybody that, but the crowd of injured and sick that had overwhelmed the hospital made it mostly impossible to track anyone down.

I'm sorry I don't. But if you leave me his name, I can try to find out more information about your friend.

This was more than anyone else had offered. He had her write Max's name and a brief description of him on a piece of paper.

In this level of chaos, and provisional behavior, she thought, as she looked out the window of the bus; what happened to Max if he died there in the parking lot?

Monica couldn't get herself to ask the man this blunt question, because he probably figured she couldn't bear the truth, so she wouldn't get much out of him. Her hand went up to her face, which she saw reflected in the grit-stained window.

The bodies most likely went into mass graves, if they were buried at all, or were perfunctorily cremated to prevent the spread of disease.

This was the fate of the dead, when in one week, hundreds of thousands perish. She thought of grizzlies and wolves in the forest, the cruel, cold endgame of Mother Nature's doing, the bitter calculation of what survives and what doesn't.

She thought of her baby. She wondered if it was a boy. Clearly, she had a new mission, to survive, for *two* now. She grimaced, looking out the window at a bank of trees going by, dark branches etched against a white sky, as still as paintings; a river flowing over rocks beneath them.

She closed her eyes and thought of Max with his arm around her, on a beach on the Bahia Concepcion, in Baja, California. Get her to the coast, she thought, just get her away from the ash, to the Pacific sea.

CHAPTER 45: TIVA

Tiva sat in the hallway of the large Portland medical center, sipping on a spiked coffee in a Styrofoam cup and toying with her cellphone.

She'd heard from her father, Zeke Sanchez, by text; he'd dashed south on a motorcycle to connect with Tiva's mom, but Tiva hadn't heard anything more from him in the last 24 hours.

She expected the unpredictable from him. She'd go a year without seeing him, then he'd suddenly show up at her work, asking whether she wanted to spend a long weekend in Miami (he had a hotel suite on South Beach, on a veteran's discount...), or Sedona, Arizona (fancy wellness spa that included "a guided peyote trip"), or wherever, the location was never boring, or not unique.

She couldn't stay angry at him for long, even though

he hadn't made it to Amitola yet. She knew he was alive, because he always emerged from the mayhem of his lifestyle, which was almost like the modus operandi of an unpredictable, wildly talented artist, in one piece.

He'd make it home when he was good and ready to, like a stray, yet loyal dog.

She sipped the coffee again, spiked with bourbon; nurses and doctors rushed back and forth, as if Tiva wasn't there. Greenhorn, the helicopter pilot, had dribbled some whiskey in from a flask he had in the inside pocket of his flight jacket.

She didn't feel an ounce of guilt drinking her cocktail, despite the medical setting–it had been a long, perilous week. In the end, she'd taken responsibility for this injured lady and her two children, who were nearby in a waiting room, feasting on kiddie yogurts and playing iPad games. Everybody had made it through fine, and for that she deserved a stiff drink, as people were fond of calling them.

She stretched out her legs, her trousers were soiled and torn, and her shoes still caked with ash, as if she'd tramped through concrete before it had set. She didn't feel pretty anymore. If they were, in fact, being transferred to southern California, she was going to shower, have a wonderful swim in the sea; then find a warm place outside, wear a dress, and dance to some music.

She would feel like herself again, the attractive Latina with bits of Native American, with the bright eyes and long, jet-black hair, who men flirted with so often that it became tiresome.

Tiva had done what she was trained to do. She had stabilized Kiatsu and kept her alive, all through the turbulent helicopter ride. Now Kiatsu was in a specialized burn unit in the hospital. She was going to make it. Some people did, Tiva thought, when they were that badly injured and the odds were stacked against them, and you couldn't predict who were going to be the lucky ones.

She'd seen it in the ER; miraculous recoveries among old people, inexplicable fatalities among the young, barely newborn infants who had no business surviving their infections, but still pulled through against the odds.

She mused, because the alcohol quickly went to her head: they'd all beaten the odds after Yellowstone's debacle. Which was ongoing, and people had been talking about how bad the upcoming winter was going to be.

Portland wasn't hit too bad, but was still getting a dusting of ash, up to 10 mm, Greenhorn said. That didn't mean much to her–what's 10 mm if only a centimeter or 0.4 of an inch? But as Greenhorn put it, as long as it struck the right place, you could disable a car's engine by tossing a tiny fistful of sand onto it.

The rumor was, they were all, including Kiatsu, going to being taken by Red Cross hospital ship, with about 1,500 other injured and traumatized refugees, to a bay in San Diego.

Tiva left text messages with her mom and Zeke:

meet me and Shilah, her brother, in San Diego. Just drop everything and meet us; we have to get our family together again.

She wondered what had happened to...what were their names?...Monica and Max? Her dad's pithy message hadn't even mentioned them. They were on the ground. Damn, she hoped they made it.

The prevailing winds were west to east across the North American continent, and way down in Southern California would be like: *There is no eruption...it never truly took place...there are only beaches, palm trees, a slow-paced vibe, a blessed break from the non-stop survival mode they'd all been trapped in.*

From now on, she wouldn't be so career-oriented and driven, she mused. She'd like to meet a good man and have a child or two someday, make an honest man, a grandfather, out of Zeke Sanchez.

You don't have a limitless amount of time to do these things. Life is fleeting. Oh so fleeting, so fast.

CHAPTER 46: ZEKE

The dudes and the hippie maidens who'd made the bonfire and concocted their own Naked Man in the desert, didn't know what to make of this bedraggled figure who'd limped out of the desert.

When he came out of his peyote trip, there were three main things he wanted to accomplish, all of them attainable: get his knee professionally wrapped (better treatment, like surgery, could come later); get his KLR 650 back; and drive the bike back to Arizona, into the loving arms of his wife.

He knew exactly where the bike was, that discarded piece of fine machinery, covered in dust and lying amongst some old barbed-wire fencing on an endless, almost nameless road in the Nevada desert.

That guy with the beard, who'd first greeted him out

of the desert, was explicitly Jesus-like, but then again, Zeke was on peyote. The others seemed to know what to do with him, because some of them were tripping, too. They got him water, and a place to lie down, then they had made some really good tea, which he drank when he had retained coherency.

He made them promise that the tea, which was something like chamomile-mint-jasmine-chai, was *not* spiked with hallucinogens. He had to get straight; he wondered if the whole aftermath of the volcanic eruption was part of his peyote trip.

Some of the skirmishes he'd had reminded him of fighting in Fallujah about 19 years ago. He'd acquired a strange sixth sense on that mission, if he hadn't already possessed it: who to trust, and who not to trust; when it was okay to pull the trigger or brandish the knife, and have no misgivings afterward, because those dudes were evil. They were trying to kill *you*.

Of course, if he had his druthers, life wouldn't involve any of that: it could all be love-making, tripping on a motorcycle, seeing the sublime places in the world, and watching his two kids grow up, discovering the amazing adults they had become, like Tiva.

He'd had nothing to do with molding the woman she'd become, except for thinking that, she'd inherited some of his *chi*, his life force.

You couldn't bottle that, or make it out of artificial substances; you either had the *chi* or you didn't. He thought of all these things, after he'd gotten the sore, swollen knee wrapped up in an out-of-the-way urgent-care clinic the hippies drove him to; then he bought them a tank of gas and they went a little farther to where the KLR 650 lay in the dirt, out in the middle of desert nowhere.

They waited for him to start it up, the handsome Jesus-guy and his good-looking, sweet-tempered girlfriend. *Damn, people could be nice,* Zeke thought, as he used his good leg to start up the bike. *The more people he met on the road, the more he thought that Americans were, in general, a good-hearted crew.* It was just that war experiences had scarred him; but at times like this, he felt he was healing.

He swerved onto the open road, as the two others waved goodbye at him.

Healing was a process, a journey like so much else, he thought, the wind flowing through his hair again, sunglasses on, the clear sunlight off his right shoulder baking the land that stretched in seemingly endless plateaus and mountains, all the way to the sea.

CHAPTER 47: KATY

April 2027, 18 months later, Bahia Concepcion, Baja, California

The sky was achingly blue, the hills white with coarse patches of dry plants, even tall cacti sprouting from the sand, looking out of place by an ocean. There were rolling hills and a row of brown, furrowed mountains.

The Baja was a desert that ended abruptly on an aquamarine sea, as still as glass.

Katy and Roy had driven a Sienna van up from La Paz, where they'd flown in from San Diego. The beaches along the way were pretty, with white sand and flat, tropical waters, and not too many people scattered across their crescents. They'd been stopping at most of them, camping, swimming, watching sunsets over the dunes and mountains (the beaches actually faced east, the Sea of Cortez, which separated Baja California from the Mexican mainland), until they reached Mulege, where they'd planned to meet Monica.

Monica had suggested the Bahia Concepcion, because it was a "happy place," out of the way, which she knew well from a previous trip there with Max Slater.

Katy had married the British Army officer Roy Hinson, who had plucked her off the battered terrain of Montana 18 months before. Chris Farnsworth was turning nine years old. Months ago, they'd failed to locate his parents, who were missing and presumed dead. When the time seemed right, Katy formerly adopted Chris, Roy became his dad, and they settled in San Diego, where Katy got a teaching post at the university. Roy got a job with a private security firm.

They all loved the beach and tried surfing together. Chris settled in well with the young couple; he'd formed a strong bond with Katy as they fought to survive a cataclysmic disaster. Like youngsters from war-torn regions, however, he'd witnessed violent death and the loss of parents and companions, at a young age when he couldn't be expected to rationally process the experience (if that was at all possible), and this trauma had led to occasional extended periods of silence, punctuated by rage, which all three of them were working to salve and heal.

Getting him outside, in the sunlight, and on the water or in the mountains, was the best remedy for him,

Katy thought.

Katy and Roy were also planning on having another child together. Katy wanted to return to Yellowstone, but its devastation was so profound and toxic that the immediate region was considered virtually a dead zone. One could fly over it and drive heavy-duty trucks and machines there, but the land could no longer sustain human habitation, for now. Birds and insects had returned, as well as microscopic life, robust bacterium or "extremophiles" that could survive any harsh environment.

She would return to Yellowstone someday. She vowed that she would be part of the first wave of specialists to help reclaim the region for wildlife, and take samples and develop extensive research on the aftermath of giant eruptions.

The three Yellowstone calderas should be quiet for hundreds of thousands of years, she thought, but one never knew.

Right now, returning to the West Yellowstone region would be like colonizing the surface of the moon. The region was buried in dust. Even the air, a year and several months post-eruption, was still contaminated with trace levels of poison gases. Yet the most resilient wildlife made valiant efforts to return.

They parked the van in a dirt lot, near a scrubby dune and the beach. The air was hot and humid, the glittering water flat and bright. Monica stood down on the edge of the water of the Bahia Concepcion. She held hands with a tiny male infant, who wore a baseball cap, and whose head only came up to Monica's knee. She turned, smiled, and waved, wearing sunglasses, and some flimsy layer over a bathing suit.

A man was sitting in a beach chair lodged in the sand nearby.

The beach had a few straw huts built on it. They were supposed to take money for staying in them, but no one seemed to be around.

Monica had traveled there with her fiancee Gavin Smith. They'd been seeing each other for about a year. She'd had Rafe Slater Lovato about seven months after she was evacuated from that hospital in Boise, Idaho, lucky to be alive, grateful to still have a thriving infant inside of her. A boy, Max's son, she'd told Katy.

She and her infant son had also settled north of San Diego; she was teaching geology and earth sciences at a college there. Katy and Roy Hinson walked down to the beach. Gavin stood up when they neared; he was a lean, tall, amiable guy with sunblock smeared on his body, and a baggy pair of shorts.

He seemed much different in demeanor than the intense, cerebral Max. That was the first thing Katy thought, comparing the two, then she had a sad moment recalling Max's death, and the better times they spent together at the YVO.

Monica was smiling, and she had a backpack slung over her shoulder, with a baby's drink container shoved into its pocket. Katy thought that she looked mostly the same, with a few gray streaks in her hair. Roy stayed with Gavin, and Katy walked down to join Monica at the edge of the water.

They had the beach completely to themselves, except for a group of local Mexican men who were playing mariachi music on a boom box back in the parking lot.

Monica hadn't seen Katy in person since Katy had refused the helicopter ride back on Hebgen Lake near Yellowstone. Eighteen months had passed. They'd actively communicated via email and cellphone, however; they wouldn't allow the disaster and its chaotic aftermath to drive a kind of wedge between them. Some people leave disasters behind them, by leaving the associated people behind as well. Not these two.

"You look wonderful," Katy said. "And so this is Rafe? He's cute!" She stepped into the water and reached down, and Rafe took hold of her index finger with his little fist.

"How's Chris?" Monica asked.

"He's fine. He's staying with a friend and playing on his soccer team." She shrugged. "He didn't want to go on this trip with us."

"That was wonderful that you adopted him."

"He's easy. It's been good, really worked out. He gets along with Roy."

"You know, I'll always remember when we left you and took off in the helicopter. We were really guilty, Max and me. To put it mildly. We thought we'd never see you alive."

"That was my decision, and hey, it all worked out." She paused a moment. It was boiling outside. She wanted to go swimming, and she tore off the T-shirt she wore over her one-piece bathing suit. "I'll get burnt to a crisp down here!" she exclaimed, then she looked down at Max's son. She wondered if Max knew, and then Monica read her mind.

"You know, I never told Max, about being pregnant. We'd broken up and...well, I was toying with the idea of having the child alone, for at least a short period. It didn't seem to change anything, so I don't beat myself up over it. He died saving me, and Rafe. That was his supreme achievement."

"I was really sad, when you told me. He was such a smart guy, and he cared so much, about everything. Well..." Katy dived into the sea; it was warm as bathwater.

She tasted salt on her lips right away; the sun dappled the surface of the bay. She swam out a bit, and she could see rocks on the bottom, and the same white sand, with her shadow moving over it. She surfaced, and stroked to shore. She stood up, wading through the water.

Two of the men walked down the beach from the parking lot, shirts off, tattooed; one of them carried the boom box on his shoulder. The music was too loud. Katy watched as Monica picked Rafe up and set him down on the dry part of the beach. Monica reached into her backpack and removed a small handgun; her left hand, still gripping the pistol, dropped to her side. She was turned away from Katy.

The men hadn't noticed this, but they began to walk, with the loud mariachi playing, up the beach in the southern direction. Monica watched them go, warily, then she glanced back at Katy, who noticed something fierce yet faintly ashamed in her expression.

This was a Monica she didn't recognize from the days at the YVO. Monica put the pistol carefully back into the backpack, then gently grasped Rafe's little hand.

It was going to take a while for all of them to get over the fear of that week, Katy thought. She looked up into the blue dome of the sky, sensing relief, but vividly recalling the funnels of exploding magma outside the windows of the YVO, when the sky was full of a darkness that seemed everlasting.

They both walked back up the beach together, with Rafe waddling beside them.

"Monica, let's get together soon," Katy said. "Up north, for coffee. I want to work with you again. We can discuss the research I'm planning to do." She sounded more earnest than before.

"We should put our brains together. The work at Yellowstone isn't finished–in fact, it's only just started. We could be part of the scientific teams going back into the plateau. What do you think?"

"I'd love it." Monica said. "I'd love to be on the same team with you again." They kept walking.

"The USGS wants us back," Katy said, sounding fortified and psyched. "It's a new mission. The funding is there; the political will. They want Yellowstone back; all the land, Wyoming, Idaho, Montana. The Senators and congressmen, the ones that are still alive, that is, want to know whether the region can sustain human habitation again. They want teams to go in there, take soil and air samples, and spend weeks, not just days. Homeland Security will also fund it, I hear. The Canadian government. They want a sort of colony set up."

"When does this project start? This new mission?"

"ASAP."

Monica stopped walking for a moment. "You're serious, aren't you?"

"Dead serious."

Monica admired the Bahia, the way the sun reflected off its calm, blue-green surface. Given her family life right now, she thought, the last thing she should do is consider any return to blighted Yellowstone.

But the idea intrigued her. She knew that ultimately, she'd never be able to say no.

She looked at Rafe, playing in the sand. He looked tiny and vulnerable. She felt no small measure of guilt, and fear.

No person could spend any serious time in the Yellowstone region, without a complete artificial life-support system. Consequently, she knew why many of the agencies, including the Defense Department, were interested in this mission: they wanted to use it as a platform for artificial intelligence and robotics; synthetic humans.

Military applications...security applications..."They've just been waiting for this opportunity," Monica said, refusing to mask her anger. "It's just fallen into their laps."

"What?" Katy said. She didn't know what Monica was getting at.

"It's a set-up," Monica said. *They want to test synthetics in Yellowstone, to prove they're superior to humans, to prove they're bulletproof. It will be the perfect testing ground. They want to demonstrate that synthetics will be able to replace humans, in most applications.*

Rafe's generation will be the first one to be forced to integrate with synthetics; forced to compete with them, on an unfair playing field.

How can I stop this?

THE END

Printed in Great Britain
by Amazon

48344901R00192